Lost River

Grace Hawthorne

A few words from readers about *Lost River*

Lost River is a snapshot in time.

Lost River flows swimmingly.

Lost River took me back to my childhood.

Lost River was a fun read.

Lost River could be a small town anywhere in 1949.

"Loved the back stories of the characters. *Lost River* really got me to thinking about my small town in Arkansas and wondering what hidden stories lurked there."

B. Davis

"*Lost River* could easily have been my home town. I grew up in upstate New York. My father's partner in his medical practice was a Dr. Nichols. My dog, Chudney was just like Boot. My parents were friends with a Conti family. Our mayor embezzled a sizeable amount of money from the village and skipped town. It was all there just with a southern accent."

P. Pritchard

"Your writing is a dichotomy of seriousness and humor that works superbly together. I'd recommend *Lost River* to anyone who is curious about small towns and interested in people."

E. Herscher

"The back stories filled out the characters and showed how people cope with the many vicissitudes of life and manage to survive."

J. Mason

To the whole crew!.

Lost River

Shenanigans and survival in a small town.

Enjoy!

Grace Hawthorne

Grace Hawthorne

BookLocker

Saint Petersburg, Florida

Print ISBN: 978-1-64719-601-1
Ebook ISBN: 978-1-64719-602-8

Published by BookLocker.com, Inc., St. Petersburg, Florida.

The characters and events in this book are fictitious. Any similarity to real persons, living or dead, is coincidental and not intended by the author.

Printed on acid-free paper.

Booklocker.com, Inc.
2021

Library of Congress Cataloging in Publication Data
Hawthorne, Grace
Lost River: Shenanigans and survival in a small town. By Grace Hawthorne
Library of Congress Control Number: 2021910583

To Freeman

Acknowledgments

Covid changed everything. Normally I would have made road trips, met people, collected information and would have a lot of people to acknowledge. Research for this book was done almost exclusively online, so my thanks to Google.

There are some actual people who provided essential help and information. First there was my creative group SpeakEasy. Martha Tate, Betty Ann Wylie and Jeff Upshaw were my first audience. They listened patiently and offered feedback and encouragement, two essential elements when dealing with the building blocks of a new story.

My Beta Readers/editors come from all over the map. They are listed here along with their small towns and the state where they live now. Bobbie Davis (Star City, AR and CA), Ellen Herscher (Sturgis, MI and MI), Jerry Matheny (Kings Mountain, NC and GA), Cynthia Pearson (Unincorporated Lyncort, NY and GA) and Phil Pritchard (Owego, NY and GA) My hometown was St. Francisville, LA. I was surprised to find that small towns are remarkably similar all over the country.

Patrick Scullin worked for a circus in his youth. What a stroke of luck to find him. He provided me with a real-life look at life under the Big Top.

Jim Wylie shared memories of the POWs who worked on his father's farm. He also loaned me *Georgia POW Camps in World War II,* which filled in a lot of blanks.

My thanks to Rev. J. Warren Culver, a retired pastor of 47 years, who walked me through the steps for planning and hosting a successful revival.

Thanks to B.J. Abraham for her careful reading and thoughtful comments.

As with all my books, huge thanks go to my husband, Jim Freeman. For *Lost River*, he generously shared memories of characters and events in his small town in Michigan. As he has done on all my books, he keeps me grounded in time and space...not an easy task. The cover design and the map of *Lost River* are his creations.

Far too many people to name related stories from their small towns and from those bits and pieces I populated *Lost River*. I am grateful to them all.

LOST RIVER DIRECTORY

A

B

Daniel Barlow, General Manager of Stubbs Sawmill and Lumber Yard

    Earlene, wife

    Sonny, oldest son

    Archie, younger son

Percy Barns, Deputy Sheriff, Operation 23

Waylon Sidney Bethune III, CPA from Valdosta, GA

Robert Blalock, Pastor, Bethel Baptist Church

    Prim, wife

    Matt, son

Boot, Town dog

Leroy Brown, Lucille's boyfriend in Chicago

C

Carmelina Conti, Matriarch

    Anthony, (Tony), son, Conti's Grocery Store

        Sophia, wife

    Salvador (Sal), son, Conti's Ford Dealership

        Nina, wife

    Vincent (Vinnie), son, Conti's General Store

        Isabella, wife

        Adam, son, deceased

Sidney Cumberland, President of Lost River Bank and Trust

    Florence, wife, president of Episcopal Church Women

    Sonny, son

D

E

F

Morris Fullerton, Bataan Death March survivor

G
Hazel Goodman, Mayor's secretary
H
James Henshaw, Pastor, Wesley United Methodist Church
      LouAnn, wife
I
J
K
Leon Kirkland, Kirkland's Print Shop, *Lost River Herald*
      Helen, wife
      Inky, adopted son
Andrew Knox, Pastor, Trinity Episcopal Church
      Annabelle, wife
L
J.W. Latham, Sheriff
      Trudy, wife, Do-or-Dye Salon
Curtis Leland, Leland's Funeral Home
      Mildred, wife
M
Agnes Mackie, Mayor
      Warren, Jr., son
Gibby Moon, co-owner Moon's Diner
      "Granny," mother
Eudalee Munson, First-grade teacher
N
Dr. S. I. Nichols, GP
      Victoria (Vickie), wife and nurse
O
Junior Ottley, Mechanic at the Gas &Grill
P
Q

R

Charlie Russo, Gambler from New Orleans

S

Harvey Skaggs, City Council candidate

Sly Slonacher, Principal Lost River School

Zachary (Zach) Stubbs, Stubbs Sawmill and Lumber Yard
      Eden, wife
      Hank, son

Father Sullivan, Priest, Saint Philip's Catholic Church

Mike Sweeney, Former Mayor
      Rebecca, wife, deceased

Obadiah Sweeney, Mike's great, great grandfather

T

Texas Bill, Hobo

Remy Thibodaux, Med student in New Orleans

Eugene Talmadge, Three-time Governor of Georgia
      Herman, son, Georgia Governor 1948-1954

U

V

W

Lucy Washburn, Sheriff's office manager

Ethyl Williams, Manager of G&G Restaurant (Lucille)

Church Directory

Bethel Baptist Church, Robert Blalock, Pastor

Saint Philip's Catholic Church, Father Sullivan, Priest

Wesley United Methodist Church, James Henshaw, Pastor

Trinity Episcopal Church, Andrew Knox, Pastor

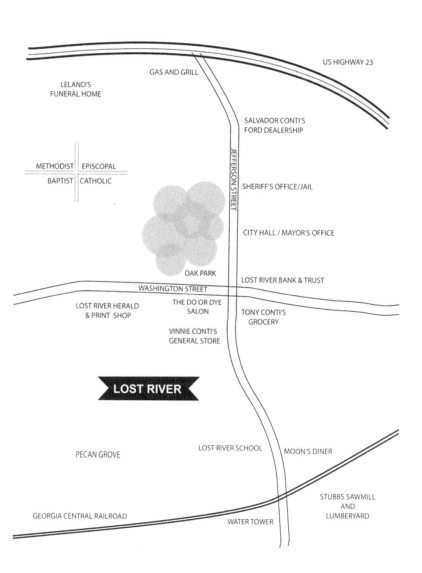

The Naked City, 1949

"There are eight million stories in the Naked City and this is one of them." As the narrator's voice ended, the screen faded to black.

The air was warm and heavy with the smell of scorched popcorn and stale butter. Hank, Sonny and Matt pulled on their coats and headed toward the exit. In the half-light, their feet made small ripping sounds as they walked across the slightly sticky floor.

"Man! That was a great movie. I wish I lived in New York City," Sonny said.

Hank scuffed his feet on the sidewalk. "Yeah, Georgia's got to be the most boring place in the world."

"You can say that again," Matt added. "Nobody in Lost River's got a story worth telling."

Story #1, Mrs. Conti (Sicily 1860)

Most of the time, Carmelina slept through the noise of the gun shots. They were part of the air like the bees buzzing through the wild flowers and the olive trees. The bees were a nuisance, but not dangerous unless you aggravated them, then their sting was deadly. Sicilians were accustomed to invaders with guns. The old women in their long black dresses rattled off the island history like beads on their rosaries. They had seen and survived it all.

"Everybody's tried to rule us starting with the Greeks, then the Romans, Byzantines, Arabs, Normans, French, Spanish, Napoleon, and now those Italians." *It was 1860, and the current trespassers from Italy were the last straw.*

For years the war had been going on in little towns nearby, but when her home town of Palermo revolted, Italy sent ships to shell the city and soldiers to deal with the trouble-makers. They executed hundreds, put many more in prison and deported others. Absolutely no one was safe. Carmelina's family talked about escaping before they could be rounded up.

Her papa made the final decision. "We're leaving. We'll each take one suitcase and you have to carry it yourself. No help." Her mother insisted that although the weather was hot, they each wear two of everything. In addition, they packed two sets of underwear, a change of work clothes, one nice outfit, three pairs of socks, an extra pair of shoes, a sweater, a heavy coat and one "special thing." Carmelina, who was six, took a book.

On the day they were to leave for America, her papa went to work at his little shop to avoid suspicion. Carmelina and her mother went to the courthouse to pick up some papers. As they were leaving to go back home, they saw soldiers dragging the school principal, Mr. Esposito, by his feet over the cobblestones in the square. They stood him up by the fountain and shot him in the head. He fell into the water and it turned red with his blood. Women screamed. Men turned their heads in disgust and shame.

"Run home! Hide!" her mother whispered.

Carmelina obeyed. She expected to see friends or neighbors along the way, someone who might help her or at least explain what was going on, but the street was completely empty and deadly quiet. When she got home, she reached out to open her front door, but she couldn't turn the knob. It was slippery. She looked at her hand; it was covered with blood. She quickly wiped it on her dress. "I've ruined my good school dress. Mama will be so angry." With no help in sight, Carmelina hid under a bush and waited for her mother to come home and let her in.

She finally got there and the family waited all night for Papa to come home, but by daybreak he still hadn't arrived. Her mother fed Carmelina and her two older brothers some milk and bread for breakfast. "Put the rest of the bread and some cheese in your pockets," she said, "and be quick about it."

As fast as they could, they left for the docks, but the streets were already crowded with people. They finally got to the port, but there was no boat in sight and it started to rain. The family found shelter in a doorway where they waited all day and through the night.

People were cold, hungry and frightened, but they were strangely silent. Even the babies were quiet. Daybreak finally came and with it a ship.

"Oh my God." The look on her mother's face was more frightening than the soldiers who roused people and hurried them up the gangplank. They were directed down into a large open area at the bottom of the boat.

The crossing took ten days and the cheese and bread they brought was soon gone. Some days they were given food, some days only dirty water. People got seasick and threw up where they were. There was nowhere else to go. Slop buckets overflowed adding to the general misery. Her family found an almost dry space and huddled together expecting to die.

On the tenth day of the trip after what seemed like an eternity, the passengers were ordered to come up on deck. No one knew what was going on. "Maybe they're going to throw us all overboard," an old man said.

Carmelina was standing next to a sailor who smiled at her. "No one is going to throw you overboard," he said. When he got no reaction, he realized she couldn't understand him. With a smile, he pointed to a large round building on the southern tip of Manhattan Island. "Castle Garden," he said, "America."

Carmelina smiled. "America! Mama, we made it."

Well, not quite yet. First the passengers were loaded onto tug boats that took them ashore. There they were met by one government official after another, each one asking questions and scrutinizing them from head to toe.

Carmelina's mother didn't understand English, but she heard the same questions over and over and guessed at what the questions must be from the answers she heard in Sicilian.

What is your name? Where did you come from? Where are you going? What is your trade?

Throughout all the questions and the medical examinations, the family stayed close to friends from Palermo. Eventually they were released and sent with their luggage to an Italian community in East Harlem. They did their best to survive, but they were fishermen and their skills were useless in the steel and concrete of New York City.

The one place where workers were needed was the rural south. The Civil War had all but wiped out a generation of young men. Recruiters combed the streets of Harlem offering jobs to anyone willing to move south. And so Carmelina's family moved to Lost River. Two brothers and some of their friends went to work logging.

When she was 15, Carmelina married Adamo Conti who had been on the boat with her family. They had three sons, Anthony, Salvador and Vincent. They were a handsome lot, those Conti boys. They took after their mama. Dark hair, dark eyes, well built. By the time she was in her 80s, Carmelina's family was a vital part of Lost River. Even into her 90s there were still traces of the young girl with flashing dark eyes and hair blowing in the wind.

Over the years, she had lost track of most of the twists and turns of her life. She had learned English, but as she got older, it was just easier to revert to the language of Sicily she had spoken as a girl. She was now one of those old women in their long black dresses. She had forgotten many things, but she never forgot the blood on the doorknob of her house back in Sicily.

Once Upon a Time... (1538)

Like a good many of its residents, Lost River had its own story going all the way back to when there really *was* a river. In the beginning, trees stretched across the country from the Texas Gulf coast to the Atlantic Ocean. They were all there: pine, beech, cypress, oak, walnut, black gum, pecan and magnolia. And there was a river, not as big as the Mississippi or the Tennessee, but a respectable size for South Georgia.

The history of early Georgia and the history of the Creek Indians went hand in hand. Members of the tribe roamed the hills, fished the river, hunted in the forest. For the most part, they were farmers who raised corn, beans and squash. Actually, the women did the farming and the men hunted.

Europeans appeared around 1538 and at first the settlers and the Creeks lived side by side in peace. Then slowly things began to change. More settlers came and they wanted to *own* the hills, the river and the forest. The Creeks didn't understand the concept of owning something. How could anyone "own" the land? It would be like trying to own the air. The struggle continued for years.

Finally, in 1813 things came to a head in an all-out war between the Creeks and the United States. The Creeks lost the battle and relinquished 22,000,000 acres of land—half of Alabama and part of southern Georgia—that had been their hunting grounds. It was the beginning of the end for the tribe. In the 1830s, the Creeks, were relocated to Indian Territory, which became Oklahoma.

As part of their mid-summer Green Corn ceremony celebrating first-fruits, every wrongdoing, grievance or crime committed within the tribe was forgiven. This act of forgiveness however, did not extend to the federal government. In a sad irony, the US referred to the Creeks, Cherokee, Chickasaw, Choctaw and Seminole as the Five Civilized tribes. The People found nothing civilized about their relocation.

With the Creeks gone, there was nothing to stop more settlers from moving in. The trees were a big part of what attracted settlers. The most prized tree was heart pine: straight, strong, beautiful and resistant to decay. In other words, living gold. Those trees stood witness to history for over a hundred years just to reach maturity. Throughout the years, ship-building, civilization and the expansion of the railroads more or less wiped them out.

However, Mother Nature frequently finds a way to even the score. On a hot afternoon near Charleston, South Carolina, a low rumble started underground. It sounded like thunder. The sound grew louder and the earth shook. Solid ground cracked and opened huge holes that sucked in everything around them.

Earthquakes weren't common in the southeast, but they did happen and the shock waves traveled far and wide. Rather than the sandy soil of the west, the rocks east of the Mississippi were older, harder and denser than they were out west. Shockwaves don't dissipate, they just keep traveling.

The South Carolina quake was felt as far away as Savannah. Although it was not Mother Nature's original intention, the earthquake was serious enough to scare a lot of back-sliding church folks into mending their evil ways. When tremors moved into southwest Georgia, they swallowed the local river whole. It slid underground, never to be seen again. Lost forever.

Through it all, the trees survived. They dug their roots deep into the earth, found the water and continued to grow as they had always done. But now they followed the course of the invisible underground river.

Even without a river, the area was beautiful. Winters were mild, the soil was rich, and government land was cheap. In scouting out a location for a new town, the settlers noticed a strange phenomenon. The oldest pine trees in the area didn't grow at random, they seemed to grow in a meandering pattern like a green river flowing through the underbrush. A group of six ancient oaks grew in a tight cluster. The settlers liked the area and so the town of Lost River was formed.

Instead of a central square and a courthouse like most small southern towns, Lost River decided to make the cluster of live oaks the center of town and to call it Oak Park. The rest of the sidewalks downtown meandered through towering pines that followed the unseen path of the river. The town might have been short on right angles and square lots, but nobody seemed to care. They felt sheltered and protected by the trees.

A Town is Born

The founding fathers decided to impose a little order and dignity on their new town by naming the two main streets downtown Washington and Jefferson. Washington ran more or less east and west on the south side of Oak Park; Jefferson ran north and south on the east side. Jefferson was the main shopping street with buildings lined up facing the park.

Lost River Bank and Trust was at the intersection of Washington and Jefferson. City Hall, which housed Mayor Sweeny's office, Sheriff J.W. Latham's office, the jail and the post office were just north of the bank on Jefferson.

When he worked in Chicago, J.W. hated the cold. He wore two sets of long johns under his uniform and a heavy overcoat in the winter. South Georgia winters were mild, so he gave the heavy coat to the moths and opted for a bush jacket with lots of pockets. Khaki pants and a short-sleeved shirt suited him fine for hot Georgia summers.

He was head and shoulders taller than most of the men in town and he was partial to a beat-up old cowboy hat. Nobody knew where it came from—Conti's General Store didn't sell them—but he was a good sheriff and since he was a Yankee, folks made allowances.

Over the years, the town continued to grow, but other than those original two, most folks didn't bother with street names. Directions—on the rare occasion anyone needed them—relied on landmarks. "It's right behind the school," or "Go up to where the ice-house used to be and turn right."

Lost River School was located near Pecan Grove a residential area most folks just called The Grove. The trees had been planted by George Washington Stubbs' son, George Freeman Stubbs. Just across the street from the high school, was Moon's Diner. It was owned by Gibby Moon and her mother and was famous for Gibby's hamburgers and Granny's homemade pies. For the kids, Gibby made sure the juke box was well stocked with all the latest records by Frankie Laine, Vaughn Monroe, Hank Williams, Ray Charles, Peggy Lee, Doris Day and Patsy Cline.

Newer houses were built in The Grove, older homes were scattered around town. Dr. Nichols owned an old house and although he maintained an office there, he made no effort to tame the yard. The house was almost hidden by oak trees, Spanish moss and head-high azalea bushes. According to the stories, the old house had once been part of the Underground Railroad, a way station for slaves headed north.

Lost River was a God-fearing community. Baptist, Methodist, Episcopalian and Catholic churches occupied four adjacent corners, close enough for the members to keep an eye on one another. Each church had a ladies' group that more or less ran things. Florence Cumberland was president of the Episcopal Church Women and she was convinced it was her *duty* to set an example of style and decorum.

Isabella Conti headed up the Catholic Women's Group. She was from one of the oldest families in the county. Trudy Latham was president of the United Methodist Women's group. She was also one of the few women in town who worked fulltime. Mildred Leland was head of the Baptist Women's Missionary Union. Her husband owned the local funeral home and Mildred supplied flowers from her garden for all burials; as well as weddings, graduations, parties and the occasional I'm-sorry-please-forgive-me bouquet.

Generally speaking, women only worked outside the home if they had to. If a husband died or couldn't take care of his family, then it was acceptable for a woman to go to work. In Trudy's case, she took over the Do-or-Dye Hair Salon from her mother when she and Sheriff Latham moved to town. She offered the latest styles and the latest gossip which came at no extra charge.

The first store built downtown was Tony Conti's grocery. Vincent Conti owned the general store across the street which stocked everything from plows to hair ribbons. Salvador Conti owned the Ford dealership north of town on Jefferson.

In contrast to the wives-don't-work rule, Sicilian wives always worked in the family business. Sophia managed the inventory at the grocery store. Isabella was in charge of displays at the general store and Nina kept books at the Ford dealership.

Every small town worthy of the name boasted a weekly newspaper. Leon Kirkland owned the Print Shop, home of the *Lost River Herald.* He always wore a felt hat with a pencil stuck in the band and smoked a cigar like Adolphe Menjou in "Front Page."

Curtis Leland owned the Funeral Home which provided services for the whole county. He was a large jovial man which didn't exactly match with his profession. However, when he put on his black funeral suit, he also put on his funeral manners and his funeral voice which he had taken great pains to cultivate.

The town's largest employer was Stubbs Sawmill and Lumber Yard which covered several acres south of the Georgia Central Railroad tracks. As a descendent of one of the original founding families, Zach Stubbs carried himself with the resignation of a man who had made peace with his destiny.

On the other side of town, was the Gas and Grill, the center of Lost River social life. It was owned by Sheriff Latham. It started as a big, rambling old house that had been empty for a number of years.

When J.W. bought the property, he added a Quonset hut garage and an orange Gulf gas pump selling Ethyl No-Nox. Then he remodeled the house and added a lunch counter and truck-stop items. Junior Ottley, in his blue uniform, pumped gas, cleaned windshields, checked under the hood and made repairs. He was a natural mechanic, but his real talent was finding parts during and after the war when parts were scarce. He was a Grade A, Number One scrounger.

Percy Barns was the short-order cook at the G&G lunch counter. Between him and Junior, the G&G more or less ran itself.

Then Ethyl Williams moved to town and J.W. hired her. It had always been his idea to hire a proper cook, expand the kitchen and convert the unused room behind it to a white-cloth restaurant and bar. He called it the Backroom. As the amenities expanded, so did the name until the establishment finely became The Good Gulf Gas and Grill Truck Stop Lunch Counter Fine Dining Restaurant Bar and Garage. Locals just called it the Gas and Grill.

J. W. offered Ethyl the rooms upstairs and gave her a free hand to decorate as she saw fit. She had worked at the Palmer House in Chicago and she decided to add a little class to the G&G. She and Junior managed to locate a 15-foot slab of marble from Tate, Georgia, for the bar. She displayed the liquor bottles behind the bar in front of a mirror and added crystal glasses—which Junior also located—on glass shelves. Junior also a found a second-hand chandelier to hang in the middle of the room.

Meanwhile, Ethyl bought a remnant of red velvet at Conti's General Store and got Morris Fullerton, the local handyman, to upholster the bar stools. "Not quite as elegant at the Palmer House bar, but damn close," she said as she admired their handiwork. The Backroom was the only fancy restaurant in the county. Once she got the bar and restaurant squared away, she moved on to the big empty room at the back of the building.

In one corner, she discovered a battered old upright piano and a couple of round banquet tables that had seen better days. She called Junior with a wish list that included a copious supply of green felt and several dozen sturdy wooden chairs with arms. With Morris's help the old tables got a new look and a new purpose.

"Sorry I couldn't find chairs with cushions," Junior said.

Ethyl laughed. "No problem. We'll call this the Back Backroom. Booze available for sale, cardplayers welcome, bring your own cushion." In addition to regular card games, Ethyl planned to host a high-stakes, secret poker game once a month. The idea caught on and the illegal game became well-known to gamblers throughout southwest Georgia and beyond. After Ethyl took over, business at the Gas and Grill picked up considerably.

Sometimes late at night when the place was closed and all the lights were out, Ethyl sat down at the old piano in the Back Backroom and played jazz. It was her secret, or so she thought.

It might not have been Chicago, or Atlanta or even Macon, but despite what the boys thought, Lost River had all the excitement anybody needed without the headaches of a big city…if you knew the right people and you knew where to look.

Story #2, J.W. (Chicago, circa 1929)

J.W. Latham was not a native of Lost River. In fact, he was a Yankee, born and raised in Blue Island, a suburb of Chicago. Like his father, uncles and brothers, he joined the police force. With only three months training, he hit the streets just in time for the St. Valentine's Day Massacre of 1929.

Gangsters, the Mafia, speakeasies, prohibition, tommy guns and bootlegging were the stuff of every Chicago schoolboy's education. Teachers talked about ancient wars, but the bloody rivalry between Bugs Moran and his Irish North Siders and Al Capone and his Italian South Side mob was much more interesting. Something illegal was always going on.

On that day in mid-February, the call came in a little past 10:30 a.m. Typical gray day, 18 degrees and snowing. J.W. and several other officers drove over to North Clark Street. When they walked into the Lincoln Park garage, they saw seven bodies from Moran's mob slumped against the wall. They had been shot with Thompson submachine guns and there was blood everywhere. Even in the cold air, the sharp metallic smell almost made J.W. toss his cookies, but he was determined not to embarrass himself in front of everyone.

J.W. hated the cold, but at least he had a job and a way to support his family, not like half the population of Chicago who were out of work. He shuddered when he saw men huddled in slow-moving lines waiting for food, but they were as much a part of the city as State Street or the Tribune Tower.

Unemployment wasn't a problem for the criminal element. Local police and federal agents tripped over one another trying to catch Al Capone, but the man was slick as bacon grease, nothing stuck to him. He held court at the Metropole Hotel and attended the opera as if he were just another successful business man.

Eventually his luck ran out and the Feds finally managed to convict him of tax evasion. He was sentenced to 11 years in federal prison, fined $50,000 and had to pay $30,000 in court costs. Whoever said crime doesn't pay obviously didn't know how things were done in Chicago.

Gangsters weren't the only force in the city, fire played a part too. The Great Chicago fire of 1871 killed 300 people and left 100,000 others homeless. The brand-new Palmer House hotel burned, but Potter Palmer rebuilt it in no time.

Less than 50 years later, the 1910 Union Stock Yard fire killed 21 firemen and three civilians. Still the city survived and grew. J.W. agreed with Carl Sandburg who said, Chicago was a "Stormy, husky, brawling, City of Big Shoulders."

Hollywood had movie stars; Chicago had handsome gangsters like John Dillinger. His spree of bank robberies and escapes put him on top of the FBI's Most Wanted List. The newspapers called him Jackrabbit because, although folks all over the city reported seeing him, the police never seemed to know where he was. Then their luck changed.

On a hot July night with the temperature topping out at 100 degrees, the police got a tip. Dillinger was planning to go to a movie at the Biograph Theatre, whose main attraction was that it was "Cooled by Refrigeration."

When Dillinger left the theatre, J.W. and about 20 other law-enforcement officers were waiting for him. Dillinger ran down an alley in a hail of bullets. Nobody knew who fired the fatal shot. J.W. secretly hoped it wasn't him. The scene was gruesome and once again there was the smell of blood.

The chaos never seemed to end. A couple of years later, five Chicago-area steel mills shut down and 22,000 workers were locked out. Ten demonstrators were killed and 60 were injured. J.W. was shot in the shoulder. It felt like someone rammed a hot poker through his body. Cops all knew they ran the risk of getting shot, but the police manual didn't mention how painful it was.

Despite everything, J.W. loved the city. As black musicians moved north from New Orleans, they brought Dixieland jazz with them and J.W. often went to Club DeLisa or one of the smaller clubs on the South Side to listen. Occasionally he made it to the Green Mill—Capone's favorite club—on the North Side to listen to Chicago jazz.

The straw that finally broke the camel's back was when J.W. killed a young man. It started out as a domestic dispute that spilled out into the street where a crowd gathered. When the man living in the apartment charged out waving a gun, it momentarily caught everyone by surprise. The police reacted quickly. J.W. fired at the man, but the bullet ricocheted off a lamp post and hit a curious teenager standing in the crowd of onlookers.

J.W. would never forget the shocked look on the young man's face or how quickly the blood soaked through the front of his white shirt. J.W. tried to help, but the boy died in his arms. Back at headquarters, he filed a report, but he never told his family what had happened. For five years J.W. sent money each month to the boy's mother.

By the time J.W.'s second son was born, he had had enough. His wife had family in Georgia and she promised him if they moved to Lost River, it was unlikely he would ever see another gangster, the chances of getting shot were slight and best of all, he would never have to shovel snow again. They left the next week.

The only thing J.W. brought with him was his love for jazz. Sometimes late at night after all the customers were gone, he would sneak into the Back Backroom, sit in the dark and listen to Ethyl play jazz. It was a long time before she realized he was there and then it became their secret.

The Georges

The old folks in Lost River referred to the family as "The Georges." The original settler was George Washington Stubbs, who came to the New World looking for better farm land than the sandy soils of Breckland, England. Next came George Freeman, George Dunbar, George Zachary and eventually George Henry. Going all the way back to GW, the Stubbs men worked the land.

George Washington Stubbs bought the first parcel of land from the Creeks, built a frame house and managed to cut enough timber and do enough farming to support his family. Rather than just farming, he saw the family's future in trees. His son, George Freeman bought more land and planted 100 pine trees and 50 pecan trees which eventually became The Grove, Lost River's first subdivision.

Twenty years later, George Dunbar began to harvest the pine trees and planted acres more. The family continued to buy land and plant trees throughout the generations. George Dunbar opened Stubbs Sawmill and Lumber Yard and eventually willed it to his son George Zachary.

As a kid, Zach enjoyed working in the woods with his father. He was tall for his age and was proud that at 12 he was doing a man's job. He wasn't strong enough to manage the saws or do the heavy lifting, but he could do what was needed to free up the rest of the crew.

Zach and his dad had a morning routine back then. Zach dragged himself out of bed and stumbled into the kitchen. Dunbar, of course, was already up sitting at the big, oilcloth-covered table, finishing his coffee and smoking his first cigarette of the day. "Get a move on, Boy, we've got work to do." Zach poured himself a glass of milk and crammed food into his mouth. He knew better than to keep his father waiting too long.

Zach grabbed their lunch boxes and climbed into the driver's seat of the old pickup truck they used to haul logs. Driving to and from the logging site was his favorite part of the day. He loved the forest and the smell of fresh sawdust, but his secret love was cars. He drew them on everything. The first time his dad paid him for a week's work, Zach ordered a subscription to *Popular Mechanics*. He eagerly read each issue cover to cover. While his classmates were diagraming sentences, Zach was diagraming cars: round ones, sleek ones, three-wheel ones, cars with wings, cars with fins, cars with no windows and cars with nothing but windows. Wisely, he kept his drawings hidden away.

He was about 13 when he saw a picture of the Duesenberg Carol Lombard gave Clark Gable. That did it. From that day forward, Zach was determined to design cars for a living. It wasn't until he was a senior in high school and started talking about going to Georgia Tech and majoring in automotive engineering that Zach came face to face with reality. Dunbar made it clear that Stubbs men did not design cars. They were in the lumber business, no if's, and's or but's about it.

It was a bitter pill to swallow, but Zach knew there was no use chasing that dream. He moped around the house for two or three days firmly convinced his life was over. Then MaryBeth Hamilton came to sit with him in the lunch room and he decided that maybe he could survive after all. He just had to shift gears.

Instead of designing cars, he started to dream about owning the fanciest car in town. No, in the state, maybe even the whole United States. He would drive around with MaryBeth by his side. In the course of high school and then college, car models changed and so did the identity of the girl beside him. But his dream of owning a fancy car never wavered. He started saving his money. Another thing Dunbar made clear to his son was that in the Stubbs family, "If you can't pay cash for whatever you buy, you don't need to buy it."

Zach saved his money, but life kept getting in the way. When he graduated from college, he was ready, but instead of a new car, he got a wife. Then there was a house and a son, Hank. Time went by and again he thought he was ready to make his move. Then his father had a heart attack and suddenly Zach found himself the President of Stubbs Sawmill with lots of new responsibilities and no time for fancy cars.

And then the war happened and Detroit stopped making cars for the duration. Zach just couldn't seem to catch a break. But he didn't give up. He drove to Atlanta in his old Ford and went to the Oldsmobile dealership where he put his name on the list for a new car after the war. No more Fords for him.

Finally, his patience paid off. The war ended, Detroit went back to making cars and Zach Stubbs got a call. His car was ready for him to pick up. He took the Greyhound bus to Atlanta, took a cab to the Oldsmobile dealership and there in the middle of the showroom floor sat his dream car! A four-door, 1949 Oldsmobile Rocket 88, four-speed Hydramatic with white walls, a deluxe trim package with lots of chrome and *a clock*. On top of that, Zach shelled out an extra $100 for a radio! The Rocket was cream-colored just like the Duesenberg. It brought tears to his eyes.

Zach could hardly believe that he'd been waiting for that car since he was 15 years old, the same age as his son Hank. He had fantasized about the car so long that actually being able to sit in it, smell the new-car scent and run his hands over the leather seats was almost more than he could handle. Almost, but not quite.

As he drove his dream car home to Lost River, Zach felt like Clark Gable cruising the California coast road with Carol Lombard by his side.

Joy Ride

It was a bleak winter Friday night in Lost River and without a football game scheduled, there was nothing to do. Hank and Sonny sprawled on the old couch in the Stubbs' den. The boys were too bored to move. For want of *something* to talk about, Hank said, "My dad just got a new car. He's been waiting for it since the war started and they stopped making new cars."

"What'd he get?"

"An Oldsmobile Rocket 88. The car's got an automatic transmission and I'm telling you he's in love with that car. He washes it off every morning before he leaves for work. He won't even let my mom drive it."

As if on cue, Mr. Stubbs pulled into the driveway. He sat for a minute breathing in the smell of luxury. When he got out, he ran his hands over the shiny surface of the car and gave it an affectionate pat before he walked into the house.

"Evenin' boys. What do you think of my new car, Sonny?"

"It's a beaut, Sir. How long have you had it?"

"Less than a month. It's still got that new-car smell. The salesman said it'd do 97, but I bet it'll do 100 easy. They don't call it a rocket for nothing, you know." Mr. Stubbs chuckled. He sounded more like a 15-year-old schoolboy than the president of Stubbs Sawmill. "You boys doing all right?"

"Yes Sir," Hank answered.

"Well, I'll leave you to it. It's been a tough week and I'm beat. Think I'll turn in early. Y'all don't stay up too late now."

As they sat in the growing darkness, one thought began to form in the mind of both boys. Nothing specific yet, just bits and pieces. Without a clear purpose in mind, Hank called Matt Blalock, his other best friend, and told him to come over. When he hung up the phone, he noticed Sonny standing at the window studying the car.

Driving the car was, of course, off limits, but just sitting in it couldn't hurt anything. Simultaneously the boys opened the door, walked out and got in the front seat. Hank slipped behind the wheel. Sonny rode shotgun. Very quietly they closed the doors. "Your dad was right," Sonny said. "Nothing smells as good as a new car right off the showroom floor." It was intoxicating and little by little, their Friday night began to have possibilities.

The whole town all but disappeared by 9:30. There might be a light on here and there, but most folks had gone to bed or were sitting in their living rooms listening to the radio. A simple "Mom, I'm going over to Hank's," was enough to set a boy free for a couple of hours.

Hank hadn't told Matt what to expect, so when he saw his friends sitting in the car, he parked his bike and hopped in the back seat. "What's up guys?"

"Oh nothing," Hank said. "We're just trying out my dad's new car. Pretty sharp, huh?"

Matt had to agree. Most of the folks in Lost River were driving the same old cars they had before the war, so having a chance to sit in a brand new one was almost a religious experience. For the next half hour, the boys tossed around words like "horse power, torque, drag coefficient and drive train" like they knew what they were talking about. It didn't take much imagination to see themselves gliding through town waving to the girls or flying down the back roads.

"You gonna start her up?" The thought had briefly passed through Hank's mind, but as might be expected, it took up residence in Sonny's brain. He wasn't one to pass up an adventure. Matt was the quieter one. He usually just watched, waited and then stepped in when things got out of hand.

"That'd make too much noise," but even as he said it, Hank's fingers were itching to turn the key just waiting there in the ignition.

Rather than let a good idea slip through his fingers, Sonny made a harmless suggestion. "We could just pretend. You could put it in neutral and back down the driveway…"

In almost every important event in life, there is a turning point. A chance to be prudent. A chance to back away from danger. Most of the time it goes unheeded, especially when there are friends on hand to offer help and encouragement.

Hank took a deep breath, eased the car into neutral, let off the hand break and very, very carefully backed down the driveway into the street. The boys sat up a little taller, just in case someone drove by and saw them.

Matt couldn't help but point out the obvious. "Hank, you do realize you're gonna have to start it up to drive back up the driveway, don't you?"

"Oh yeah, I hadn't thought about that."

Sonny waited. Better to let Hank figure things out on his own.

"I guess it couldn't hurt to start it up and let it idle a while, just to see what it sounds like." Hank thought he meant it, but once he turned the key and the Rocket sprang to life, there was no turning back. A bad idea multiplied by three can sometimes feel like a really good idea.

Hank had been driving the family's old Ford since he was 12. "I can do this, absolutely. Just around the block," Hank said to himself. He might as well have said it out loud, because that's what they were all thinking.

"Hold on, you guys," Matt said. "If this car is going anywhere, I'm not staying stuck in the back seat."

Sonny had seen that coming but there was no way he was giving up the window seat. He got out and Matt slid in to the middle of the front seat. Sonny reclaimed shot-gun and very carefully Hank put the car in gear and gave it a little gas. So far so good. However, around one block turned into around the neighborhood and that turned into around town. But the Rocket was not designed to sneak around backstreets, it was made for better things. It was made for the open road. It was made for speed.

Once again, the same thought seized all three boys and without saying anything, Hank surrendered to the siren song of the big V8 engine and headed toward the high school and the Lower Cochran Road. They all knew what that meant. A cold clear night, a bright moon, a straight road and a fast car, it was every teenage boy's fantasy come true. When they got to the final turn before the straightaway, Hank stopped.

"Doors shut?"

"Check."

"Radio on?"

"Check."

"Ready to roll?"

"Check."

"Matt since you're sitting in the middle, you watch the clock. My dad said it would get up to 60 in 13 seconds. Let's see if it will." Hank put the car in gear, took a firm grip on the steering wheel and floored the accelerator. They hit 60 in 12 seconds flat!

That did it. They had passed the point of no return. Hank tightened his grip on the wheel and kept his foot on the gas. He hadn't really planned to drive fast, but it was so easy he just kept going. The car was big and heavy, not like the rattle-trap Ford he was used to. The 88 was so smooth it hardly felt like the car was moving at all. In fact, the Rocket seemed to enjoy the ride as much as its passengers. Sixty-five, seventy, seventy-five...

Suddenly Matt reached over and turned up the radio. Patti Page's voice cut through the roar of the engine, "It's time to take the wheel, drive a Rocket Oldsmobile..."

Eighty, eighty-five. Hank was struggling to hold the wheel steady. Patti Page sang on, but what Hank heard was the little voice in his head. "Have you lost your mind!?!? The slightest movement at this speed will flip you over. You'll probably all be killed and if you survive, your dad will kill you."

Hank's knuckles were white and his arms were shaking. When they crested a hill, the road dropped out from under them. It was better than the roller coaster at the State Fair.

"Damn, this is great," Sonny yelled. "Reckon what it's gonna be like coming over the top of Superman Hill." It was the highest elevation in Bleckley County and every kid knew if you went fast enough, you could get airborne and fly just like Superman.

They were going at least 90 when they saw headlights coming from the opposite direction. They crested the hill and suddenly realized the on-coming car was crowding the center line. The Rocket was going so fast the pine trees on either side were just a green smear. The two cars whizzed by only inches apart. The other car swerved to avoid a collision and Hank got a glimpse of the ashen face of the young driver.

It all happened so fast, there was no time to think. Hank was afraid to touch the break or turn the wheel. He did at least take his foot off the gas. The next thing he knew the right-hand wheels were off the road and throwing up dirt and grass and weeds. The car finally rolled to a stop. Hank slumped over the steering wheel. Matt and Sonny slowly unfolded themselves. They stared straight ahead sucking air into their lungs. Finally, Hank asked, "Y'all OK?"

"I think I gotta change my shorts," Sonny said.

"Yeah, me too," Matt said. "I'm shaking all over."

"I'm too scared to shake," Hank said.

For some reason that struck them as funny. They sat in the car in the dark and laughed so hard they cried. Hank found a side road and turned around very slowly.

"You think we oughta check on the other car?" Matt asked.

"How're we gonna do that? At the rate he was going, he's probably in Florida by now," Sonny said.

Hank drove no more than15 miles an hour on the way home. They looked, but they didn't see any sign of a wreck. When they got to his house, Hank made sure to park exactly where his father had left the car.

Then they got busy cleaning up the evidence. They used the hose to wash the car and get the mud off the tires and the white sidewalls. Before Matt and Sonny left, they helped to clean the driveway and finally they put the tools away. "Matt, you OK?" Hank asked.

"I reckon, but every time I think about how close we came, I start to shake. I think I'll just walk my bike home."

"Hold up. I'll walk with you," Sonny said.

"You guys take it easy. I'll see you at Moon's tomorrow." Hank watched as his friends walked down the driveway. He made one final inspection before he tiptoed upstairs. He spent a long time in the shower trying to wash away the fear-sweat. When he got in bed and closed his eyes, all he saw was the stricken face of the other driver. Eventually, he fell asleep.

Spared

Moon's was the gathering place for Lost River teenagers. It was a converted railroad diner that sat on an abandoned spur across from the high school. Gibby, who owned the place, was pretty in a dramatic sort of way. She was tall and her eyes were black as midnight. Her hair was long and dark and she wore it braided and pinned up on top of her head like a crown.

Her voice was husky and no matter how busy the place got, Gibby's movements were always slow and deliberate. Nothing rattled her. There was a rumor that she kept a baseball bat behind the counter, but nobody had ever seen it.

It was a well-known fact that every boy in the county was in love with her because she made the best hamburgers east of the Mississippi. Her mother, Granny, made pies: pecan, coconut cream and peach. If you got in trouble, Moon's was the first place you went to get help.

Normally the diner was only open on week days from noon to 8:00 p.m. But the last Saturday of the month, Gibby opened for breakfast and made pancakes. As was their habit, all three boys were sitting in their favorite booth by 8:30. At first, they sat and listened to the gossip around them. "I don't hear anybody talking about an accident last night, so I guess the other guy made it OK," Sonny said.

"Yeah. I didn't see any sign of a wreck on the way home." Hank poured half a gallon of maple syrup on his stack of pancakes. "I'm telling you, I got scared all over again this morning when I got to thinking about it. Boy, we sure were lucky."

Matt looked worried. "Do you guys realize yesterday was Friday the 13th? We weren't lucky, we were *spared*. I think it was a sign from God."

"Whatcha mean?"

"You know, my mama's always saying Baptist stuff like that. Something'll happen and she'll say it's a sign that something else is gonna happen...or not. It's like a warning."

They were used to hearing stories about Prim Blalock's dire predictions and warnings. "Then we better straighten up and fly right 'cause I reckon we used up all God's grace out there on the highway last night."

Matt wouldn't let it go. "I can't stop wondering about the other guy. Hank, you think we oughta tell somebody?"

"No, no, no! There was no wreck, nobody got hurt, and thank goodness nobody saw us. Just leave it alone. If my dad ever finds out what we did, my life won't be worth a plug nickel. He'd never let me drive again. No sireebob!"

"What's the big deal? Nothing happened," Sonny said through a mouthful of pancake.

"What happened is that I took my dad's brand-new dream car *without his permission*—which he would not have given me if I'd asked—and I drove it. Fast! We can't tell anybody about this *ever*! I'm not kidding." They agreed and took an oath to remain silent.

***

While the boys were sitting at Moon's, Sheriff J.W. Latham was sitting in his office. Normally he didn't come in on Saturday morning because he knew he'd be on duty Saturday night, since it was pay day at the mill. He figured he'd get caught up on his paperwork. He should have known better.

The first interruption was Widow Mackie. J.W. could never figure that woman out. He knew her late husband had been a civil engineer in Atlanta and left her well provided for, but she always dressed like a field hand. Overalls that looked like they had been cut out of an old tarpaulin, rubber boots, a dingy undershirt sticking out of the sleeves of a faded denim work shirt and an old felt hat. She was hardly a picture of Southern gentility. But then, she wasn't Southern or genteel.

However, she *did* have her good qualities. Agnes Mackie believed in paying her way. When she came asking for a favor, she never came empty-handed. She walked into the office and handed J.W. a small bag holding warm apple strudel. According to her, it was just one of the things her ancestors back in Pennsylvania were famous for.

In her usual rapid-fire way, she started in. "Sheriff, I know you're busy so I'll get right to the point. I'm in the middle of a crisis. My boy, Warren Jr., is missing. He graduated from Georgia Tech two days ago and he's not home yet. Now that's not like him. He's very responsible. Been that way since he was a boy. Never left his toys out overnight, saved his allowance. Never gave his father and me a minute's trouble."

J.W. was paying more attention to the aroma of apples and cinnamon than he was to Agnes. "If he just graduated, don't you think he might be off celebrating with some of his friends?"

"No sir, I don't think so. You see, he doesn't drink, he doesn't smoke, and he is *not* one of those party boys. Would you please get in touch with the police in Atlanta and find out what's going on? I would be much obliged." Having stated her wishes, she left his office, got in her car and went home.

J.W. got a fresh cup of coffee, took a bite of apple strudel and went back to his paperwork. He had come to recognize Widow Mackie's concerns as just one more in a list of false alarms. Chances are young Warren was having some fun and would show up sooner or later.

Not five minutes after that, the phone rang. "Sheriff, I was bringing a load of logs in to the mill this morning and it looks like somebody ran off the Lower Cochran Road going pretty fast. All I could see from the road were some deep ruts headed back into the trees. Anyway, I thought you might wanta take a look."

So much for paperwork. J.W. grabbed his hat and headed out to his pickup. The truckdriver who called hadn't been very specific about the location so it took some time, but finally J.W. saw the tracks. He parked his pickup and tramped through the palmettoes and scrub brush until he found the car, a 1940 Ford coupe convertible. It had been a fine-looking car, but now the front end was completely destroyed and parts of the engine were sitting on what was left of the front seat. Oddly, there was no body. Without a body, he didn't have a name and without a name, how was he supposed to investigate?

Story #3, A-14 (Lost River 1933)

He never could figure out why folks thought having a name was so important. For a lot of years, he didn't have a name, just a number. He was A-14. Number 14, Cabin A on the boys' side. That's the way things worked at Saint Joseph's Home for the Mentally Ill. When a child was admitted, the nuns told them they were mentally deficient. Most of the kids didn't know what that meant, but they accepted it as a fact, because nuns never lie.

The sisters didn't consider the lie a sin because it was told for a good cause. After all, no real harm done. The truth was, it allowed Saint Joseph's to collect $2.75 a day for upkeep. That was the going price for crazies. Orphans were only worth $1.25.

In fact, very few of the children were mentally ill and some of the "orphans" actually had local families. When hard times came, families would drop off their kids and then when things got better, they'd come pick them up again. It was a system that worked for everyone.

"When I asked Sister Dominic what mentally deficient meant, she told me it meant I was dumb. She said my mamma had committed an awful sin and that's why I was simple-minded. She told me my mama left me on the doorstep because she didn't want to be bothered with a retarded kid. Sounded to me like she just didn't want me around. I didn't want to believe the Sister, so at first I waited for my mama to come and get me. Sister Dominic said if I didn't stop that, she was going to lock me in The Closet. That scared me enough to make me stop.

"We all worked hard and obeyed the nuns 'cause we didn't want to get locked in The Closet. It was a dark place, a bad place, a little room in a work shed out back. Freezing cold in the winter, scorching hot in the summer. You could scream, but nobody could hear you, and even if they did, everyone was too afraid of the nuns to come to your rescue.

"We had to follow the rules, eat everything on our plates—no matter how bad it was—learn our catechism, say our prayers, be quiet, keep everything neat and clean and never, never talk back to the sisters."

At full capacity, Saint Joe's held about 40 children. They were housed in two dorms in the big house, one for boys, one for girls and a number of cabins scattered around the grounds. Saint Joe's took all ages from babies to teenagers. When kids turned six, the nuns moved them from the dorms to one of the outlying cabins. Six was also the age when the kids were rented out to work. Girls as domestics, boys as farm workers to help planting or harvesting. Sometimes they worked for one of the merchants in town.

"Most of us couldn't remember much of anything but the orphanage. We were lucky. The kids who had families were always homesick. At first, they'd cry at night, but the nuns made them kneel down on hard rice and thank God they had a nice safe place to stay. They couldn't get up 'til they stopped crying."

A-14 stayed at Saint Joe's until a fire forced the church to shut it down. One night the water heater behind the kitchen blew up and started a fire. The timber was old and dry and the fire spread to the rest of the house in no time. The sisters got all the little children out of the big house. By the time the town's old fire truck got there, the wind had set the cabins on fire too.

The nuns padlocked the cabins at night. As the flames spread, the boys tried, but they couldn't open the doors. "I knew I had to do something, so I kicked out one of the window screens and the other boys did the same thing." The windows were only about three feet off the ground, so everyone managed to escape.

"Boys were forbidden to go over to the girls' side, but that night me and a couple of other boys went anyway. Their doors were padlocked too, so I told the girls to kick out the screens like we did."

Thanks to A-14 and his friends, everyone was saved. However, in less than two hours, the buildings were nothing but charred beams and piles of ashes. By the end of the next day, almost everyone was gone.

Sister Dominic rounded up all the nuns and any kids without families and told them they were being taken to a big orphanage in Macon. "She told me I was 16 so I was old enough to get by on my own. When I asked her what I was supposed to do, she just said God would provide."

As it turned out, it wasn't God, it was Sister Mary Joseph who provided. Everybody in town saw the fire and came over to get a closer look. She cornered Leon Kirkland and told him the fire wasn't the real story. The big story was the boys who had rescued all the kids in the cabins. "Those boys are real heroes, especially A-14. He was smart enough to kick out the screens and to get all the girls out too."

The next day A-14 and some of the boys and girls had their pictures on the front page of the Lost River Herald. *The story praised their quick thinking and bravery. In her experience, Sister Mary Joseph found that sometimes God needed a hand to get things done, so she explained to Leon that A-14 was being left behind.*

"You mean to tell me they're just gonna leave the boy here by himself!?" Mr. K. was outraged. "What the hell—excuse me, Sister—what are they thinking? That's just not right!"

Helen Kirkland was standing nearby and overheard the conversation. "Sister, you know our son Steve didn't make it home from the war. His room is just sitting there empty, maybe we could help."

"A-14 has worked with me in the shop from time to time and I could use some extra help on a regular basis," Leon said. "Don't worry, Sister. I'll pay him. It's important for a man to

feel like he's earning his way in life. Feller oughta always have some walkin' around money in his pocket."

When she told A-14 about the Kirkland's offer, Sister Mary Joseph hugged him and said, "Don't you ever let anyone tell you you're retarded or simple-minded. You are not!" Then she gave him a copy of the story from the front page. "You keep this with you to remind you how smart you are and how proud I am of you." She turned and walked away quickly before he could see the tears in her eyes.

A-14 settled into his new home with the Kirklands. Without being asked, he swept the print shop every night and every morning he swept the sidewalk out front. In fact, he started sweeping all the sidewalks nearby. After he locked up at night, he walked around testing all the doors downtown to make sure everybody was safe.

"At first I was sad because all my friends had been sent away. I was lonely too, 'cause I'd never slept in a room by myself. It took me a while to get used to having a room of my own. Mr. K. and his wife were good to me and the best part was, he gave me a name. He said A-14 was no kind of way to go through life, so he called me Inky and I've been Inky ever since."

The Search

The sheriff rounded up a couple of volunteers to help search the woods for the body. It was a cold, wet February morning when they parked on the Lower Cochran Road and hiked back into the woods. J.W. led the way to the car wedged headfirst into a pile of briars and brambles. The front end was accordion pleated against an ancient pine tree. The three men shook their heads as they surveyed the damage. "My God, that guy musta been flying to smash up a car this bad. Can't believe you didn't find a body."

One of the men crawled over the back of the car to take a closer look. "I found a couple of empty PBRs on the floor and an open pack of Camels."

"PBRs?" J.W. asked.

"Pabst Blue Ribbon cans. I'm guessing a young kid, fast car, drinking beer, nobody else on the road, he was probably trying to see how fast it would go. I'd guess 80 or 85 at least."

He pried the glove box open, took out the registration papers and handed them to the sheriff. Slowly J.W. unfolded the documents hoping the owner wasn't a local. The worst part of his job was delivering bad news to friends. "Mumford Gardner, 19. Lives on Powers Ferry Road in Atlanta."

"Yeah, I know that area north of downtown. Rich neighborhood. Well, at least now we have a name."

"You know, Sheriff, if he was going that fast, then the body might have been thrown a long way," the second volunteer suggested. "Maybe we're looking too close."

As it turned out, he was right. About 200 feet farther into the woods, J.W. stopped dead in his tracks. There was no mistaking that odor, he'd smelled it enough times in Chicago. Another 20 feet and they found the body partially hidden in a tangle of seedlings, briars and fallen leaves. The boy's face was bruised and badly swollen. He had a deep cut across his forehead and lots of dried blood on his face.

J.W. kept a stretcher in his pickup. It was a struggle to get the body untangled and loaded into the back of the truck. They covered the stretcher the best they could with an old blanket.

"I didn't recognize the name. Does he look familiar to y'all?" the sheriff asked.

None of the men knew the boy. "It's kinda hard to be sure though, with all the swelling, the bruises and the blood."

They took the body to Leland's Funeral Home. "Listen fellows, don't say anything about this to anybody until we get a positive ID," J.W. cautioned. "I'll notify his family when I get back to the office. I guess they'll have to come down here to identify him. Lord, I dread making that call."

When J.W. reached Mrs. Gardner, he tried to sound official and at the same time give the boy's mother some hope that the body might not be her son. She confirmed that their son did own a maroon Ford convertible. However, she insisted he was fishing with some friends at Indian Springs. They were staying at a cabin, but there wasn't a phone and she had no way to reach him. J.W. knew the area well. The Creek Indians believed the water from the springs had healing powers.

Mrs. Gardner didn't seem too worried. "His father and I will leave within the hour. We'll meet you at your office. No doubt there has been some terrible mistake. The sooner we clear this up, the better." She hung up before J.W. could say anything else.

He decided to use the time waiting for the Gardners to finish some of the paper work. He found what was left of Widow Mackie's strudel, got his third cup of coffee and settled down. Two hours later, the boy's family arrived in a long, black Lincoln. Mr. Gardner was a big man wearing a three-piece suit and a frown; about what J.W. expected. His wife was short, with gray hair curled tightly around her face. She was equally fashionably dressed. Neither of them seemed sad or worried. J.W. directed them to the funeral home.

Normally people coming to identify a body were hesitant, but not the Gardners. J.W. got the impression they were not hesitant about many things. Leland's was not set up for families to view bodies outside of a coffin, but Curtis Leland had done the best he could to be sensitive to the family. He cleaned the blood off the boy's face and covered the purple bruises. He arranged the body as naturally as possible and covered it with a sheet. Curtis slowly rolled the gurney into the room and turned back the cover so the parents could see the face. He and J.W. stood back to give them some privacy.

The couple looked at the body and Mr. Gardner said, "Just like I expected. This is not my son." There was no mistaking his attitude. He was put out that he had wasted his time to confirm something he already knew to be true.

His wife was only slightly more sympathetic. "I don't know who this poor boy is, but as my husband said, he is definitely not our son Mumford."

The sheriff could tell the Gardners were anxious to be on their way but he had a few more questions. "I'm glad this isn't your son, but he's somebody's son and I need to find out whose. Since he was driving your son's car, that makes him my best source of information. Please have him call me as soon as he gets back from fishing or as soon as he gets in touch with you."

They agreed and left in a hurry. The sheriff was frankly glad to see them go, but now he had a new problem, an unidentified body. J.W.'s stomach rumbled and he wondered if he was hungry or just annoyed. Either way, he decided to go by the G&G and grab a sandwich and a cup of coffee.

The minute he sat down at the counter, Ethyl handed him a cup of coffee and a piece of pecan pie. "I just ordered this from

Moon's, but you look like you need it more than me. Before he realized it, he was telling her all his problems. During her years working at the Palmer House bar in Chicago, she had learned to be a good listener. "At first, I had a name, but I didn't have a body. Now I have a body and a name, but they don't match."

Story #4, Lucille (Chicago 1945)

Lucille was hired to wash dishes in the kitchen of the Empire Dining Room at the Palmer House in Chicago. The pay wasn't too bad, but she hated the job. Scrape, rinse, wash, disinfect, rinse again, dry, shelve. Over and over with no end in sight. She had about worked up the courage to leave, when the assistant bartender quit and she was offered his job.

That was not only a solution to her problem, it was a great opportunity. She would now work behind the elegant bar in the main lobby with dark wood paneling, crystal chandeliers, red velvet bar chairs and marble-topped tables. The Palmer House was first class all the way.

It was definitely a sweet job. No more drab uniforms for her. The bartender wore a tux. Lucille wore black slacks with a satin stripe down the side, a starched white shirt with a black bow tie and a short black jacket with satin lapels.

Lucille knew her light skin worked in her favor. But she had a problem. Having frizzy hair might have been all right for washing dishes, but working up front demanded something more sophisticated. She knew she could never look like Lana Turner, but with the help of Madam Walker's pomade, she smoothed her hair back and tucked a flower over her ear like Billie Holiday. That worked.

Instead of looking at dirty dishes, she watched all the high-society guests and the entertainers who came to perform at the Empire Room. Not just people like Sinatra and Garland, but her people: Fitzgerald, Belafonte and her all-time favorite, Louis Armstrong.

Lucille stocked the bar, cut the garnishes, prepared the mixers and washed glasses. The one thing she hated was taking out the garbage. The metal cans were heavy and the alley was long, dark and narrow. In contrast to the glitz and glamor of the lobby, all the restaurants and night clubs along State Street and Monroe dumped their garbage in the same place. The ground was slick with grease and the air smelled like rotting meat.

The worst part was trying to lift the heavy metal can and pour the garbage into the bin. Lucille was strong, but still some garbage always ended up on her shoes. Damn. Lucille spent good money on shoes. Sturdy shoes that fit. She was determined not to end up like the old colored women who shuffled along walking on the backs of their shoes.

"One of these days I'm gonna have my own bar, maybe even a fancy restaurant and then I'm gonna hire somebody else to take out the damn garbage." She envied her boyfriend Leroy because he had a trade and a good job working in the press

room at the Chicago Defender. *It was the largest weekly black newspaper in the city. In fact, it had readers all across the country because Pullman car porters smuggled it to customers all along their routes.* The Defender *went everywhere. Folks knew "if it wasn't in the* Defender, *it didn't happen."*

Leroy was a good man. He was a quick study and a whiz at math. On top of that he was a natural mechanic. He joined the Defender *as an apprentice doing cleaning and upkeep of the huge presses. Eventually he worked his way up to pressman and on the first day of his new job, one of the old hands showed him how to take a page of yesterday's newspaper and fold it into a square pressman's hat. Not only did it provide protection from the ink, it was a symbol of pride. It set pressmen apart from everybody else working for the paper. The head pressman was the only man who could actually stop the presses—not even the owners could do that.*

Leroy breathed in the smell of ink. It was kind of a combination of cedar, musk, and some unknown spice that hung in the air. He loved the power of the big presses with the river of paper flying along at 300 feet per minute. Raw newsprint came off the huge rolls at one end and a newspaper came out the other end, printed, folded and trimmed. As soon as the papers came hot off the presses, they went to the newsboys waiting on the loading dock. The boys filled their canvas bags and hit the streets hawking the latest headlines. Being a pressman was a good job and it paid well. Leroy liked fancy clothes and he made sure when he and Lucille went dancing at the Club DeLisa, they both looked sharp.

The club dominated State Street on the South Side. Unlike the Palmer House, it was a black and tan club, so everybody came to listen to jazz, blues, swing and soul music. And they came to dance! Mostly the black folks danced and the white folks just watched.

There were no signs saying "Black Only" or "White Only," but there were some unwritten rules. Basically, you danced with your own kind. Lucille and her friends laughed at that. Why would any of them want to dance with a white guy when everybody knew white men got no rhythm.

But there is always an exception. Enter Darnell Hines. He was an ordinary looking white man, a little taller than average, blond hair cut short. He came in wearing a suit—like all the other men—but very quickly he was down to his white shirt, fancy tie and suspenders. Nothing unusual there, but on the dance floor, that white man had moves!

People stopped dancing to watch, but it was soon clear that none of the girls at his table could keep up with him. Darnell had been watching Lucille and very politely he approached their table and asked Leroy if it would be all right if he asked Lucille to dance.

"Sure, if that's what she wants," Leroy said. Lucille had no doubt she could keep up, so they walked onto the floor. The band played "Jump, Jive and Wail" and Darnell cut loose. Lucille held her own and folks crowded around to watch. Jitterbug and swing were all right, but when the band played a

tango, and Darnell pulled Lucille close to him, Leroy had had enough.

At first people thought Leroy was just trying to cut in, but it quickly turned ugly. Punches were thrown, blood was shed. Without thinking, Leroy grabbed a champagne bottle from a nearby table and swung it at Darnel. The man went down and didn't move.

At that moment, Lucille realized she had just witnessed the one thing no black woman ever wants to see, her man standing over the body of a white man.

One of the men with Leroy bent over to check out the damage. "He ain't dead, but you don't wanta be here when the cops come."

No argument there. Lucille and Leroy ran out of the club, stopped by their apartment to pick up some clothes and the money they kept in a coffee can. Then they left Chicago.

They rode buses and hitched rides when they could to save money. One morning Lucille woke up and Leroy was gone. He left half of the money and a note. "You didn't do nothing, so there's no need for you to be on the run. I can travel faster by myself. Take care of yourself. Love, Leroy."

Because both of them had heard stories about coloreds traveling in the South, they borrowed the Green Book from Leroy's brother. The real name was The Negro Motorist Green Book Compendium. *It was a list of establishments in the South where they could safely eat, sleep, get a car repaired and shop.*

Recommended accommodations varied from hotels to families who were willing to rent out a room for a night or two for a small fee. That's how Lucille and Leroy ended up on the outskirts of Lost River. When Lucille asked about breakfast, her hostess pointed down the road to Moon's. Lucille took her suitcase and walked over to what looked like a railroad dining car. She was surprised to see a white woman dumping garbage. Cautiously Lucille asked, "Excuse me, but can I get some breakfast here?"

Gibby looked at the young woman standing in front of her. Simple dress, but quality shoes. Gibby appreciated good shoes. "Don't serve breakfast but one Saturday a month," she said, "but I can make you a burger. Best burgers east of the Mississippi. Everybody says so. Come on in."

The room was empty and Lucille sat at the counter. The burger was the best she'd ever tasted and she told the woman so. "Listen, I need a job. Is there anything I can do around here?"

"What do you know how to do?" Gibby asked.

"I'm a bartender..."

"We don't serve liquor here, but I might be able to help you out. I'm going over to the Gas and Grill, so I'll give you a ride. Ask for J.W. Latham and tell him Gibby sent you. He's the sheriff, and he owns the place."

Lucille wasn't sure how things worked down South, but she was pretty sure she didn't want to get mixed up with any sheriff. On the other hand, she didn't have much choice.

When they got there, J.W. was standing out front. "This girl is looking for a job. I thought maybe you could help her," Gibby said.

J.W. invited Lucille inside. "Where're you from?" he asked and before she could stop herself, she said, "Chicago."

"Me too. Gibby says you need a job, what do you do?"

"I was assistant bartender at the Lobby Bar at the Palmer House."

"Fancy place. I've been meaning to fix this place up, maybe open a restaurant, get a cook and hire a regular bartender. You reckon you could handle running a restaurant and being the bartender all at the same time?"

Lucille smiled, "Yes Sir."

"You got a place to stay?"

"No Sir."

"Well, you'll probably be working late most nights. There's a bedroom upstairs and a bathroom at the end of the hall. Comes with the job if you decide to take it. I can't pay you what you were making at the Palmer House, but I reckon we can work something out. By the way, what's your name?"

Lucille suddenly realized she had already told this law man more about her business than she should have. She looked through the plate glass window at the gas pump outside and a sign caught her eye. "Gulf No-Nox Ethyl, stops knocks."

"Ethyl," she said. "My name is Ethyl Williams."

Mistaken Identity

While the sheriff was eating pecan pie at the G&G, Hank and his friends were eating burgers at Moon's. The boys had agreed not to tell anyone what they'd seen Friday night and J.W. had cautioned the volunteers not to discuss the accident, but the word got out anyway and now everybody was talking about what happened and filling in the parts they didn't know with gossip. Somehow that didn't seem right.

Hank halfway wished his father had caught them so he could come clean about that night, but as far as they could tell, they had gotten away with it. Gradually he realized that getting away with it was not the same thing as being innocent or being forgiven.

Sonny couldn't understand why Hank was making a mountain out of a molehill. It wasn't like they had stolen the car or wrecked it. They just drove it, maybe a little too fast, but nobody got hurt. What was the big deal?

Matt, of course, was still talking about being *spared* and following his mother's example, he started seeing signs everywhere. His dad had mentioned cars at his Wednesday night prayer meeting and Matt took that as a sign they should confess. On the other hand, it rained the next day and he took that as a sign they should keep quiet. Matt's signs didn't always make a lot of sense.

It didn't help matters any that not only was the accident the main topic of conversation all over town, but Leon Kirkland had made it the front-page story in the *Lost River Herald.* He had taken pictures of the tire tracks that plowed through the mud and the underbrush and added a couple of shots of the smashed-up car. A major wreck with an unknown victim broke the tedium of talking about the weather and politics, and folks intended to chew on it 'til all the flavor was gone.

In the midst of everything else that was going on, Widow Mackie called the sheriff to see if he had made any progress in finding Warren Jr. He assured her he was working on it, but had nothing to report at the moment.

Finally, he got a call from the Gardner's son, Mumford. Yes, he drove a 1940 maroon Ford coupe convertible. No, he didn't have the car with him. The sheriff kept asking questions until the story started to come together.

"We were all at a fraternity party here in Atlanta and I decided to spend the night with…well, I decided to stay with a friend. Skeeter asked if he could borrow my car to go home. I knew he'd been drinking, but I figured it would be OK since we were only a couple of miles from campus. I had no idea "home" meant driving half way down to Florida. What did you say the name of that little town was?"

"Lost River and we're not that far from Atlanta. Who exactly is Skeeter? Is that his real name?" As soon as he asked, J.W. wished he hadn't.

"No, it's Mack. Ahh Mackie, Warren Mackie."

And there it was, the name J.W. had dreaded hearing. Like gears meshing, all the pieces fit seamlessly into place. Fraternity party, drinking, driving, recklessness and senseless loss. The boy in the car was Warren Jr. and J.W. now had to tell Widow Mackie the truth. Well, part of the truth. He could see no reason to tell her about the alcohol. She'd lost a son, no need to destroy her image of who she thought her son was.

Small towns can be notoriously small minded, but they can also be incredibly compassionate. When the women of Lost River heard Widow Mackie's only son had been killed, the community came to her rescue. There was hardly a woman in town who hadn't lost a child, a father, a husband or a brother. Each death left a hole in somebody's heart.

Since Widow Mackie was now alone, it was hardly necessary to bring food, but they brought their casseroles anyway and they brought something more important. They brought their stories. They brought their companionship. They brought their time. They brought their gentle touches and their soft voices.

They had all known Warren Jr. since he was a baby, actually way before he was born. It was common knowledge that Agnes and Warren Senior had wanted children. The problem wasn't that Agnes couldn't get pregnant; she just couldn't carry a baby to term. After the third miscarriage, she learned not to tell anyone she was pregnant. She was five months along before she allowed herself to believe it might actually work this time. Everyone celebrated when she gave birth to a healthy, seven-pound boy. The town watched him grow up and they relived those memories with Agnes. Some folks thought that might be hurtful, but those who had been through a death, knew how important it was to hear people talk about the loved one. It kept them alive just a little while longer.

Confession is Good for The Soul

Having a name to go with the face of the other driver, made Hank, Sonny and Matt rethink their decision to remain silent. Warren Jr. was a school generation ahead of them. He had gone off to college when they were still in grammar school, so they didn't know him personally, but in a way, they knew him better than anyone else.

They were the last people to see Warren Jr. alive. Each of them had a memory of the terrified look on his face as the two cars flew past each other. They sat longer than usual at Moon's.

Finally, Matt put his burger down, "We gotta tell somebody. If that truckdriver saw the tracks, then how do we know somebody else didn't see them and know we were out there too?" They all agreed, but they were not exactly sure how to go about it. In the time-honored tradition of teen-age boys, they decided to put it off a while. They turned their attention to eating, but they were careful to avoid eye contact. When the food was all gone, they realized they had to do something.

They had huddled in the booth so long, it got Gibby's attention. She was used to rowdy conversation, but silence made her curious. Time to see what was going on. "How's it going, boys?"

Their stricken faces told her something was wrong, something more serious than the usual teenage trauma. In her quiet, deliberate way, she pulled up a chair and sat down. "Why don't y'all tell me what's bothering you, maybe I can help."

They looked at one another, but nobody was willing to be the first one to speak up. Finally, Hank said, "You know my dad got a new car, a Rocket 88?"

Gibby nodded, everybody in town knew that, although she couldn't see where the story was headed.

The boys traded off telling the story a little at a time. "Well, Friday night we were hanging around with nothing to do…

"and we sorta drove the car…"

"without asking permission…"

and we went kinda fast."

The light was beginning to dawn.

"We were driving out on the edge of town…"

"on the Lower Cochran Road…."

Gibby was almost afraid to hear the rest of the story. But knowing how hard it was to get them to open up, she sat quietly and gave them her undivided attention.

"You heard about the wreck out there?"

"The one where Warren Jr. was killed?"

Gibby nodded.

"Well, we saw it. I mean we didn't actually see the wreck…"

"…but we saw the car go by and he was going really fast."

"We both were."

Sonny took the lead. "He swerved to miss us and then I guess he kinda lost control and went off the road. It took us a couple of miles to slow down and we had to find a side road so we could turn around. That's when we headed back to town."

Hank helped him out. "But we didn't see any sign of a wreck on the way back to town. We didn't know anything had happened until…later."

"You reckon we oughta tell somebody what we know?" Matt asked. "Even though we don't really know anything," he quickly added.

In her usual unhurried way, Gibby took time to consider the situation. "None of your folks know anything about this?"

"No," Matt answered. "We took an oath not to tell. But now we're not so sure that was a good idea."

"Well, Hank, since it was your dad's car and you were driving, I think you better go home and talk to him. And you two," Gibby looked at Sonny and Matt, "don't think you're getting off scot free. You go with Hank to talk to Mr. Stubbs. Then go home and talk to your parents."

"Do we have to tell the sheriff we were there?" Matt asked.

"Tell your parents first and let them decide what to do after that. And do it now! You've been sitting on this information too long already." They hesitated. Gibby never raised her voice. She didn't have to. "Now means right now. *Go*."

They went.

When he came home from work, Zach Stubbs was more than a little surprised to find the three boys sitting in his living room. Rather than their usual energetic selves, they sat entirely still, looking like three deflated balloons. Apparently, they had already talked to his wife, Eden.

"Honey, the boys have something to tell us. They said it was serious and insisted we both be here." Zach sat down cautiously and Eden perched on the arm of his chair. They waited.

Hank realized there was no escape and it was up to him to do most of the talking. As the story started to unfold, the other boys backed him up from time to time.

Neither of the adults spoke when the story ended. Eden reached out to take Zach's hand. Since the boys had directed most of the confession to him, she waited for him to speak first.

Zach forced himself to go slow and take time to analyze the situation. On the one hand, they hadn't done anything illegal or seriously wrong. On the other hand, the possibilities for disaster were overwhelming. He realized the boys were upset and they had come clean, even if it had taken a while. On other the other hand, he could not believe his son had done something so dangerous and just plain stupid! He was having a hard time controlling his temper. But somewhere in the back of his mind, he realized just a matter of inches separated him from the grief Widow Mackie was going through.

"You boys go home, talk to your folks and then y'all meet us at the sheriff's office. You're going to tell Sheriff Latham everything you just told us…and I do mean everything."

Confession may be good for the soul, but nobody ever said it was easy. Less than half an hour later, the adults sat together on a hard, wooden bench in J.W.'s office. The boys were lined up, standing at attention in front of the sheriff's desk. J.W. looked each one of them in the eye and just shook his head.

"Sheriff, we're really sorry," Hank began. "We didn't see the accident, but if we had, well then maybe we coulda done something…"

"Maybe we coulda helped."

"At least we coulda stopped and…"

The sheriff knew the boys couldn't have done anything at the scene of the accident, but he wasn't about to let them off that easy. He made sure they realized what a colossally stupid thing they had done. One person was already dead and they had come damn near killing themselves. Their young faces told him they already felt bad enough.

"I appreciate the fact that you're telling the truth even if it did take you a hellava long time to do it. However, let me warn you, if I ever catch any of you speeding, even if you are only five miles over the limit and you're stone-cold sober, I'll arrest you on the spot. Is that clear?"

It was.

"Don't think you're walking out of here free and clear. All three of you will attend Warren Jr.'s funeral and from now on you will present yourselves at Widow Mackie's every Saturday morning and do whatever she says needs doing around her place. Do you understand?"

They did.

Dogs and Funerals

Dogs are one of the things that distinguish small towns. In big cities, people own dogs, but in small towns, dogs own themselves. Even if they have homes, they come and go at will and more or less fend for themselves. No self-respecting dog would allow someone to put a harness on him and lead him around on a leash.

For some reason no one could ever figure out, the dogs in Lost River attended funerals. Whenever one was held, they congregated at the church, sat respectfully outside until the service was over, then went home. Warren Jr.'s memorial was no exception.

When Agnes Mackie reached Trinity Episcopal, Boot and the rest of the town dogs had already begun to gather under the shade of the big oak trees in front of the church. It reminded her of other things she had once found strange about the South.

She was born and raised in Pennsylvania Dutch country and was proud of the fact. Only later did she realize in Lost River that made her a Yankee. Not a pretend Yankee from north

Georgia, but a real, honest-to-goodness northern Yankee. Some folks still took that kind of thing seriously.

She also realized early on she was probably the only Lutheran within a hundred miles. Given the choices available, she decided to become an Episcopalian because everybody had to go to church somewhere. It took her a while to get used to the South and to the citizens of Lost River. First of all, there was Mrs. Conti.

She was from the Old Country. She looked ancient and even in the heat and humidity of South Georgia, she always wore widow's weeds. A black dress, high neck, long sleeves, her skirts hanging down to her ankles. Hot.

But that wasn't the strange part. Mrs. Conti refused to touch a doorknob. She would stand in front of a closed door until someone came along and opened it for her, which they always did. No one seemed to know why. Germs, someone said and that seemed as good an explanation as any.

On top of the characters in town, there was the language. Agnes thought all that, "I love her to death, but…" and "Bless her heart she's doing the best she can…" was just a waste of time. Why not say what you mean, plain and simple? "Pitchin' a fit" or being "mad as a wet hen," were at least descriptive and the meaning fairly obvious.

The phrase she never did figure out was the one she heard mothers say to their children all the time. "Y'all play nice now, don't be ugly." As if being ugly was a choice. Agnes knew for a fact that it was not.

Nevertheless, she worked hard to be a good neighbor and to fit in. She adopted the habit of taking food to people for no discernable reason. Sickness, new babies and funerals she could understand, but Southerners were always exchanging food. And when someone gave you a dish of something, you were obliged to fill the container before you returned it.

There were other mysteries too. The name for instance. She had expected a river, but she found that as far as anyone could remember there was not, nor had there ever been, a river in or near the town of Lost River. There were some old Indian legends about lost rivers, but nobody put much store in them. Given all that, dogs attending funerals no longer struck her as unusual.

What was unusual that day was Widow Mackie's appearance. It was common knowledge that Warren Jr. had been a late-in-life, miracle baby and Agnes doted on him. In honor of her son, she wore a reasonably stylish black dress, with a matching hat and gloves and polished black pumps. The congregation understood and approved.

Pastor Knox, the young rector of Trinity Episcopal Church helped Agnes lay out the service, chose the music and the scriptures. Kirkland's printed the Order of Service and Inky delivered the cards to the church. Eudalee Munson, Warren Jr.'s first grade teacher delivered the eulogy. Six of his ATO fraternity brothers came down from Atlanta to serve as pallbearers.

As was the custom, the cemetery was adjacent to the church and the grave-side service was short. The high school *a cappella* choir sang *Abide with Me*, Pastor Knox recited a final prayer and the service ended. The dogs went home.

The next morning Hank, Sonny and Matt showed up at Widow Mackie's to rake leaves, trim the hedges, weed her garden, wash her car and do any other odd jobs she gave them. She wasn't exactly sure why they came, but she was glad to see them and they continued to come by every Saturday from then on, just like clockwork.

Story #5, Boot (1932)

Boot was one of those independent small-town dogs. He considered himself a handsome animal, all black except for his right front leg which was white up to his knee. It looked like he had pulled on one boot and forgotten the other three. He was of uncertain parentage, part German shepherd, part boxer. He thought he owned himself, but actually Lost River owned him.

The local vet gave him a collar, a tag and a rabies shot every year. Boot decided to be Ethyl's dog because she made him a nice warm bed in the storeroom next to the Back Backroom.

She also showed him an opening in the corner where he could come and go on his own. Housewives were accustomed to hearing him scratch politely at their back doors where he waited patiently for a bowl of whatever leftover table scraps might be available. Boot's only bad habit was digging in Mrs. Conti's garden. He was very selective and only dug up her garlic plants. The garlic might have accounted for the fact that he never had fleas.

The butcher at Conti's Grocery could be counted on for a juicy beef bone from time to time and Inky left him a bowl of fresh water by the print shop door every morning. Friday was his favorite day because he met Hank, Matt and Sonny at Moon's. They each chipped in and bought him a hamburger all his own. It was a good life, not like the old days riding the rails with Texas Bill.

Bill found him when he was just a puppy wondering around a hobo jungle looking for food. He had followed his nose to the cooking smells coming from the camp near the railroad yard. Bill claimed him, but the whole camp decided they should be in on choosing a name. The men spent a lot of time deciding on the perfect one. They rejected Peg Leg—sounded like a pirate— and Hopalong—sounded like a washed-up cowboy and Spats, well he'd need four white paws for that. They were about to run out of ideas when someone suggested Boots. "Too bad he's only got one," Bill said.

"Then just call him Boot," Rounder suggested. "Let's give 'er a try. Come here, Boot." The puppy knew who had the treats, so he happily trotted over to Rounder. Everyone laughed and the name stuck.

One night the bulls raided the camp. To avoid the police, Bill stuffed Boot in his coat when he hopped a fast freight out of town. From then on, they were inseparable.

Traveling with a puppy was easy, but when Boot grew up, it demanded a bit more dexterity. Bill would wait for a train moving kinda slow out of the yard, throw Boot through the boxcar door and then jump in himself.

The hobos traveled light but they all had a load of stories. After dark they'd sit around the campfires and swap tales of their adventures which always began the same way, "When I left home..."

Riding the rails was a matter of choice and a matter of pride. The men on the road were quick to explain. "Hobos like us are looking for work. Mostly we follow the crops. We go wherever we can find work for a couple of days or weeks. Now tramps ride the rails too, but generally they're just traveling, not looking for work. A bum don't do nothing. Don't travel, don't work. Nobody wants to be called a bum."

When Boot was about a year old, the bulls caught Bill late one night and beat him severely. Boot took a bite or two out of one of the cops before the man threw him under one of the box cars. When the police finally left, Boot crawled out and stood guard by Bill all night but the next morning Bill didn't wake up. The rest of the riders said he had "caught the westbound." They buried him and did their best to remember all the words to the Lord's prayer. Then they moved on. Without Bill, Boot was stranded. He had lost his best friend. He hung his head and slowly started walking along the tracks. Lost River was the first town he came to.

His only experience was with the men on the road so he didn't know what to expect from people who lived in houses and never went anywhere. Tony Conti was setting up vegetable bins *in front of his grocery store. "Well hello, feller. Where'd you come from? You hungry? Sit over there and I'll see if I can find something for you."*

Tony came back with a bowl of dog food and a bowl of water. Boot was glad to see the water, but he wasn't so sure about that other stuff. It didn't smell like real food, but he was too hungry to be picky. It was dry and crunchy, but it didn't taste too bad and he ate every bite.

"You got a name?" Tony looked at the dog's one white leg. "Looks like you stepped in a can of paint, but we can't call you Paint. That sounds too much like a horse. How about Boot?" Boot wagged his tail. It was a miracle. Somebody already knew his name, and that was important. Maybe he'd found a new home.

Idle Gossip

Widow Mackie knew there was no such thing as idle gossip. Even with all the kindness the town had shown her after the accident, she still heard whispers about Warren Jr.'s drinking. She ignored them, but she was sure if he had not died, the whispers would have gotten stronger and louder because gossip is never idle. It is always busy looking for new converts to spread the word. That's just human nature.

Gossip comes in two basic forms. There is vicious gossip created to inflict serious damage and then there is titillating gossip that can be—let's face it—fun. But even the innocent kind has to be handled properly. It's important not to scuttle your own reputation as a good person in the process of besmirching someone else's. The best approach is to test the water with a question. That way, if no one chimes in, you can back away unscathed.

Like all good teachers, Eudalee Munson—Lost River's perennial first grade teacher—had eyes in the back of her head and could hear things nobody else could hear. She had just turned 22 when she was hired to teach first grade at Lost River

School. The big red brick building that housed all 12 grades looked imposing, but she never hesitated.

As she prepared to go to work, she pulled her long brown hair into a knot and pinned it at the back of her head. She put on a no-nonsense gray suit with a white blouse. Next she laced up her brown oxfords with sensible one and a half inch heels. Finally, she added a pair of black horn-rimmed glasses for effect. She was pleased with her reflection in the mirror. She was now "Miss Munson." She wore that basic settle-down-and-pay-attention outfit every week day for the next 40 years.

On Sunday, she wore a hat and white gloves and a different suit. Navy blue with white trim. It was a sunny March day and a perfect time to test out her theory that gossip is never idle. That morning she had heard something interesting from a group of kids playing outside the church when they should have been in Sunday School.

She caught up with a group of her friends as they were walking home after church. They were all there, Eden Stubbs, Earlene Barlow, Florence Cumberland, Helen Kirkland, Trudy Latham, Ethyl Williams and Mildred Leland. She carried a Leland Funeral Home fan summer and winter because the church was always too hot for her liking. "Preacher outdid himself this morning, didn't he? I always like his sermon on Ruth and Naomi," she slipped the fan into the outside pocket of her purse. "By the way, did y'all hear anything out of the ordinary from your children this morning?" When there was no response, she offered a little hint. "Anyone missing from Sunday School? Or coming in late? Or something like that?"

Earlene Barlow said, "Well, now that you mention it, my youngest, Archie, did say something about not having Sunday School because Annabelle Knox didn't show up to teach their class. I didn't think anything about it at the time, I just supposed Annabelle was late. You reckon something's wrong?" Despite her best efforts to keep her voice neutral, the others heard a slight note of hopefulness.

That's the way it began. "As a matter of fact, I heard Zach Stubbs tell my Sidney that Annabelle wasn't at church at all this morning. That's a little unusual for the Episcopal pastor's wife. And on top of that, *Pastor* Knox didn't come in until just before the service was about to start." Florence Cumberland could always be counted on to contribute.

"You're right. I saw him as he crossed the street, and he looked like he had *slept* in his clothes. It's a sign, I'm telling you. For a man like him, *that's* unheard of. He's so precise and proper he probably sleeps in pajamas with a handkerchief in his breast pocket." Prim Blalock could spot a sign a mile away.

Helen Kirkland chimed in, "You know I hate to be the one to say it, but it wouldn't surprise me one bit if there *was* something going on over there."

"I've always wondered how Annabelle does it," Eden said. "Nobody can be *that* nice all the time. Lord knows I sure couldn't manage it. It's hard to imagine her doing something… *wrong*." The word dripped with possibilities.

The ladies settled down to a more serious discussion of what might be going on. Although "bless her heart" entered the conversation from time to time, there was no shortage of catastrophes that might be hidden behind closed doors.

As soon as he could get away, Pastor Knox left the church and headed home. He tried not to show it, but he was dealing with his own cloud of hypothetical situations. Never in his wildest imagination had he envisioned a situation like the one he found himself in at the moment. His wife, Annabelle, was missing and he didn't know where she was or what to do.

He remembered his seminary professors stressing the fact that as an ordained Episcopal priest he was held to a higher standard. People looked up to him and he was supposed to act accordingly. Not only was he expected to avoid all forms of wrongdoing, but he was also expected to avoid even the *appearance* of evil. How the hell was he supposed to do that when he had no idea what Annabelle might be up to?

Normally, he lived a well-ordered life free of turmoil or histrionics of any kind—except maybe that dust-up over the slipcovers. But this situation was different. Annabelle was gone and he was totally bewildered. He didn't know what he should feel: fear, anger, sorrow, confusion? Helpless, that's what he felt. Totally alone and helpless.

Annabelle often told him he didn't pay attention to her and maybe she was right. Oh Lord, what if she told him her plans and he just didn't listen? If that were the case, he'd have to spend the rest of his life trying to make up for it.

He went into the kitchen, opened the refrigerator and reached for a beer. Oh no! That would never do. What if someone came over and smelled liquor on his breath? He settled for a cup of coffee, sat down at the kitchen table and forced himself to go over what he knew...or thought he knew. It had all started Saturday.

Annabelle hadn't been home when he got there around noon. That was a little odd because she was always there to welcome him home. But she could have been out shopping, so he didn't worry too much about it.

When she hadn't come home by 5:30, he called his mother-in-law in Macon. No, Annabelle wasn't there and she hadn't seen her for a week or more. Before Mother Carpenter could go off on a tangent, Andrew made some lame excuse and hung up the phone. Having his mother-in-law on the warpath was more than he could cope with at the moment.

He drained the last of the cold coffee and considered his options. He couldn't start calling church members without admitting that he had no idea where his wife was. He certainly didn't want *that* information to start circulating through the congregation. That was definitely not the way to go.

As an only child, Andrew was accustomed to being alone, but at that moment what he wanted more than anything else in the world, was a friend. A best friend, someone he could be honest with; someone he could ask for advice. However, he realized of all the people he knew in Lost River, there was not one of them he considered a close friend.

He had been a pretty good poker player in seminary, but he was never invited to join the Lost River poker club, nor did he expect to be. Even in casual situations, he was an outsider. If someone told an off-color joke in his presence, they always apologized. The jokes didn't make him uncomfortable, but the apologizes did.

He made another pot of coffee and lit a cigarette. "My God, I never thought I'd be one of those desperate, lonely men drinking coffee and smoking one cigarette after another." One by one, the hours crawled by. By the time it got dark, he was in sad shape. The kitchen was thick with smoke and the inside of this mouth tasted like an old sock. He opened the windows to let in some fresh air and went into the bathroom to brush his teeth. That made him feel slightly better, but still the phone did not ring.

He sat at the kitchen table, waiting. Part of him said he should be doing something to find her. Part of him said don't make a fool of yourself. Just sit tight. Finally, he forced himself to take two Aspirin and go upstairs to bed. He didn't even bother to undress.

By early Sunday morning he knew something was seriously wrong and things just *did not* go wrong in Andrew's predictable life. Although he was nursing a splitting headache, he managed to change his pants and was looking for a clean shirt, when Deacon Daniel Barlow knocked gently and opened the front door. Andrew had to smile. Of course the man walked right in, nobody in Lost River ever locked their doors.

He called up the stairs, "Andrew, we're expecting you over at the church." Andrew stumbled downstairs and one look at him told Daniel something was amiss. "What's wrong?"

Andrew had been debating whether or not to call the sheriff, now he just threw caution to the wind. "It's Anabelle. She's gone."

Daniel took a minute to digest that information, then he smiled slightly. "Andrew, how long have you two been married?'

Andrew didn't seem to understand the question. "Ah…. a little over a year."

Daniel sat down and lit a cigarette. "Listen, Earlene and I have been married 30 years and I couldn't count the number of times she went home to her mother when we were first married. In the beginning, I panicked, but eventually I learned to just sit tight and be ready to apologize when she came home, which she always did. I wouldn't be too worried. Have you checked with her mother?"

"Yes, but she's not there."

"What about friends?"

"I'm not sure who that would be."

"Did you and Annabelle have a fight?"

"No, we never fight."

Daniel found that unusual. How was it possible to be married and not fight from time to time? Not only did it clear the air, but making up was half the fun. At any rate, he let that go for the moment. "Was Annabelle upset about anything?"

"No. Yes. Well, maybe. There was that business about the slipcovers, but I'm sure that couldn't be it."

Daniel looked at the bright orange covers on the couch and remembered that one of Earlene's departures had been over a can of beans.

Andrew started to explain, "Well, you see, Annabelle wanted to do some decorating and the Episcopal Church Women had already..." All of a sudden, he changed directions. "Oh my Lord, Daniel, I bet you're right. The ECW group tend to take over sometimes and that makes Annabelle... well she doesn't like what she sees as interference. I'll bet she's trying to avoid them and just needs some time to herself.

"Look, give me a few minutes to freshen up and I'll meet you over at the church. Daniel, don't say anything to anybody about Annabelle being gone. You're probably right and I'm just making a big deal out of nothing. Right after the service, I'll go look for her."

Andrew thanked God he had made some notes on Moses and the burning bush earlier in the week. It wouldn't be his finest sermon, but frankly he didn't think anybody would notice.

Daniel Barlow agreed to keep Annabelle's disappearance a secret because he was sure she would turn up in her own good time. However, he did happen to mention it in passing to his wife Earlene while they were having Sunday dinner later that afternoon. She told him not to worry about keeping it a secret, she already knew all about it.

"Yeah, Miss Knox didn't show up to teach our class this morning," his son Archie volunteered. He saw no reason to confess that he and his friends had pocketed their offering money. He thought of it as manna from heaven, a gift from God like they'd talked about in Sunday School.

Now that she had some hard facts to back up her story, Earlene got on the phone to Helen Kirkland who mentioned the news, in confidence, of course, to her husband Leon. You never know when it might turn into a story for the paper.

Helen also passed the word along to Mildred Leland, who mentioned it casually to her husband Curtis. Of course, Mildred cautioned him to keep it under his hat. Mildred wouldn't dream of telling a stranger, but she did call her best friend Florence Cumberland. As president of the Episcopal Church Women, she had a right to know.

Florence thought that might explain why Annabelle hadn't gotten back to her about Andrew's birthday celebration. In strictest confidence, of course, Florence called Eden Stubbs. The ladies chatted a few minutes and Eden promised to keep the news to herself. Of course, that didn't mean she couldn't share it with Trudy Latham.

Far be it for any of them to spread idle gossip. They only discussed it with their close-knit circle of friends. The circle included husbands, of course. That was to be expected. Keeping secrets between husband and wife was never a good idea. Adding the husbands—and any children who happened to be within earshot—that brought the number of people sharing the secret up to more than 20.

It was clear that no one remembered Ben Franklin's wisdom that, "Three people may keep a secret if two of them are dead."

Slipcovers

Now that Andrew thought about it, maybe it was the slipcovers. The whole scene came back to him in technicolor and at full volume.

"They're *orange*, Andrew. Not burnt orange, but bright Halloween orange, glow-in-the-dark orange. That avocado green chair was bad enough, but *orange slipcovers* all in the same room. I'm sorry, but I can't stand to have those things in my house." Annabelle stood in the middle of the living room giving off sparks. Her eyes blazed, her fists were clinched, her face was bright red and she was shouting. Andrew had never heard her raise her voice before.

"Annabelle, Honey, remember we've talked about this before. The house really isn't ours. It belongs to the church and the ECW, that's Episcopal Church..."

"I *know* what it stands for! When I married you, I didn't realize I was trading my mother for the Church Women. I thought I was finally going to be able to do things on my own, to make a nice home for you, something we could be proud of.

But there's no way anybody could be proud of those ...." She bit her tongue to keep from cursing, "...those horrible slipcovers. They're ... bilious!" She dissolved in tears. Andrew reached for her, but she moved away from him.

She was tired of hearing people describe her and Andrew as the perfect pair even though she knew they made a striking couple. Andrew was tall with light brown hair and incredibly dark eyes. His good looks and his clerical collar made an intriguing combination. Annabelle was pretty in an understated way. Her hair hung in soft curls around her face. Her eyes were the color of well-washed denim. They did make a handsome couple, but *perfect*? She thought she would scream if she heard that word one more time.

However, because she loved Andrew, she eventually came to terms with the slipcovers. She bought a lovely beige throw which hid most of the couch and could be snatched off whenever the ECW showed up.

She even managed to grit her teeth and smile when "*the girls*"—there was no one in that group under 50—showed up carrying matching Easter outfits. A stylish, three-piece suit for Andrew and a blue-and-white, polka-dot outfit with a peplum for her. *Nobody* wore jackets like that anymore.

All that paled in comparison to the latest invasion. For weeks Annabelle had been planning a romantic, candlelight dinner for Andrew's birthday. She was going to cook all his favorites. She bought a sexy nightgown and an expensive bottle of wine for them to share...alone.

However, on Saturday morning just as she was leaving to do the grocery shopping, Florence Cumberland, the president of the ECW called. She made an effort to speak with the same modulated tones her favorite soap opera star used on "Our Gal Sunday."

"Annabelle, dear, I just wanted to remind you—in case you might have forgotten—it has been the tradition of the ECW to plan the birthday celebration for our minister on his first year with us. I know the pastor's birthday is coming up sometime soon. Don't worry, we'll take care of everything, the cake, the candles, even the wine and some decorations. You don't have to lift a finger. Just let us know when you want us to arrive and the girls and I will be there."

That did it. As soon as Annabelle hung up the phone, she grabbed her purse and stormed out of the house. She didn't have a destination in mind when she started, but by the time she got downtown, she had a plan. She walked into Conti's General Store and made her way back to the Greyhound ticket counter. Thankfully she didn't recognize the young man working there. She bought a ticket on the next bus which was leaving in ten minutes.

As the bus pulled away from the front of the store, Annabelle sat back in her seat and tried to relax. It would take several hours to get to Savannah, so she had time to do a lot of thinking. Her mother had always wanted her to have a position in society, well, now she had one. Outside. It didn't take long after she and Andrew moved to Lost River to figure that out. She had no interest in being one of "the girls" in the ECW.

For one thing, they were all too old. But she didn't fit in with the younger crowd either. They were always on their best behavior around her, nobody ever let their hair down and just talked. Most of the time when they did talk, it was about babies and diapers and croup and colic.

Once she had said something about Andrew wearing a handkerchief in his pajama pocket. She meant it as a joke, but she could tell by their subdued reaction that even a glimpse into her personal life made them uncomfortable. She never did that again. She wondered if Andrew dealt with that kind of thing too?

As she watched the landscape slide by, she realized no one in the world knew where she was. She liked the feeling.

Before she checked into a hotel, she stopped by a department store downtown and spent Andrew's birthday surprise money to buy a change of clothes and basic supplies to get through a couple of days. She couldn't bring herself to eat alone in the dining room, so she ordered room service and went to bed early.

The next morning, she woke up with a nagging feeling that she was going to be late for Sunday School. Then she remembered where she was, looked at the clock, rolled over and went back to sleep. She was smiling.

Story #6, Annabelle Carpenter Knox
(New Orleans 1942)

Annabelle had always been a patient, cooperative child and she grew up to be a soft-spoken, polite, agreeable young woman.

Her mother, Regina Carpenter, was fond of saying, "Annabelle, you know your father and I only want the best for you. We want you to find a young man who will love and cherish you. Someone who is reliable and steady. Someone who will be a good provider. And when he comes along, you must be ready to take your place by his side, to provide a calm and cheerful home, to encourage him in his chosen work and to help him in every way to succeed."

Annabelle could never remember a moment when her mother wasn't there scolding and molding her.

"Annabelle, don't slouch."

"Annabelle, don't squint."

"Annabelle, don't fidget."

There were lots of rules and for every "don't," there were as many "dos." Talents every proper Southern girl must master if she wanted to marry well. She must know how to play bridge, how to set the table for a formal dinner, how to preside at tea, how to dance, how to play the piano, to dress modestly, to make introductions... Good God, the list was endless.

Always on the lookout for ways to broaden Annabelle's horizons, her mother decided to allow her to spend a summer with her wealthy cousins in New Orleans. After all, she was a senior in high school. They called it a graduation present.

"Annabelle, it will be a wonderful opportunity for you to be exposed to life in a big city and to have a chance to meet the right kind of people." They went to Atlanta to buy new clothes and Annabelle was looking forward to the trip.

New Orleans was everything she had dreamed it would be. She went to dances and parties and wore her new two-piece bathing suit to go swimming at Audubon Park. She explored the French Quarter with her cousins and their friends. They drank Jax beer and had café au lait and beignets at Café du Monde. No one questioned her age and she loved pretending to be grownup.

The city was a world apart from Macon. The houses were different, the food was different, the language was different, even the boys were different. Especially Remy Thibodaux. He had black curly hair and the bluest eyes she had ever seen. He was in pre-med at Tulane, he spoke French and was a great dancer. She told him she was 19 and in no time, he swept her off her feet. Theirs was a whirlwind romance.

For two months they were inseparable. One afternoon they drove to a secluded spot along the levy to have a picnic. Remy put down a blanket, unpacked lunch and a bottle of wine. They ate and drank and when he kissed her, she kissed him back. When he laid her down, she smiled. When he unbuttoned her blouse, she didn't resist. When he touched her, she thought she would die of happiness. She wasn't quite sure how it happened, but before she knew it, they were both naked. She knew she ought to cover herself, but she was proud of her body and she wanted Remy to look at her.

On the other hand, she had never seen a naked man before and although she tried not to look, she couldn't take her eyes off of him. He smiled, "I'm all yours if you want me."

"I do want you, but I don't know…I mean I've never…"

Remy looked at her. "Are you telling me this is your first time?"

She hesitated. "Yes. I'm sorry I wish…"

"Oh Annie, don't be sorry. This is a gift. It's an honor to be your first lover and don't worry we'll take it slow. I won't do anything until you're ready."

Annabelle had dreamed of this moment since the first time he danced with her. She was scared, but she was ready. It never occurred to her to wait. After all, he had called himself her lover. Wasn't that enough? They were in love and the summer was short.

The rest of the afternoon was like a wonderful dream. Every place he touched her, made her want more. When he asked if she wanted him to stop, she said, "No, don't stop." Eventually they lay side by side and Annabelle laughed. "Oh my God, I had no idea..." Remy couldn't help but laugh with her. The next few weeks were the happiest in her life.

But love came with a price. Toward the end of summer, she realized she was pregnant. This couldn't be happening. This was not part of her romantic dream; this was a nightmare. She was afraid to tell her cousins and she didn't dare call her mother. She had to do something, but she didn't know what. Every morning she looked at herself in the mirror and she was sure she could see her belly getting bigger.

Finally, she broke down and told Remy. She expected him to take her in his arms, say he loved her and tell her they'd get married and everything would be all right. But instead, he asked, "Are you sure?"

Annabelle was shocked. He didn't sound angry, in fact, he didn't sound any way at all. She was afraid if she tried to speak, she would cry, so she just nodded.

"Poor Baby," he said. "Well, don't worry, we'll take care of it."

Annabelle relaxed a little until she realized that "taking care of it" meant one thing to her and something quite different to Remy. He made a phone call to one of his friends in med school. "I'll make all the necessary arrangements. By tomorrow afternoon, it'll all be over. Don't worry, Cher, you'll be in good hands." He put his arm around her shoulders, more like a brother than a lover. "I wish I could go with you, but I've got a big exam. Connie, she's a friend of mine, will drive you there."

Annabelle couldn't believe what she was hearing. He had been so loving before and now he was treating her like an inconvenience. And worst of all, he was sending her off with some girl he knew! It was too much to deal with. In a haze, she just nodded her head.

The next morning Connie picked her up. Annabelle refused to speak to the girl and sat as far over in the front seat as possible. They drove to a grand old house in the Garden District. Connie talked to the woman who answered the door. "Annabelle, this is Miss Irene. She'll take care of you." That was it. Connie was gone.

Miss Irene was a large woman with soft features. She didn't talk much. After all, what was there to say? Annabelle kept her jaw clinched and her eyes closed throughout the procedure. Remy was right, by afternoon it was all over. Miss Irene called a cab, walked Annabelle to the curb, gave the cab driver some money and the address and sent her on her way.

Annabelle told her cousins she wasn't feeling well and wanted to lie down for a while. As she lay in the big canopied bed, she couldn't decide whether she was more embarrassed or hurt or angry. Maybe all three. Thank God no one knew. She pushed the memory to the back of her mind and swore she would never think about Remy or anything else about New Orleans ever again.

When she got home, her mother insisted on hearing all the details. Annabelle knew what her mother wanted to hear and that's what she told her, that and nothing more.

A year later, while she was attending Agnes Scott College in Atlanta, Annabelle met Andrew Knox. He was an Episcopal seminary student at the University of the South in Sewanee, Tennessee. Her parents not only approved of him; her mother was delighted.

After they both graduated, they planned to be married in the rural church where Andrew had been working. But Mother Carpenter was having none of that. She planned a small, but exquisite ceremony to be held in her very own rose garden in Macon. It was the perfect setting and although she would never brag, she knew it was the envy of everyone in her garden club.

Mother Carpenter hoped Andrew would be assigned to a big church in Atlanta, but she had to settle for a small church in the rural town of Lost River.

Nevertheless, the young couple would have a proper place in society—such as it was. Her mother took comfort in the fact that they would live in the rectory, a lovely old southern house supplied by the church. She could just picture Annabelle hosting dinner parties, presiding over teas and impressing all the Episcopal Church Women with her social skills. Mrs.

Carpenter's years of training would not go to waste. Annabelle had turned out to be the perfect daughter and now she would be the perfect wife.

Lady Luck

The March wind was living up to its reputation. Men came in clutching their hats and complaining about the cold. The Back Backroom at the Gas and Grill was beginning to fill up with players anxious to try their luck in Ethyl's monthly high-stakes poker game. It wasn't long before a thick cloud of smoke hung over the room. Three black oscillating fans made an effort to clear the air a little, but they didn't help.

The Lost River Poker Club was assembled: Tony, Sal and Vinnie Conti, Sheriff Latham, Zach Stubbs, Daniel Barlow, Sidney Cumberland, Leon Kirkland, Curtis Leland and Mayor Mike Sweeney. A number of visitors were also present. Most of them had sat in on games before with one notable exception, Charlie Russo, who said he was from New Orleans on his way to Savannah.

There was no need for the usual catching-up conversation among the locals because in Lost River everybody already knew what everybody else was up to. At least they thought they did. In fact, the mayor was barely holding things together. He signaled for Ethyl to bring him a double bourbon. Maybe that would help.

No one paid any attention to him because all their attention was focused on Russo, an unknown element. He was polite, but not forthcoming with information. When Sal asked him directly what he did, he said he was in the import-export business. That caused some raised eyebrows. Idle gossip said lots of the New Orleans Mafia was in the same business.

As the night wore on, Russo proved to be a reasonably good poker player, nothing flashy. It was Mayor Sweeney who was always the wild card. He never worried about percentages or probabilities. He played his gut, with predictable results.

But that night turned out to be anything but predictable. Most of the visitors dropped out of the game by midnight, but hung around to watch the action. The mayor won a hand, then he won another hand when he drew to fill an inside straight— 5,6,7,8,9! Not an easy thing for anyone to do and for the mayor to have such luck was totally unheard of. Even Ethyl, who had been busy serving drinks and emptying ash trays, stopped to watch the action.

It was past 2:00 in the morning, when they decided to play one more hand. By that time, the game was down to four players: the mayor, Zach, Sid and Russo.

It was Zach's deal and when the mayor picked up his cards, he couldn't believe his eyes. He knew staying for one more hand hadn't been a smart move, but—oh my God—it might just pay off. He stared at his cards, but he wasn't looking at what he *had*, he was looking at what he might *get*. He just needed one card for a Jack high straight flush. If the pot was high enough, it could solve all his problems.

In the real world, there was a better chance of Ethyl taking Holy Orders and entering a convent than of the mayor getting the one card he needed.

The dealer asked, "Can anybody open?"

Sid said, "Yeah, I'll open for $10," and everybody else stayed.

"Who needs cards?"

Mike held his breath. "One here," he said. Sid asked for two cards, Zach three and Russo just one.

When Zach delt the cards, Mike was afraid to touch his. If it was the right card, he'd be home free. As casually as possible, the mayor picked up the card and play continued.

Sid tossed in his hand on the first round and after a couple more rounds Zach dropped out. The pot grew as the mayor and Russo kept raising each other. The peanut gallery figured the mayor's luck must be holding.

"Reckon what he's got?" Vinnie asked.

"Whatever it is, it must be good," Curtis said.

J.W. snorted, "Not necessarily."

The mayor and Russo continued to bet and raise until the mayor realized he couldn't cover Russo's last raise of $250.

"Hell, I can't quit now, not with this hand," he thought. He looked lovingly at his cards and then looked at Russo. "I'm feeling lucky, will you take my marker?"

Russo was skeptical. He glanced around the room. "I don't know this guy, is he good for it?"

"Yeah, he always pays off his markers." Zach said.

The prudent move would have been to simply call the bet. But the gambler in Mike Sweeney's soul led him astray. He counted on the fact that all his past bad bets would make Russo think he was bluffing. But this time it wasn't a bluff. He covered Russo's raise and raised another $250! A $500 marker.

The spectators fell silent. What the hell was the mayor up to? What if Russo raised again? Instead he said, "This is getting too rich for my blood. I'm gonna call."

Every eye was on the mayor as he laid out his cards. Lady Luck had delivered the 8 of diamonds. Slowly he fanned out the cards. Diamonds 7,8,9,10, Jack. "Read 'em and weep. A straight flush, Jack high. Let's see you beat that!"

Then Russo laid out his cards. 8,9,10, Jack and Queen of Clubs, a straight flush *Queen high!*

"No, no, no. This can't be happening, not when I was so close." The mayor's mind was racing, but he couldn't speak. "I can't just sit here," he thought, "I have to do something... Think! Buy time, I need to buy time." He took a deep breath and made a supreme effort to sound casual. "Well damn. Listen, I'll need a couple of hours once I get to my office, but if you come by tomorrow afternoon, I'll have your money. Is that acceptable?"

Russo shrugged. "Yeah, sure. No problem."

That broke the tension. Ethyl served another round of drinks and around 3:00 a.m. everybody headed home. Everyone, that is, except the mayor. He made it to his car before he broke down. In the darkness, he cried like he hadn't cried since Rebecca passed away. His world was falling apart. His wife was dead, he was broke, worse than that, he was deep in debt. And he'd just lost the best poker hand he was ever likely to get.

For years the Sweeneys had been robbing Peter to pay Paul to keep up appearances. His father sold off most of his family's land and took lumber leases on the rest. By the time he died and Mike came home to take over, the family was up to their eyeballs in debt. Mike borrowed against his life insurance and took a second mortgage on the big house from an out-of-town bank in an effort to pay off the family debts.

It was only a temporary fix. A smart man would have stopped, but that's not the way a gambler's mind works. As Mike saw it, all he needed was a big win to straighten things out. That's when he decided to play in the high-stakes game. He "borrowed" the $500 buy-in for the game from the Fire-Truck Fund in his office safe. It had taken the community over a year and countless bake sales, cake walks and donkey polo games to raise $1,200 toward replacing their old fire truck.

If the situation he was in now had come up in a regular weekly game among friends, he might have confessed and thrown himself on their mercy. Given enough time, he could have paid the money back. Russo, on the other hand, didn't strike him as the forgiving type. He might not be Mafia, but then again, he might. That was one gamble the mayor was not willing to take.

He couldn't bring himself to go home to his empty house, so he drove out into the country, found a side road, parked, lit a cigarette and sat there trying to figure out what to do. He couldn't run the risk of stiffing Russo; besides that, he had a reputation to maintain. He had no choice, when the man showed up, he'd have to pay him. There was just enough money left in the Fire-Truck Fund to cover the $500 marker. But then what?

Friday afternoon was the monthly Town Council meeting and the first thing on the agenda was the Fire-Truck Fund. Once the Council figured out he had stolen the money, he would be finished as mayor. J.W. would probably arrest him on the spot. He was glad Rebecca wasn't still alive. She had always been his anchor. This kind of scandal would have broken her heart. In the pre-dawn hours, he drove home and drank enough bourbon to pass out.

About 8:00 the next morning, his alarm clock jarred him awake. He forced himself to get up. His mouth was dry, his eyes burned, his head hurt. Somehow, he managed to take a shower, get dressed, throw some clothes in a suitcase and head to his office. Rather than wait around for Russo, he took $500 from what was left of the Fire-Truck Fund and put it in an envelope on his desk. Then he stuffed the rest of the fund and all of the office petty cash in his pocket. Stealing the last couple of hundred dollars couldn't make the situation any worse.

He told Hazel Goodman, his secretary, a Mr. Russo was coming by to pick up the envelope. He explained that he was leaving for a meeting in Macon but he'd be back in time for the council meeting that afternoon.

His head was pounding and his hands were shaking, but he made it to his car. He thought about going by the G&G to fill up his tank, but he decided against it. He could stop somewhere down the road. At the moment, the most important thing to do was to put as much distance between himself and Lost River as he could.

The Plot Thickens

When Sheriff Latham walked into his office early Monday morning, he was surprised to see the entire City Council waiting for him. Lucy Washburn, his office manager, had made coffee and was trying to keep order.

"The mayor didn't show up for our Friday afternoon council meeting," Daniel Barlow announced. "He was supposed to be back from Macon, but he didn't make it. Hazel called the guy she thought he was meeting over there, but nobody had seen hide nor hair of him."

"That's not the worst part, we've been robbed," Zach Stubbs said. Then everyone started to talk at once.

"Cleaned out."

"The Fire-Truck Fund's all gone."

"Every red cent, wiped out."

"Along with a whole lot more."

"Even the petty cash is gone."

Eventually J.W. sorted things out enough to get the gist of the story. At their regular meeting on Friday afternoon, the council discovered the mayor had stolen the Fire Truck money. That prompted a look at the books. They weren't sure, but it looked like His Honor had been siphoning funds for years.

When J.W. called the mayor's office, Hazel filled in some more details. She explained that the mayor had left an envelope on his desk and Mr. Russo, a very handsome man, had picked it up. She specifically remembered him because he was so polite and he complimented her stylish suit—which just happened to be new. "Frankly, Sheriff, I'm more than a little confused. On his way out the door Friday morning, the mayor said he was going to Macon and I'm sure he said he'd be back in time for the meeting. The council is saying some awful things about the mayor. They say he stole money, but I can't hardly believe that. He always gave me flowers on my birthday and let me leave early every Wednesday to get my hair done. This whole thing has got me so upset, I'm just beside myself."

J.W. thanked her for the information and started adding things up. Russo had picked up his winnings. The Fire Truck money was missing. The mayor was gone. It didn't take a genius to figure out what happened. He looked at the group clustered around his desk. "Damn it, why didn't you call me about this when you found out on Friday?"

"Ahh J.W. you know how Mike's been since Rebecca passed on. We figured after the shellacking he took at the poker game he might have tried to drown his sorrow and was just sleeping it off. I guess we hoped he'd show up with an explanation…or something."

"Well, that didn't happen, did it?" J.W. was doing his best not to show how angry he was. Welching on a bet was one thing, but stealing city funds was a lot more serious. "Are y'all making this an official complaint?"

That caused a fair amount of discussion, but in the end they agreed. "Yeah, I guess we are."

"Then there's nothing I can do but swear out a warrant for his arrest and circulate it around the county."

"I reckon you oughta make it the whole state," Sid said.

"Maybe farther than that," Zach added. "After all, he's got a three-day head start. No telling where he could be by now."

It had to be done, no doubt about that, but it wasn't an easy decision. Mike Sweeney was their friend. They were angry, not so much that he had stolen the money, but that he had been doing it for years right under their noses.

The meeting was about to break up when Lucy remembered a call she took earlier that morning from Andrew Knox. "I hate to add to your problems, Sheriff, but according to Andrew Knox, Annabelle's missing." That stopped everyone in their tracks. "What do you mean *missing*?" J.W. asked.

Lucy walked over to her desk and picked up a yellow legal pad. "She's been missing all weekend, I think. Andrew was so upset it was hard to get it all straight. Anyway, I took it down in shorthand to make sure I got the facts right." She consulted her notes, "OK, here's what he said. 'Annabelle is missing. She's been gone…well, she may have been gone since Saturday morning. I left early to make house calls, so I'm not sure. I know she didn't come home Saturday afternoon or Saturday night and Sunday was my birthday. She missed that too and she's *still* not home. It's like she just disappeared. Nothing here is out of place, she didn't have access to the car because like I said, I was making house calls. Her clothes and her suitcase are still here, she didn't leave a note. She's not at her mother's. She's just gone and I have no idea what to do.'"

Lucy glanced at the sheriff. "I told him you'd look into it. As a matter of fact, I kinda did some checking on my own. I called a friend over at the bank, but she said there hadn't been any recent withdrawals from their account. I hope I didn't do something wrong. I was just trying to find out what I could."

The men exchanged looks. Although no one said anything out loud, this information put a new spin on things. One person missing was certainly unusual in Lost River. But now the mayor, the city's money and the Episcopal minister's wife were all missing…at the same time. *That* was a whole different kettle of fish.

Runaways

Andrew had waited all Sunday night hoping the phone would ring. By 8:00 Monday morning, he gave in and called the sheriff's office. He tried to keep the panic out of his voice as he explained to Lucy that Annabelle had "been away" since some time on Saturday. Lucy told him not to worry and that she would have the sheriff look into it and call him back. But here it was mid-afternoon on Monday and Andrew hadn't heard a thing. He knew calling the sheriff's office again was probably a bad idea, but he did it anyway.

When J.W. answered the phone, he apologized to Andrew for not getting back to him. "I'm sorry Annabelle hasn't come home yet and I'll get on it right away. It's just that I had my hands full this morning. When I got here, the whole City Council was camped out in my office telling me that the mayor is missing too. He cleaned out the Fire-Truck Fund and we're pretty sure he's been stealing from the city for a long time. But don't worry, I haven't forgotten about Annabelle. Just sit tight, we'll find 'em." Before Andrew could respond, the sheriff hung up.

Andrew stood there holding the receiver. "What does he mean 'missing too?' He said 'We'll find *them*.' Them?! He makes it sound like they're together. Oh my God!"

Imagination is a powerful thing. It can invent ideas that transport a person into a new and exciting world, it can create a symphony, it can amuse children with fantasies and magic. But left to run wild, it can also create a world of demons.

Once again Andrew's seminary training came back to haunt him. He vaguely remembered a lecture during which the professor described imagination as a "prelude to action" and the action in question was usually some kind of transgression, major or minor. A plot that led to a plan of action.

"I've got to stop this," Andrew told himself, but the mental images just kept coming. It wasn't that he mistrusted Annabelle, he didn't. He knew her. She would never do anything wrong. She was the perfect wife…

But what was it people said? Nobody's perfect. Was there a side to Annabelle he didn't know anything about? She *had* gotten pretty mad about the slip covers. But she had been right, they were horrible.

"Get a grip, Man. You're making yourself crazy worrying about…nothing. You have no proof there is anything going on between Annabelle and the mayor." The real problem was Andrew knew just enough about the Sweeny family to make him concerned. If he was being truthful with himself, he had always thought the mayor was a little bit too friendly, a little too charming around the ladies.

To distract himself, Andrew reached over and turned on the radio. The voice he heard was unmistakable. "Great! That's just what I need." He was so angry he started to turn it off, and then he had to smile. "Maybe that *is* what I need."

Instead of turning the radio off, he turned it up full blast and sang along with Hank Williams, "Your cheatin' heart will make you weep…"

$2 + 2 = 5$

The only thing that travels faster than gossip, is bad news and the fact that the mayor had gambled away the Fire-Truck Fund, stolen money from other city accounts and left town, was certainly bad news. But that wasn't all. When you combined the news that the mayor was missing, the money was missing and *Annabelle Knox was also missing*, you had the makings of a real, live, honest-to-goodness scandal.

No one would ever admit such a thing, but a good scandal was like a summer rain on a hot day. It might be inconvenient, but everyone enjoyed it while it lasted. The facts were enough to tempt a saint to sin. In no time, rumors were flying as thick as gnats in August.

In the beginning, everyone agreed that Annabelle might have run away, but the idea of her running away with the mayor was preposterous. However, the more folks thought about it— and they did think about it—the more they began to admit it might be possible. After all, the mayor was a reasonably good-looking man. He hadn't gone to fat like a lot of men his age. His hair was beginning to gray a little bit, but that just made him look distinguished. He was a likable fellow and he could be a charmer when the occasion called for it.

The Episcopal Church Women, the Women's Missionary Union at the Baptist church, the United Methodist Women and the Roman Catholic Women's Organization each called a special meeting to "discuss" the situation.

"Girls, I asked you to come over so we could talk about the terrible rumors about Annabelle. It just breaks my heart," Florence Cumberland sighed. "It's not like she's a member of…one of those *other* churches. Annabelle is an *Episcopalian!* And Episcopal Church Women like us do *not* run off with some man, even if he is the mayor. This is the worst thing that has ever happened to me. You realize if the stories turn out to be true, I'll never live it down. I can't believe this happened during my reign as president." Florence was fit to be tied. The girls sympathized.

The women from all the other churches were discussing the situation too. Prim Blalock said, "Do you remember the fuss Annabelle made about those orange slipcovers? Now that was a sign if ever there was one. She had to be upset about a lot more than just slipcovers. I'm telling you it wouldn't surprise me if the ECW didn't have something to do with this."

Sophia Conti added her two cents. "We all know Florence can be bossy from time to time. Don't forget that awful polka-dot outfit the ECW gave Annabelle for Easter. As far as I know, she only wore the thing once and I'm pretty sure I saw it hanging in the thrift shop over in Macon. That suit by itself would have been enough to send me over the edge."

After they danced around the facts long enough to empty two pots of tea, Sophia Conti finally spoke up, "As a kid, they taught us that all good Catholics were supposed to give everybody the benefit of the doubt, but the truth of the matter is, Annabelle never did really fit in here. Once I asked her when they planned to start a family, and she looked at me like I was crazy. 'We're way too young to be saddled with kids right now.' *Saddled*, that's what she said. Like having kids was some kind of burden."

"I met her mother once," Earlene Barlow added, "and if you ask me, I think a lot of her standoffishness comes from that woman. Mrs. Carpenter never thought Lost River was good enough for her daughter. I mean, it's not like she's part of New York High Society. She lives in Macon, for heaven's sake."

There is a long-held misconception that men don't gossip like women. And it's true up to a point, they don't gossip like women, but they *do* gossip as evidenced by the group gathered after work in the Back Backroom at the G&G. It was early for serious drinking, but a beer or two seemed in order given the present circumstances. Ethyl opened a Schlitz and poured it carefully into a glass before she handed it to Dan Barlow.

"I wouldn't have figured Mike was smart enough to embezzle money," he said. "Take the Fire-Truck Funds, yes, but embezzlement?" Before he could order it, Ethyl handed

Leon Kirkland a Pabst Blue Ribbon. She knew her customers' preferences well.

"What puzzles me, is how he managed to talk a pretty young woman like Annabelle into running away with him." Leon shook his head. "I really can't figure that one out."

"Wonder where they're headed?" Zach Stubbs added. "New Orleans maybe? Or Memphis? Gotta be somewhere he can find some action."

Sid Cumberland brought two more beers to the table. "I'd say he's got more action on his hands right now than he can handle." Everyone laughed.

When All Else Fails

Monday was April Fool's Day and Andrew Knox was still at his wits end. If only the whole thing could somehow be a joke. It was bad enough that Annabelle hadn't come home, but the idea that she might have deliberately run away with the mayor was unthinkable. It had to be a terrible mistake, a misunderstanding. All he had to do was to talk to her and she would clear everything up. It all hinged on a telephone call. He stared at the phone as it sat silently on the hall table.

He considered calling the Greyhound office to see if they knew anything, but he was afraid to tie up the line. What if Annabelle called and got a busy signal?

To get his mind off his troubles, he decided to clean the house, but he couldn't take a chance on running the vacuum cleaner. What if Annabelle called and he didn't hear the phone ring?

He kept remembering Annabelle laughing with the mayor at a recent church meeting. No, no, he had to clear his head. Maybe a walk would help. But then he couldn't take a chance on leaving the house. What if Annabelle called and he wasn't there to answer?

Maybe a shower would help. A nice long, soothing shower. But he couldn't do that. What if Annabelle called and the water drowned out the sound of the phone?

He finally dissolved into a helpless heap on the couch. He was physically and emotionally exhausted and totally out of ideas. "I give up. Dear God just let her be safe." Suddenly he sat bolt upright. "Pray! That's what I need to do. I recall there's some scripture that says the fervent prayers of a righteous man availeth much...or something like that. I don't know why I didn't think of that sooner. What I need now is a fervent prayer."

He tried to remember if he had ever preached on the power of prayer. He believed in prayer, of course—in an intellectual way—but the idea of getting down on his knees and pleading with God seemed excessive and a little silly. But at this point he was desperate. If someone had suggested he get naked, paint himself blue and dance in the moonlight he probably would have tried it.

He ran to his office and started searching his book shelves for the *Book of Common Prayer*. In the index he found Prayers for Various Occasions. It listed prayers for the world, the church and the nation. He kept looking and found prayers for family and personal life. He was getting closer and Number 52 was *Prayers for the Absent*. He wasn't able to find a prayer for a missing wife who may have run off with the mayor, but she was definitely absent, so that would have to do. He took the book back into the living room and The Reverend Mr. Andrew Knox got down on his knees, clasped his hands and began to pray.

"O God, whose fatherly care reacheth to the uttermost parts of the earth: We humbly beseech thee graciously to behold and bless those whom we love, now absent from us. Defend them from all dangers of soul and body; and grant that both they and we, drawing nearer to thee, may be bound together..." He was interrupted by a knock at the front door.

One of his legs had gone to sleep, but he hobbled to the door as quickly as he could. When he opened it, a young man thrust a telegram at him and waited for a tip. Andrew paid him and ripped the envelope open. The message was short. "Marshall House Hotel, Savannah." It was signed "Annabelle." Andrew was shocked. "Wow! I had no idea prayer could work that fast."

He charged upstairs, stuffed some clothes in a suitcase, found his car keys and was nearly out the door when he realized he should contact the sheriff. He dialed the number and was relieved when Lucy answered the phone. "Annabelle's OK, I'll explain later." He hung up and ran out the door. During the drive to Savannah, he flip-flopped from the joy of knowing Annabelle was all right, to the dread of the unknown. He tried to keep the thought of the mayor out of his mind. It was the longest two and a half hours of his life.

Doing his best to look calm and composed, he presented himself at the front desk of the Marshall House Hotel. When he asked if Annabelle Knox was registered there, he was directed to the honeymoon suite on the third floor.

"Oh my God!" He didn't wait for a bellboy or an elevator, but bounded up three flights of stairs, found the appropriate door and knocked. When Annabelle answered, he said the one thing he was determined not to say. "Is the mayor here with you?"

Annabelle looked at him as if he had lost his mind. "*What?!* No! Why would you ask me such a thing?"

Andrew smiled weakly. As calmly and quickly as he could, he explained what had been going on in Lost River.

Annabelle looked at him, "The mayor took all the money and so you thought I must have run off with him. Is that it?"

"Well, no. I never believed that for a moment," he said hurriedly. "But you just disappeared without a word and I didn't know why. I was worried. No, I was scared. I panicked. I was desperate." He was talking faster and faster. "I was at my wits end, so I prayed. Yes, yes I did. I found a prayer in the *Book of Common Prayers* and I got down on my knees and I prayed and prayed and then the telegram came and I left as fast as I could and I think I forgot to lock up the house and I may have left the stove on. The house will probably have burned to the ground by now."

He finally ran out of steam and when he looked at Annabelle, she was laughing. "Oh Andrew," she threw her arms around him, "I love you. Come here, I want to show you something."

She led him out to their private wrought-iron balcony with the lights of Savannah twinkling in the distance. On a small table was an ice bucket with a bottle of champagne and two glasses. "Just sit down, I'll take care of everything."

She expertly popped the cork and filled their glasses. Andrew watched in amazement. This was a side of Annabelle he had never seen. After they finished their first glass of champagne, she ordered room service, had it delivered to the balcony and tipped the waiter.

She chatted casually during dinner about the history of Savannah and the art galleries she had visited. After dessert, she suggested he take the last of the champagne into the bedroom and climb into bed. She disappeared briefly and returned wearing a black satin nightgown that took Andrew's breath away. When he reached over to turn off the bedside lamp, she said, "Leave it on. This is my night. I'll handle everything." And she did! Much later, she kissed him sweetly on the cheek and whispered, "Happy birthday."

Once he was sure she was asleep, Andrew slipped out of bed and got down on to his knees again. "Thank you, God!" He carefully got back into bed and went to sleep with a smile on his face.

Upon their return to Lost River, Andrew threw the orange slipcovers in the garbage. Then he worked up the courage to have a long talk with the ECW about boundaries.

From then on, every once in a while, Annabelle would disappear and Andrew would get a telegram telling him where to meet her. It was their own private charade. She always wore a black satin nightgown and sometimes Andrew left his collar on...just for fun.

A World of Hurt

Andrew may have unraveled his problem. On the other hand, the City Council had spent several hours bellyaching about the extent of Mayor Sweeney's larceny without coming to any conclusion. After sorting through stacks of files, they finally admitted the situation called for a more intense investigation. They called in an outside auditor from down south in Valdosta. The man recommended for the job was Waylon Sidney Bethune III, from the firm of Baggarley, Aldridge and Bethune. He showed up wearing spectators, a seersucker suit and a bow tie. He had a full head of white hair combed straight back. He looked more like a traveling evangelist than a CPA.

The first thing he did was to ask Lucy to bring him a pitcher of sweet tea, a tall glass with lots of ice and a big ash tray. Then he spent the better part of the day huddled in the mayor's old office going over the books. When he finally emerged from the smoke-filled room, he was shaking his head. In a town of colorful slow-talkers, Waylon gave a new dimension to the word 'drawl.'

"I declare Boys, y'all got yourselves in a world of hurt. I know y'all figured out part of the mayor's most recent chicanery, but that does not amount to a hill of beans compared to the reprehensible behavior he's been up to all these years. The evidence is all here, plain as the nose on your face, you just gotta know where to look."

"Like where?" Zach asked.

"I'm fixin' to tell you. Here's a good example." He pulled a bunch of invoices out of the pile of papers on the desk in front of him. "Y'all have been paying $50 a month for termite inspection. It does not take a genius to figure that one out. I mean, think about it. This here's a *brick building*. Paying for termite treatments makes about as much sense as tits on a bull." Waylon laughed and lit a cigarette from the one burning down in his fingers.

"Lord love a duck, y'all oughta know bettern' to buy a pig in a poke. Now I can easily spend the rest of the day—at my hourly rate, of course—and no doubt I could come up with copious other obvious examples, but the long and short of it is this. He's been playing fast and loose with city funds so long that by now y'all ain't got a pot to piss in. Pardon my French." Waylon made out a formal report in standard English, handed them a bill for $200 and headed back to Valdosta.

"Does he always talk like that?" J.W. asked. "And what the hell is a pig in a poke?"

Leon laughed. Being from up North sometimes put J.W. at a disadvantage. "I've known Waylon for years and he told me once he talks that way on purpose. He thinks it makes him sound intelligent and colorful at the same time. A poke, by the way, is a bag. Means you're buying something you can't see."

So now they knew the worst. Waylon Sidney Bethune III was right and, in a way, they had brought this on themselves. They liked the mayor and despite all the stories about the Sweeney family, it never occurred to them to distrust him. "That's not how things are supposed to work in a small town. We know our neighbors. We leave our doors unlocked, we help one another," Tony Conti started to pace back and forth. "The fact that Mayor Sweeney pulled the wool over our eyes for so long, makes me feel like a fool."

The City Council was a roster of the town's leading citizens. Tony was the president, Sidney Cumberland was vice president, Leon Kirkland was the secretary and Daniel Barlow had been treasurer for as long as anybody could remember.

Up until that point, the Council had considered themselves successful, intelligent businessmen. Tony had spent years building his business from a pushcart to the best-stocked grocery store in the county. Sid was president of the Lost River Bank and Trust. Leon, had owned Kirkland's Print Shop and published the *Lost River Herald* for more than a decade and Daniel was the general manager of Stubbs Sawmill. How had they missed all the signs?

The facts painted a bleak picture. The mayor was long gone and apparently had no intention of returning. The idea that he might come back to make things right, was a pipe dream. The town was broke. Like it or not, Waylon Sidney Bethune had spelled it out. They were in a world of hurt and they had to do something to get the town back on track.

"I don't see any way around it. There's nothing for me to do but resign." Tony looked around the room, "Do we have some kind of official resignation form, Leon?"

Before Leon could answer, Daniel spoke up. "Hell, I'm the treasurer. I'm the one who should have been on top of this. If you resign, I should resign too."

"I don't know about any form, but I think Tony's right. We oughta *all* resign," Leon said. "I sat right here, listened to reports, took minutes at every meeting and never suspected a thing. No way I can stay. But who are we gonna give our resignations to?"

"We'll give them to Sid, he's the vice-president," Tony suggested.

"Don't leave me holding the bag," Sid said. "Vice-presidents aren't supposed to have to do anything. I can't run the town by myself, even if I wanted to…which I don't."

J.W. looked at the men sitting around the table. "The way I see it, we've got no mayor, no money, no council. Before y'all officially walk away from this, you've got to call a special election and try to talk somebody else into running for mayor and the City Council, which, under the circumstances, isn't going to be easy."

Daniel Barlow, who had been married longer than most of the men in the room said, "You know, 30 years of marriage has taught me one thing. Women are better at sorting out problems than we are. Maybe we oughta turn this over to our wives. They could probably straighten this whole Sweeney fiasco out in no time." Everyone laughed and the meeting broke up without finding a solution to their problem.

Story #7, The Sweeneys (Georgia 1760)

The Sweeney family had a long and sordid past. It began when Lost River was just a small community trying to coexist with the Lower Creek Indians. One of Mike's early ancestors was named "keeper of the stores" for the colonists. But he mismanaged the funds and supplies and when word of his conduct got back to England, the Magistrates ordered him to account for the missing money and goods.

History said Old Aaron Sweeney thumbed his nose at the Crown, resigned his position, moved off the Crown land and never looked back. He didn't really need their money. He owned cotton fields throughout the county. In those golden days when cotton was king, more than half a million farms in the South were producing two-thirds of the world's cotton, thanks in part to Eli Whitney's invention of the cotton gin. Money was no problem.

Aaron Sweeney built Riverview, a Greek Revival house that had columns made in Savannah and mirrors and cornices shipped over from England. A custom-made poker table was shipped up from New Orleans and the rest of the furnishings came from New York and Chicago. Rumor had it that the poker table was rigged somehow. Nothing was ever proved, but Ole Man Sweeney had a favorite seat and no one else was ever allowed to sit there. Other rumors said that folks who won big at one of his frequent poker games had an unfortunate way of disappearing.

Stories were always circulating about the shenanigans at Riverview, but no matter how much crap they stepped in, the Sweeneys always came out smelling like a rose. During the War of Northern Aggression in the 1860's, the Sweeneys survived a typhoid outbreak and General Sherman left their house untouched as he burned his way to Savannah. Emancipation and Reconstruction ruined many old Southern families, but again, the Sweeneys managed to prosper.

There is always money to be made during war time if you aren't too choosey about the kind of people you do business with. Emancipation meant plantation owners could no longer depend on slave labor, so the Sweeneys converted their cotton fields to tree farming and concentrated on timber. Trees paid better and you didn't have to feed and house them.

Under a section of the state constitution labeled "Offenses Against Public Health and Morals," all forms of gambling were outlawed in Georgia back in 1877. The Sweeneys never paid attention to laws they considered a nuisance. If you got caught playing poker, it was only a misdemeanor, so they continued to host poker games which were legendary throughout the region. Players were housed at Riverview. Food was sumptuous, moonshine was brought down from the north Georgia hills and *girls were imported from Storyville in New Orleans. It was common knowledge that duels were fought and men died, but again, nothing was ever proven. The rest of the Sweeny story was more or less lost to ancient history and rumor.*

However, the darkest story of the family was a rumor about Obadiah Sweeney, Mayor Sweeney's great-great-grandfather. The old man was hard as nails and when he was drunk, he was mean as a snake. One night he pulled his wife out of bed at 3:00 in the morning and demanded that she fry chicken for him and his friends.

When she didn't work fast enough, he grabbed the skillet full of hot grease and hit her with it. She was severely burned and the blow was fatal. As the story goes, Obadiah surveyed the damage, threw his cronies out, cursed and staggered up to bed. The next morning, the cook found the body and called the sheriff. Obadiah claimed to have no memory of what happened. No witnesses were ever found. So, no witnesses, no trial, no punishment. Same old story, the Sweeneys weren't accountable.

At his wife's funeral, the old man fell to his knees by the coffin and swore to God and all present that he would never drink again. His resolve lasted a couple of years and then he died. His temperance pledge didn't carry over to his son Edward.

On the first day of school, Edward's youngest son Lawrence showed up for the first grade with his left arm hanging useless at his side. Eudalee Munson had just started teaching, but she had a pretty good idea about what happened. All Lawrence said was, "Daddy was drinking."

"I'm not going to stand by and let that man hurt his son." The older teachers cautioned Eudalee not to mess with the Sweeneys. She didn't listen. She questioned Lawrence and although he never admitted that his father had hurt him, Eudalee was convinced it was no accident. Rumors said it wasn't the first time one of the Sweeney boys had come to school with an unexplained injury.

Miss Eudalee was young enough to think she could right the wrongs of the world. Although she knew there would be hell to pay, she broke the unwritten law that said you never interfere with the way parents discipline their children. And you certainly didn't interfere with the Sweeneys.

Nevertheless, she called the boy's maternal grandparents over in Alabama. They didn't ask questions they just came to the school and took Lawrence home to live with them. Eudalee expected to be fired, but she wasn't. Years later Lawrence moved back to Lost River, married a local girl and they had one son, Mike.

By that time, most of the stories of the Sweeneys had faded into myth and legend. The famous poker table was long gone and the family did their best to avoid talking about the old days.

Mike went away to college and had no intention of ever coming back to live in Lost River. But fate had a different plan. Mike opened a law office and worked in Savanah for several years, but then his father died of a sudden heart attack and Mike became the sole survivor of the Sweeney clan. He and Rebecca had no choice but to move back to Lost River.

The Circus Royale

In all the years since its founding, Lost River had never been in a situation like the one it found itself in now. For over a month, city workers weren't getting paid, the garbage wasn't being collected and their one and only stop light wasn't working either. April showers had turned into April storms and the whole town was under a cloud like the one Al Capp drew over Joe Btfsplk in *Li'l Abner*. The character caused bad luck wherever he went. Of course, no one had ever seen him outside of the funny papers, but folks in Lost River still felt like he was lurking in the shadows somewhere. They were ashamed to have been taken in and cheated by *one of their own*. It was just down right embarrassing.

Then overnight the skies cleared. May blew in with warm breezes and the town was transformed from RKO black and white to MGM technicolor. Huge posters with bright colors and big words like "stupendous" and "colossal" appeared on every flat surface big enough to hold one. No doubt about it, the circus was coming to town and not a moment too soon.

Ringling Bros. and Barnum and Bailey might be the Greatest Show on Earth, but it was by no means the only show. In the pre-dawn hours, 15 trailer trucks of the Circus Royale rolled down Highway 23 and pulled into the grounds where the orphanage used to be.

The morning mist was pushed aside and like a colony of busy ants, a town began to take shape. The canteen tent was the first thing to be set up. When Boot and his friends heard all the commotion, they went to investigate. As far as they were concerned the grounds of the old orphanage were their private park. They had plenty of space to run, an inexhaustible supply of squirrels to chase and an occasional rabbit to add extra excitement.

They stood on the edge of the field and watched. To Boot, the big trailers looked like train cars and the smells coming from the canteen tent reminded him of his days on the road with Texas Bill. That seemed like a good enough reason to hang around and see what was going on. Boot and his buddies had plenty of company because pretty soon almost the entire population of Lost River had gathered to watch.

Unemployed men eager for work and boys eager for excitement showed up hoping to get hired. The lucky ones were signed on as roustabouts which promised a safe place to sleep, good food and maybe a dollar or two in their pockets. If their luck held, some of the men might even get hired on a permanent basis.

Mr. K and Inky were on hand to cover the tent raising for the paper. The crowd watched anxiously as the center poles were set with ropes dangling from pullies at the top. One end of the rope was attached to the canvas and the other end was attached to the elephants' harnesses. On a signal from the trainers, all 12 elephants started to walk outward and the Big Top rose up like a giant toadstool after a hard rain.

Boot and his buddies gave those big animals a wide berth. When the main tent was finally in place, the onlookers whistled and applauded. The circus had officially arrived. Mr. K. took a series of pictures which appeared on the front page of that week's edition.

Having the circus in town gave the grown-ups permission to momentarily forget their troubles, to act like a kid again, to laugh at clowns and marvel at the lady in pink tights flying through the air. The dirt and weeds of the grounds around the old orphanage became a magical place of color and lights, music and the smell of popcorn and spun sugar. Where else could you eat dusty cotton candy, candied apples and hot dogs and gape at the bearded lady, the tattooed man, the sword swallower and a gaggle of trained geese—all in one place?

Otherwise prudent businessmen and penny-wise wives gladly laid their money down to toss rings over bottle necks and shoot pop guns at cardboard ducks hoping to win a stuffed animal or a plastic bag with two goldfish swimming around inside. No one seemed to notice—or care—that Boot and his friends mingled with the crowd and wandered into the main tent without tickets.

Adults and little kids welcomed the circus every year. But the Big Top offered a different kind of excitement for the teenagers. For Hank Stubbs, Sonny Cumberland, and Matt Blalock, it was the height of the social season. People—that is to say girls—from all the nearby towns came to the circus. The three friends slicked their hair, puffed out their chests and practiced their best moves.

They explored the midway early in the day and scouted out the games of chance where they were most likely to shine and the side shows where they could show off their bravery. When the main tent started to fill up, they held back waiting to see where the prettiest girls were sitting. Spotting three in a row took some time, but it was worth the effort.

The next step was for the boys to saunter in one at a time and take a seat by the girl of their choice. They moved with the precision of a well-trained team, in matching uniforms: denim jeans with the cuffs rolled up one turn, white T-shirts, white socks and penny loafers. It was all right to *be* different as long as you looked like everybody else. Thank goodness Mother Nature provided some variations. Hank was tall, Sonny was short and Matt had red hair.

The boys weren't the only ones checking out the crowd. Three girls from Empire, a town just over the line in the next county were on the look-out too. They knew the rule: spread out, no boy was going to approach three girls bunched up together. The problem was, they did everything together. Before they started first grade, they pricked their fingers, shared their blood and promised to stay together and to be best friends forever. Their mothers all lived on the same street, went to the same church, shopped at the Piggly-Wiggly and loved movies. When their daughters were born, the women named each girl after a movie star: Olivia, Ingrid, and Rita.

Before they left Empire, the girls solved the question of "what are gonna wear?" by choosing white blouses with Peter Pan collars and summer cotton skirts all made from Simplicity pattern 8458. Olivia and Ingrid wore espadrilles so they would look taller, Rita wore ballerina flats so she wouldn't.

On a normal evening, the chances of three eligible guys finding three pretty girls were slim, but this was circus night so anything was possible. Hank went first and sat down beside Rita. In no time, Matt and Sonny squeezed in by Olivia and Ingrid.

For the next two hours they had a great time. So did Boot and his friends. They sat under the first row of bleachers with a great view of all the acts. Everything was going fine until the wrangler with his trained geese entered the ring. Boot had kept a respectful distance from the big animals. But geese? He'd chased a few of them in his time and found it great sport.

Without a second thought, he bounded out from under the bleachers and launched himself into the middle of the startled birds. It looked like fun, so his friends joined him. The idea was to round up the geese and chase them out of the tent. But they wouldn't cooperate. They had strength in numbers. They stood their ground, hissed and flapped their enormous wings.

Boot was shocked, but he wasn't stupid. He turned tail and ran with the other dogs and a flock of very angry geese right behind. The crowd laughed, applauded and the wrangler—being a trained showman—took a bow on his way out. The act was definitely a hit. Trapeze acts and big clowns in tiny cars followed and when the show was over, the teenagers didn't want the evening to end.

As they were leaving the tent, Hank saw his parents ahead of them and suddenly got an idea. "I'll be right back." He hurried to catch up with his folks. "Hey, Dad, wait up! Great show, huh? Listen, can I borrow the car?"

His father had not quite gotten over the episode with his new car and he was certainly not thrilled about handing over the keys. No surprise there, but Hank was ready to plead his case. "We just met these real nice girls from over in Empire, and I was wondering if we could drive them home. All three of us, you know, me and Sonny and Matt. Rita's dad—she's the girl I was sitting with—drove them over, but I was hoping maybe you could talk to him and…."

Hank was prepared to keep talking until his dad gave in, but to his surprise, his mother spoke up. "Zach, why not let him use the car? We could walk home, it's a nice night for a moonlight stroll… What do you think?"

Zach looked at Eden and slowly realized his night might have possibilities he had not originally considered. It should take Hank a couple of hours to drive to Empire and back…

"OK, if your mother thinks it's a good idea, here." He handed Hank the keys. "Take your time, no speeding!"

The plans were made. Hank went to join his friends and the girls. Rita talked to her dad and he gave his permission. The teenagers piled in the Rocket 88 and Zach and Eden walked home arm in arm.

Without a specific deadline, Hank decided they had time to stop by the Dairy Queen in Empire and still get back to Lost River before midnight. So far, it had been a great night. About 11:30 the boys dropped the girls at Rita's house and said good night. On the way home, Sonny blurted out, "I wish Lost River had a swimming pool."

"Why?"

"Because if girls wear white bathing suits, and they get wet, then you can see right through them."

"No way."

"Yeah, it's like they're invisible. You can see everything. And that's not all. Did you know you can't get a girl in trouble if you do it in the water?"

Hank nearly drove off the road. "Where'd you hear that?"

"Around."

Matt shook his head. "That's dumb. How are you gonna lie down in a swimming pool without drowning?"

"You don't have to lie down," Sonny said.

"You don't?!" This was clearly a new idea for Matt.

"Most folks can do it standing up. Course you can't 'cause you're a Baptist and somebody might think you were dancing." Hank and Sonny burst out laughing.

Matt didn't think it was so funny. "You guys are getting way ahead of yourselves. You haven't even gotten to first base yet."

"Never hurts to be prepared."

Meanwhile, the girls sat on Rita's front porch talking too. "I can't believe we met three cute boys all at the same time. And one of them has a car... at least he can borrow his dad's big car. I'm so glad Hank picked me because he's tall. That means I can wear heels with him. You know, I could never date a boy shorter than me. You have to be able to look up to a guy, like they do in the movies."

Olivia chimed in, "Wouldn't it be great if we all fell in love at the same time? We could triple date and invite them over to the fall dance. It would be perfect."

"And after a while we could all get engaged..." Ingrid added. "And get married. We could have a triple wedding. That would save our folks a lot of money."

"My dad would love that," Rita said. "I've got two older sisters to marry off before Dad gets to me and by that time there probably won't be any money left."

"It would be the best thing ever. We could build our houses close together…"

Ingrid picked up on the idea, "It would be just like we planned when we were all in first grade. And we could raise our kids together and…

"Oh, slow down," Olivia said. "I think we're getting way ahead of ourselves. We haven't even kissed the boys yet."

"That's true, but it never hurts to be prepared," Ingrid sighed with a far-away look in her eyes.

Being prepared is a good thing, but nobody was prepared for what happened next.

A Little Doohickey

The speculation that surrounded the disappearance of Annabelle and the mayor was initially exciting, but the citizens of Lost River were a lot more upset about the mayor running off with their money than about his running off with the Episcopal priest's wife.

The circus had been fun, but now they had to get down to brass tacks and *do* something. The question was what. The town had looked forward to a new fire truck, but now they were back to relying on the old one which only started when the spirit moved it. Hazel came to work every day in the mayor's office, even though all she could do was to keep repeating "I'm sorry, I don't know where the mayor is. Yes, he took all the money. No, I don't know if he's ever coming back." She said that so often, she was reciting it in her sleep. And on top of that, she had no idea who was going to pay her salary.

Sheriff Latham was the only official left, so after they talked to Hazel, everyone called him with their problems. Thank the Lord, Lucy was in the office and she and J.W. did their best to keep things under control. However, as the problems mounted and the complaints went unanswered, it was clear something had to be done—and quickly.

With everything else that was going on, Lucy had forgotten about Andrew's call saying Annabelle was all right. She already knew that because she had seen Annabelle around town, so she was a little bit surprised to look up and see the young woman standing in front of her desk. "Lord have mercy, Annabelle. What brings you in here?"

"Nothing much. I just thought I ought to come by in person and apologize for any trouble my trip to Savannah might have caused y'all. It was just a spur-of-the-moment thing and Andrew and I got our wires crossed. You know, just a silly misunderstanding." She could tell by the look on Lucy's face she was talking too much and not saying anything helpful. She took Andrew's arm and smiled sweetly. "We just wanted to let you know everything is fine now."

After they left, Lucy looked at J.W. "Was I that scatter-brained when I was her age?"

"Maybe. I didn't know you at that age." He ducked just in case Lucy took offence at his remark. Scatter-brained or not, J.W. was glad at least one problem was solved, but everything was far from fine.

Andrew and Annabelle left in a hurry and nearly tripped over Morris Fullerton and his cane. They apologized and made a hasty exit. Morris took a minute to regain his balance. He favored his right leg and was a little unsteady on his feet.

It's a well-known fact that every small town has an oddball or two and Morris was one of Lost River's. He was a quiet little man who always wore a white shirt with the sleeves rolled up and a string tie. He lived with his mother in a big old Southern house. Behind the house was a separate building where Morris had a repair shop. He re-caned chairs, did upholstery and the men in town all knew him well because he could fix anything. Morris was shy about his lopsided walk. His mother's arthritis made it hard for her to get around too, so they mostly kept to themselves.

Their standoffishness didn't sit well with the mothers of Lost River. They considered the Fullertons odd, maybe even dangerous. To be on the safe side, they warned their kids to "stay away from that Morris Fullerton." When they asked why, kids got the standard adult answer, "Because I said so, that's why."

Morris would have been surprised at his reputation. He was a gentle man and went out of his way not to attract attention. He had gotten so good at it, sometimes people didn't notice him at all. Like now. He stood in front of the sheriff's desk holding his hat in his hand, waiting politely.

Finally, J.W. looked up, but even then, it took him a second or two to place the man. As far as he could remember, he'd never seen Morris in the office before. "Well, Morris, you're a surprise. What can I do for you?"

"I reckon it's something I can do for *you*. I want to give y'all some money."

"Here, sit down."

Morris eased himself into a chair.

"Morris, I don't understand."

Morris placed his cane across the arms of the chair. "Everybody says the city's broke, so I wanta pay the bills until y'all can get back on your feet."

J.W. tried not to smile. "That would take a lot of money, Morris."

"That's OK, I got a lot." He took a deep breath and then began an explanation that he had obviously rehearsed beforehand. "Long time ago Mr. Tony Conti asked me to fix his lawn mower. You see it would work fine as long as it was running full on, but when he let it idle, it would cut out. Then he'd have to crank it again and he didn't like having to do that." Morris shifted his weight, took a deep breath and continued.

"Well, I made a little doohickey that fixed the problem. Mr. Tony was real pleased and one day he ran into the Briggs and Stratton salesman at Mr. Vinnie's General Store and showed it to him. That feller was real impressed too and wanted me to give him one to show to his engineers." He took another deep breath. J.W. resisted the urge to interrupt. Instead, he lit a cigarette and settled in for what was shaping up to be a long story. Lucy joined him.

"Mr. Tony said we could talk about that the next time the feller was in town. When he left, Mr. Tony told me I needed to patent that little doohickey. That way nobody could use it unless I said it was OK. And that's what we did." Another deep breath.

"Later on, the Briggs and Stratton Company gave me a contract. Now every time they put one of those things in one of their motors, they pay me two cents. I know it don't sound like much, but they make lots of motors for all kinds of stuff. Mr. Cumberland over at the bank helped me open a savings account. Now he tells me I'm the richest man in town, but I think he's just funning me. Anyway, those fellers at Briggs and Stratton have been sending me checks for a lotta years. What I need is for you to tell me how much money y'all need to keep things going for a while."

By this time both J.W. and Lucy were listening spellbound. Nobody had ever heard Morris say more than two or three words at a time. And certainly, nobody ever dreamed Morris Fullerton was rich. J.W. finally came to. "Morris, if you're serious, you might be able to save the town! But Lord, Man, I've never heard you talk that much before."

"It's because ttttalking make me nervous. That's the reason I don't do it much."

"Well, you did it fine just now."

"That's because I was explaining something. When folks just stand around ttttalking, I can't ever ttttthink of anything to say. That's why when I see folks, I just cross the street so I don't have to ttttalk."

"Well, that explains a lot," J.W. thought.

"We can go over to the bank whenever you've got the time," Morris said. "You just let me know." He heaved himself out of the chair and started to leave. Then he turned around. "There's just one more thing, Sheriff. I don't want anybody to know where the money is coming from because then they might want to ttttalk to me. You gotta promise not to ttttell anybody."

J.W. and Lucy readily agreed. J.W. shook Morris' hand and Lucy gave him a kiss on the cheek. Morris hung his head and turned four shades of red. After he left, Lucy said, "I hope I didn't embarrass him too much. I just kinda got carried away. It's just that he's the first person to come in here with good news…"

J.W. smiled. "Don't worry about it, Lucy. Hell, I was ready to kiss him too."

Keeping Morris' secret was a small price to pay for the funds it would take to get the town momentarily sorted out. Bright and early the next day, J.W. and Morris sat down with Sid Cumberland at the bank. They met in the conference room.

As befitting his position as President of Lost River Bank and Trust, Sid made it a point to look prosperous. The bank was the only building in town with air-conditioning which allowed Sid to wear his three-piece suits in comfort. His vest added a note of dignity and hid his expanding waist.

Sid had personally prepared all the necessary papers. Of course, he trusted his staff, but you can't be too careful with a secret of such magnitude. When all the signatures were in place, J.W. breathed a sigh of relief. At least for the moment, the town was saved. Lost River had a temporary reprieve, Morris Fullerton had gotten his first kiss and ventured out of his shell just a little bit.

Story #8, Morris Fullerton
(Philippines Circa 1941)

On December 8, 1941, the day after Japan bombed Pearl Harbor, the Japanese invaded the Philippines. Within a month, they had captured Manila and the American and Filipino soldiers stationed there were forced to retreat to the Bataan Peninsula. For the next three months, they held out alone. Because of the devastation at Pearl Harbor, there was no naval or air support available, no supplies or ammunition. Forces on the ground soon realized they had no hope of getting any reinforcements.

By April 9, 1942, the situation was critical. The troops were crippled by starvation and disease and General Edward King, Jr. reluctantly faced the unavoidable decision that he must surrender the combined forces of 75,000 American and Filipino troops to General Masahara Homma of the Imperial Japanese Empire.

General King knew his men were not quitters and he recognized the sacrifice he was asking them to make. "As you know, we have no further means of resistance. We are low on ammunition, have virtually no medical supplies and our food is all but gone. If I do not surrender my forces to the Japanese today, Bataan will be known around the world as the greatest slaughter in history." Even so, many of the sick and wounded cried as they laid down their arms.

"Men you must always remember that you *did not surrender, I ordered you to surrender."*

The Japanese troops saw the situation in a totally different light. They believed in Bushido, *the Samurai code that said a true warrior would rather die than surrender. All they saw were weak men who gave up rather than fight to the death as honorable soldiers. With that as the background, the Bataan Death March began. The prisoners were marched approximately 50 miles north to the closest rail head at San Fernando. Their ultimate destination was Camp O'Donnell. It had originally been a Filipino training camp that the Japanese took over and turned into a prison. From the very start, the Japanese treated the inmates with utter contempt.*

The inhumane treatment started on that march north. If a prisoner asked for food, he was shot. If anyone got malaria or dysentery, he was shot. If someone fell behind, he was shot. If anyone stopped to help a buddy, they were both shot. There were free-flowing artesian wells along the road, but anyone who tried to get water was shot.

When the captives got to the railhead at San Fernando, they were stuffed into sweltering metal boxcars. The prisoners were packed in so tightly nobody could move, not even if they passed out. If men had to relieve themselves, they did it where they stood. The stench was overwhelming. It was an added indignity.

The end of the line meant freedom from the boxcars and a breath of fresh air. Bodies were pulled out of the train cars and piled on the ground, but the torture wasn't over.

Finally, the prisoners were forced to walk another ten miles to Camp O'Donnell. Along the road, soldiers wrapped buddies in blankets and carried them suspended between two bamboo poles. The Japanese shot anyone who couldn't walk and left them by the side of the road.

In the camp, Americans were separated from the Filipino soldiers. The first day, the Japanese ordered the American prisoners to empty their pockets. Anyone found with Japanese money or souvenirs was shot. Their captors assumed the items had been stolen from dead Japanese soldiers. Americans weren't treated like Prisoners of War; they were considered the scum of the earth.

Prisoners were routinely beaten and tortured. One favorite punishment was the sun treatment. In the 110-degree heat, men were forced to strip and sit for hours in the direct sun with no protection. Japanese soldiers stood in the shade and passed around a jar of water. Sometimes they would hold the jar up, pour the water on the ground and laugh. The abuse went on day and night.

One young soldier woke up in the middle of the night with a piercing pain in his right leg. He reached down and touched it; it felt warm and wet. When he opened his eyes, he saw a Japanese soldier shaking blood off a bayonet and laughing with his friends as they walked away. Other prisoners came to his rescue. They stopped the bleeding because they knew if the young man couldn't walk, the Japanese soldiers would kill him without batting an eye.

There were 7,000 Americans and only one spigot of drinkable water in their part of the camp. Food was one cup of watery rice a day, no medical care at all. Prisoners died like flies. Some of those who managed to survive the Death March were sent to Japan to work in the mines, on the docks or in the factories. The brutality continued.

In October, 1944, General Douglas MacArthur finally made good on his promise to return to the Philippines. Four months later in February 1945, US and Filipino forces recaptured the Bataan Peninsula.

The war ground on and finally in September of 1945, General Masuhara Homma was arrested by Allied troops. He was convicted of war crimes relating to the actions of troops under his direct command. He was executed by firing squad on April 3, 1946.

The exact number of Americans and Filipinos who died in the Bataan Death March and the three and a half years that followed will never be known. Too many men simply died and were left by the side of the road. Estimates range from 6,000 to 18,000 deaths.

Morris Fullerton was one of the few survivors.

Bridge

From the very beginning, the women of Lost River were a force to be reckoned with. When Estelle Sweeney, Mike's great, great grandmother heard from her friend in Richmond that all the aristocrats in her social circle were playing whist, she immediately organized a group of her own. Later when the game evolved into bridge, she formed the Lost River Bridge Club.

Throughout the years, nothing interfered with The Club. Marriages, births—and some folks said, even funerals—were scheduled around the sanctity of the second Saturday of each month. Vacancies were created by death and in some cases by senility. There was a rumor that a member could be expelled for adultery, but only if it involved another member's husband.

In the light of the recent municipal malfeasance and temporary financial deliverance, the group gathering for the July meeting was unusually serious. They trooped into the Back Backroom one by one: Widow Mackie, Eden Stubbs, Florence Cumberland, Earlene Barlow, Helen Kirkland, Mildred Leland and the Conti wives: Sophia, Nina and Isabella. The church group was made up of Annabelle Knox, Prim Blalock and LouAnn Henshaw, the Methodist minister's wife and Bridget Ward, Father Sullivan's cook and housekeeper. The women with full-time jobs included Eudalee Munson, Trudy Latham, Gibby Moon, Ethyl Williams, Lucy Washburn, Vicki Nichols and Hazel Goodman. Just enough for five tables of four players.

All rank and religion were dropped at the door. Lost River was too small to allow proselytizing. The religion you started out with was what you ended up with. Exceptions were made for a husband or wife to change churches so the couple could attend together. Once in a while a bunch of Baptists got crossways with their preacher and swarmed off to start a new church, but that hadn't happened for a long time.

Although they weren't meeting at Florence's house, she took charge of the group. "Ladies, before we settle down to play cards, I think we need to discuss what's going on with the City Council. I know that we are all thankful for our anonymous benefactor, but that money will probably run out sooner or later." Before she could continue, Lucy Washburn spoke up.

"Do y'all remember the story about the Little Red Hen? When she needs help getting her wheat ground into flour to make bread, everybody's too busy. Well, that's about what's going on with the City Council. I've heard 'em talking in the sheriff's office. Everybody wants the town to prosper, but nobody wants to get involved. The present Council's trying to keep it a secret, but they're all gonna resign and they're scraping the bottom of the barrel to find somebody else to run for office."

Florence started to continue, but Lucy cut her short. "Just listen. Let me tell you who they've come up with so far! Mr. Slonacher, the school principal for mayor. And their choices for City Council are even worse than that. Harvey Powell, for Council President, Billy Bob Meachum for Secretary, Percy Barns has *volunteered* to be Treasurer and Buster Hornby wants to be vice-something. Mayor or president, he doesn't care which."

Everybody started talking at once. "Slonacher is older than I am, and I'm older than dirt," Eudalee said. "That man just sits in his office and sleeps all day. And Billy Bob!?! I taught him in the first grade and I didn't think he'd ever learn how to write. His penmanship was terrible. When I talked to him about it, he said he did it on purpose so nobody would know he didn't know how to spell."

Eden spoke up. "I can't believe they're suggesting Harvey Powell for Council President. For heaven's sake, everybody knows why he took 'early retirement.' It was either that or get run out of town."

Prim took over. "Let me tell you a thing or two about Percy Barns. He's a nice enough fellow, but his problem is that he's too smart for his own good. He gets a job and in no time he gets bored. That's when he starts *volunteering* for everything. Over at Bethel Baptist, we call him Mr. Yesbut. No matter what the deacons suggest, the first words out of his mouth are always, 'Yes, but...' I'm telling you he'll find something wrong with anything, anybody suggests. They'll never get anything done. We are in deep trouble, no doubt about it."

"And then there's Buster," Helen said. "If the newspaper printed a list of the biggest drinkers in town, he'd be right on top. Buster's the town lush and everybody knows it. What are these men thinking?"

Eudalee chimed in. "There was a time when Buster was more or less respectable. Maybe he's reformed."

"Maybe," Lucy said. "J. W. says Buster has given his word to sober up once a month for the Council meeting. The way Buster figures it, it's the least he can do to repay the city for providing him room and board all those Saturday nights."

"Lord have mercy," Florence said. "if that bunch of lay-abouts gets elected, Prim is right, we *are* in serious trouble."

Silence descended.

Finally, Ethyl spoke up. Paying attention to what the men were talking about in the Back Backroom gave her an inside track on what they were planning. "I'm just going to throw this out to see what y'all think about it. The other night the sheriff and a bunch of the men were drinking and talking and somebody said they ought to turn the whole thing over to their wives and let them work it out. Of course, he was just joking, but considering what they've come up with so far, I'm thinking that might not be a bad idea."

More silence.

"Well," Mildred said cautiously, "let's see what we might have to offer. Lord knows, we couldn't make things any worse."

They went around the room listing their experience, but mostly that was having babies, helping out in the family business and running a home. Sophia Conti finally said, "I've been writing about this town to my Italian relatives for years. I think I could handle taking notes at the Council meetings."

Mildred made a note. Sophie Conti for secretary.

That gave Annabelle courage to speak up, "I know I'm a newcomer, but I was treasurer of my sorority at Agnes Scott the year we got a $10,000 grant. I was responsible for keeping track of the money and writing all the reports. And I didn't steal a penny."

Mildred added her name. Annabelle Knox for treasurer.

Trudy looked around the room, "I'm pretty busy over at the Do-or-Dye, but I reckon I could be vice-president 'cause they don't really have to do much. Right?"

Another name went on to the list. Trudy Latham, vice president.

"God knows I've worked behind the scenes with Zach to run the mill for years. I may live to regret this, but if nobody else wants to take it on, I guess I could be president," Eden Stubbs said hesitantly.

That rounded out the ballot. Eden Stubbs, president.

Mildred read the list. Everyone agreed it was a great improvement over the roster the men had come up with. "All we need now is a candidate for mayor…"

That was greeted by a long empty silence.

Finally, Widow Mackie spoke up from the back of the room. "I have a bachelor's degree in business from Penn State." Every head in the room turned to look at her. Nobody had ever thought to ask about her life before she came to live in Lost River.

She hesitated a minute and then stood up. "Warren and I always worked together. He had the ideas, but I was the unofficial project manager. I was good at sorting out the details and making sure we met deadlines."

While the others were thinking their way through this new information, Ethyl clearly saw the handwriting on the wall. "Hot damn! This'll work. We've got it. We can do this!" She started to laugh. "I think Mayor Mackie's got a real nice ring to it."

It only took a moment for the idea to become a plan. After their initial excitement died down, Gibby spoke up. "But how are we gonna get our names on the ballot? The men will never stand for us running against them."

Widow Mackie walked slowly to the front of the room. "Ladies, I think it's time we took a page out of Eugene Tallmadge's playbook of Southern Politics."

Just One Little Problem

"Come on Ladies, y'all ought to remember this story," Eudalee said. "For a couple of months after the election just a few years ago, we had three men all claiming to be the governor. The crisis was basically caused by our state's complicated county-unit system. It was supposedly designed to keep the big cities from overwhelming the rural communities. Eugene Talmadge, who was born over in Forsyth, was fond of telling everybody, 'I can carry any county that ain't got street cars.'

"Here's the way it works. We have 159 counties. The eight big city counties get six unit-votes each. The rest of the 30 town counties get four unit-votes each. That leaves 121 counties classified as rural and they each get two unit-votes. To win, candidates have to get a majority of *unit votes*—not to be confused with a majority of the popular vote. That was right up Talmadge's alley.

"Eugene's supporters were pretty sure he would win, but there was just one little problem. He was 62 and in very bad health. His political backers were afraid he would win the county-unit vote, and then die before he could take the oath of office. They needed a back-up plan and they found it in the Georgia Constitution.

Eudalee went on to explain. "That document says if no person wins the majority vote, the legislature gets to pick a governor from the other leading candidates. The way the Talmadge crowd saw it, if Eugene died, he couldn't be considered a person. That would leave only the two remaining candidates: James Carmichael and D. T. Bowers. But that wouldn't work. What they needed was *another Talmadge* and they found him in Herman, Eugene's 33-year-old son.

"There was just one little problem. Herman wasn't on the ballot. The solution to that problem was simple, make Herman a write-in candidate. Just to be on the safe side, they lined up what they thought would be enough legislative votes to insure his election if it came to that.

"Sure enough, Eugene died on December 21 before he could be sworn in. So, they went to plan B. There was just one little problem. When the legislature counted the write-in votes, Carmichael had 669 votes, Bowers had 637 and Herman had 617. Then a miracle occurred. An extra 56 votes for Herman were found in Telfair County. That's Herman's home territory.

"Shockingly 34 of the ballots had been cast in alphabetical order and on top of that, some of the voters had been dead for years while others swore they had never voted at all. Minor technicalities. When the official totals were finally announced, Herman Talmadge won with 673 county-unit votes.

"There was just one little problem. For the first time, we had a lieutenant governor. Officially, he became chief executive if the governor died in office. However, the constitution was a little fuzzy about what happened if the governor-elect died *before* he took the oath of office.

"Ellis Arnall was the sitting governor and had every intention of staying in office. The new lieutenant governor, M.E. Thompson thought he should become acting governor. And as the majority winner of the county-unit votes, Herman Talmadge thought the victory was his.

"As it turned out, Herman was right. He was elected governor by the legislature, just like his cronies had planned. There was just one little problem. When he went to claim the office from Arnall, the guy refused to leave the premises. The next day, Georgia had three governors. Arnall sitting in the official office, Talmadge sitting in an anteroom and Thompson walking the halls.

"That afternoon, Herman told a state trooper to make sure that Mr. Arnall left the office and got home safely. There was just one little problem. His home was in Newnan, 40 miles south of Atlanta, down in Coweta County.

"The next morning Arnall was back at the Capitol. There was just one little problem. During the night, Hermon had the locks changed. Arnall didn't give up. He commandeered an information desk in the rotunda and governed from there.

"The wrangling went on for a while and in all the hubbub, someone realized the state seal, needed for all official documents, was missing. Secretary of State Ben Fortson said he had no idea who the legitimate governor was, so he just hid the seal under the cushion on his wheelchair. The turmoil went on for a while, but finally, Herman wore down the competition."

"So that's how Herman Talmadge got to be governor," Trudy said.

"Hummon—that's what his goodoleboys call him," Earlene corrected.

Helen chimed in, "I knew part of the story, but I'd forgotten some of the details. I remember his daddy, Gene, campaigning around here. Always in a long-sleeved white shirt, a tie and both a belt and suspenders."

"My father-in-law still says Gene Talmadge was the best entertainment in town," Hazel added. "He fancied himself the voice of the farmers. At some time in every speech, he'd say, 'Y'all got only three friends in this world: The Lord God Almighty, the Sears Roebuck catalog and Eugene Talmadge. And you can only vote for one."

"All this is fascinating, but we need to get back to business. I still want to know how we're going to get on the ballot," Gibby said.

Several voices spoke up, "Write-ins. It's a proud Southern tradition."

Gibby wasn't convinced. "I think you're leaving out a couple of steps. I don't see how this is going to work."

"First of all, we'll go house to house and explain to women that in this election they have a choice. We just have to make sure they get out and vote," Widow Mackie said.

Next, they wrote some simple instructions and made sample ballots to show voters how to handle the write-in candidates. They also printed some facts about each of the women candidates. Chances are nobody knew that Widow Mackie graduated from Penn State.

They settled on the Do-or-Dye as their headquarters. Women would feel comfortable coming there and no self-respecting man would show his face in a beauty shop. The meeting broke up by 2:30 to give everybody time to get home in time to cook supper.

As they were leaving, Eudalee said, "Ladies, this reminds me of one of my favorite Mark Twain quotes. He said, 'Politicians and diapers should be changed often and for the same reason.'"

Everyone laughed. For the first time in the history of the Lost River Bridge Club, politics trumped bridge. Not a single card was dealt and nobody seemed to care. They were on a mission to save their town.

Vote Early and Vote Often

Leon Kirkland was beside himself with excitement. He had a real news story worthy of a banner headline ready for the next edition of the *Lost River Herald*. Big city newspapers like the *Macon News* or the *Atlanta Journal* ran major stories all the time, but weekly newspapers generally had to make do with reporting high school football games or the price of hog bellies.

Since the first time Inky came from the orphanage to work in the shop, Leon had been teaching him how to set type and lay out the paper. Leon's son, Steve, had never shown the slightest interest in the shop. He couldn't get away fast enough to go hunting or fishing. Even if he had made it through the war, Leon knew Steve would never have been interested in taking over the business. Inky, on the other hand, was a natural. Now Leon and Inky stood side by side making up the paper.

"Entire City Council Resigns!" The banner head stretched all across the front page.

Secretly, Leon had always wanted to run a headline with an exclamation point at the end. His first draft of the story was purple prose, no doubt about it. Even Inky gave that one thumbs down. Leon had to admit he had gone a little overboard with the adjectives. The solution was to get back to basics, who, what, when, where, why and how.

The story reminded readers of the mayor's involvement in the events leading up to the crisis with a reference to inside pages for more details. It also directed readers to the editorial page where Leon explained that the Council had not resigned as a sign of any involvement on their part, but rather to express their regret at having let the citizens of Lost River down. In an effort to set things right, they had scheduled an election and agreed to stay on until the new council could take office. To round out the story, Leon listed the roster of candidates.

Sly Slonacher, Mayor

Harvey Powell, City Council President

Buster Hornby, Vice-president

Junior Ottley, Secretary

Percy Barns, Treasurer.

Although it was common knowledge by the time the paper came out, Leon couldn't pass up the rare opportunity to go over the details of the real-life scandal about the mayor and the Sweeny family in general. After all, he figured it was his civic duty to at least make sure folks got the facts straight. He and Inky laid out a double-page spread on the inside pages.

It took some time, but Leon finally found a quote from Waylon Sidney Bethune III that was fit to print. "I declare Boys, y'all got yourselves in a world of hurt." Inky searched old photo files and found some pictures of the mayor in better times. He even found some really old pictures of Sweeny's ancestors. He also included a shot of the old, run-down fire truck, just in case anyone missed the significance of the theft.

Once that was complete, they turned to inserting local advertising, setting up the want-ads and fitting in other news. Like most weekly papers, the *Herald* was a family affair. Helen was in charge of features like sewing tips and favorite recipes. She was also responsible for obituaries and the society page in which she published engagements, weddings, anniversaries and other local social gatherings. What the readers really looked forward to was news about the comings and goings of their neighbors. Who went where, when, why and with whom. The staff of the *Herald* finally "put the paper to bed" and the next morning Inky got on his bike and delivered them to one and all.

When the women from the Bridge Club read the paper, they smiled. They had printed a sample write-in ballot with instructions. These were bundled, labeled and delivered the day before the citizens got their weekly newspaper. If the woman of the house had any doubts about the importance of voting, Leon's editorial about the Sweeneys and the two-page spread with pictures outlined the problem. Listing the candidates running for City Council had an unexpected consequence. Women read it and suddenly realized why the write-in votes were so important.

The one thing that was missing was the excitement of an actual race. There were no political speeches, no one was casting aspersions or making promises they couldn't keep. Where was the fun?

Trudy called a meeting. "We need to get the women together, get them talking, build up some excitement. I've got an idea."

She showed them a brand-new, 24-cup coffee maker and several cases of Coca-Cola. "I'm going to serve the Cokes like the society ladies in Atlanta. You ice the bottles down in a silver punch bowl and serve them with fancy napkins and straws."

"That's a great idea," said Ethyl. "How about putting out a sign? Something like, 'Stop by for a wash-n-set, free refreshments and local gossip.' That ought to draw a crowd."

Trudy's idea paid off. Women talking and sharing ideas in small groups worked so well Sophia Conti suggested each of the church groups hold a tea. The invitation made no mention of politics, just fellowship, tea, cakes and, of course, cucumber sandwiches. Working on the idea that "it may not help but it couldn't hurt," each tea party ended with a prayer for divine guidance.

The men—who were all running unopposed—saw no reason to waste time making speeches and campaigning in the heat and humidity of late August. However, they did plaster huge posters all over town. "Vote Early and Vote Often. Elect Slonacher and a New City Council." J.W. had always appreciated Mayor Dailey's approach to democracy and at least the signs added a little humor to the world's most boring election. On election day, the Wednesday after Labor Day, a storm rolled in. "I hope this isn't a sign," Prim Blalock said ringing her hands.

The voting was overseen by Rev. Robert Blalock from Bethel Baptist —better known in Lost River as Brother Bob. He and Rev. James Henshaw from Wesley United Methodist Church took the first shift. Andrew Knox from Trinity Episcopal and Father Sullivan of St. Philip's Catholic Church took the late shift. Some folks might have questioned the separation of church and state, but given the town's luck with politicians so far, they decided to leave the voting in the hands of God or at least in the hands of the clergy. The polls closed at 5:00 and the counting began at 6:30.

It was Wednesday night so Brother Bob left early to set up for prayer meeting. That left James Henshaw, Father Sullivan and Andrew Knox to count. J.W. was on hand to make sure everything was legal.

The country might have a two-party system, but in South Georgia, there was only one party. Democratic. You'd have to go out-of-state to even find a Republican. Since the voters only had one choice, nobody was taking the counting too seriously. However, they were keeping a running tally.

Father Sullivan read the first ballot. "Mayor, Sly Slonacher. City Council President, Harvey Powell; Vice-president, Buster Hornby; Secretary, Junior Ottley and Treasurer, Percy Barns." Andrew marked the tally sheet.

And the second. "Mayor, Sly Slonacher. City Council President, Harvey Powell; Vice-president, Buster Hornby; Secretary, Junior Ottley and Treasurer, Percy Barns." Andrew marked the tally sheet.

And the third. "Mayor, Agnes Mackie. What?! Mackie? What's her name doing here?" He glanced down the page, "My God, all the names are different. Somebody's written in a whole new slate of officers. City Council President, Eden Stubbs. Secretary, Sophia Conti. Treasurer, Annabelle Knox..."

Andrew smudged the tally sheet. "What!?"

"That's right. Your wife is listed as the candidate for Treasurer and Trudy Latham is running for Vice President." Now it was J.W.'s turn to be shocked.

Father Sullivan paused a moment to shuffle through more ballots, "Saints preserve us, they're all women!"

Quickly the men shook the remaining ballots out of the box onto the table and started sorting through them. "Here's another one. And another one."

"Heaven help us, they're all over the place."

It took several hours, and the numbers on the tally sheet told a shocking story. "What does this mean?" Father Sullivan asked.

J.W. looked over Andrew's shoulder at the final totals. "I thought Chicago politics were wild, but this takes the cake."

With just the slightest smile he said, "Gentlemen, I'm afraid this means we've been hornswoggled."

Extra!

Voters Elect All-Female City Government

In an unprecedented move in yesterday's voting, the following candidates were elected to the City Council by an overwhelming majority. Mayor, Agnes Mackie. City Council President, Eden Stubbs; Vice-president, Trudy Latham; Secretary, Sophie Conti and Treasurer, Annabelle Knox.

The situation came about as a result of a list of write-in candidates being added to the official ballot. The election committee was taken completely by surprise and Sheriff J.W. Latham was heard to say, "Gentlemen, we have been hornswoggled."

The new Mayor and City Council will take office immediately. Preliminary research indicates that this election makes Lost River the first town in the state of Georgia to have an exclusively female city government.

The male candidates, Sly Slonacher, Harvey Powell, Buster Hornby, Junior Ottley and Percy Barns, refused to comment.

Story #9, Agnes (Allentown, Pa, 1909)

There were no two ways about it. The baby was ugly. Not deformed or disfigured, just...not pretty. Friends and family were at a loss for what to say to the parents. Lutherans were not prone to flowery speeches, but new babies were usually fawned over. After all those months of being pregnant and then all those hours in labor, the mother deserved to hear some kind words. In this case, visitors talked about perfect little fingers and toes. They made encouraging remarks about how healthy the baby looked. Her grandmother predicted that the child would be smart. Everyone hoped she was right. They named her Agnes, which didn't help matters any.

Agnes' father, who was in his late 50s, was every bit the Proud Papa. He carried his new daughter everywhere and introduced her to all his friends. "We make a handsome pair, don't we? Look just alike. Neither one of us has any hair or any teeth." He laughed and so did Baby Agnes.

As she got older, her features filled out some. She had nice dark eyes; they were just a little too close together. Her hair, when it finally came in, was thick, although it was just a little too curly. Her nose, well, it was just a little too prominent.

Agnes, however, lived up to her grandmother's prediction. By the time she was five, she was reading. She was also wearing glasses. Turns out one of her ears was slightly lower than the other so her glasses never sat straight on her face. Agnes didn't care. As long as she had books to read, she was happy.

Wisely, her mother dressed her simply, no fancy dresses, no ribbons and bows. Again, Agnes didn't care. All those fancy clothes would just have gotten in her way. As long as she could run and play and climb trees, she was happy. When she started school, she quickly proved to be the smartest one in her class, much smarter than all the boys.

Her mother was concerned. "Agnes, it's fine to be smart, but you don't want to be too smart. You don't want to show off, because then people will think you're a smart aleck and nobody likes that, especially boys. Boys don't like smart girls."

Papa listened and then he and Agnes had a long talk. "Your mama means well, Sugarfoot, but the truth is, she's not very well qualified to tell you what boys like. Smart boys like smart girls. You don't want to waste your time on some knuckle-head who's dumb as a post and proud of it.

"You're going to go to college—first one in our family to do that—and you're going to learn everything you can about everything you can. That's going to make a difference, you wait

and see." Agnes looked doubtful. By high school she had learned two things. Pretty went a long way in the world and she was not pretty.

Papa didn't give up. "Now you listen to me, I know you may not believe this now, but you have something that can't be painted on your face with powder and lipstick. You have a brain. Just be your smart self, and everything will work out fine."

Agnes had plenty of proof to the contrary. In junior high, the local church ladies organized a dance and all the kids were invited. Agnes wore her school clothes, but all the other girls were wearing pretty party dresses. Nobody asked Agnes to dance.

Her junior year in high school was a leap year and there was a big school dance. Agnes wasn't going until her mother explained that during leap year, everything was turned around. The girls asked the boys to the dance. If the boys weren't invited, they couldn't come. "This is your chance, Dear. You get to invite a boy you like, and it's the girls who ask the boys to dance."

As an added incentive, Agnes and her mother went shopping and bought her a beautiful, blue taffeta party dress. For once in her life, Agnes felt...well, not beautiful, but pretty. She asked Teddy Hopgood, the shyest boy in her class, because she was sure no one else would invite him. Everybody met at the school gym.

When Agnes walked in wearing her new dress, everyone laughed. One of the pretty girls said, "Oh Agnes, you got it all wrong, again. This is a Sadie Hawkins Dance, you know like in Li'l Abner. Everybody dresses like hillbillies just to be silly. Nobody tries to be pretty." She flipped her long blonde hair and went back to her group of friends. They laughed and Agnes fled forgetting all about Teddy. She never tried to look pretty again.

Papa was true to his promise, Agnes went to Penn State. She was never popular, but she did meet a few other smart students. Warren Mackie, from Georgia, was smart and handsome. Agnes fantasized about him, but she had long since stopped believing in fairytales. Then by some miracle she was assigned to be his lab partner in biology.

She remembered Papa's words, "Smart boys like smart girls." Agnes liked working with Warren and she allowed herself to dream just a little bit. Then Warren asked her out and she said no. It was a trick and she wasn't going to fall for it and have everybody laugh at her again. She was smarter than that.

Warren was puzzled. In fact, he was shocked. Girls never turned him down. "Why won't you go out with me?"

"Why would you want me to?"

Warren shrugged. "I like you."

Now it was Agnes who was shocked. "Why?" The minute she said it, she knew it was the wrong thing to say. She should have said, "Why, I'd love to," Not just "why?" She'd done the wrong thing again.

Warren laughed. "Because you're not just an empty dress. You've got ideas and opinions. You cut that frog open and never batted an eye. You're fearless and that makes you interesting and that makes you beautiful."

Agnes almost believed him.

The next time he asked her for a date, she said yes. Although they went out from time to time, Agnes always kept him at arm's length. She simply would not allow herself to believe the best-looking boy in her class really liked her. A year later, when Warren asked her to marry him, she was shocked. But she had learned her lesson. Without a moment's hesitation, she said yes. Yes, a thousand times yes.

Warren's mother was not pleased. She had assumed her son would marry the daughter of one of their rich Southern friends, not some homely girl from up North. But Warren and Agnes were married anyway. On her wedding day, as her father walked her down the aisle, Agnes knew three things: her father was the smartest man in world, at that moment she was beautiful and sometimes miracles really do happen. Shortly after the wedding the young couple moved to Warren's home town, Lost River, Georgia.

Now Comes the Hard Part

The trouble with miracles is that folks sometimes have a hard time believing them even when they see the proof right in front of their eyes. The first meeting of Lost River's new, all-female City Council was a good example. The ladies had pulled off the take-over, but now they had to take over and that was a whole different story.

They were good at raising money for special projects or various charities. However, the sheriff made sure that they understood Mike Sweeney had not only stolen the Fire-Truck Fund, he had more or less cleaned out all the accounts. The city was broke and the anonymous benefactor couldn't be counted on forever. J.W. dropped that bombshell and then pleaded urgent business elsewhere.

The Council knew the situation was bad, but they didn't dream it was that bad. Cake walks and donkey polo weren't going to solve the problem this time. They realized what they needed was a source of income and the quicker the better.

Raising taxes was out of the question and they already charged fees for all the normal things like licenses and permits. The city didn't own anything anybody wanted to buy, nor could they think of any new services anybody would be willing to pay extra for.

They were deep into a discussion when Sophia Conti burst into the room. "Sorry I'm late." She practically spit out the words mixed in with a string of curses. The Sicilian language has elements of Greek, Arabic, French, Catalan and Spanish and it sounded like Sophia was trying to use all of them at one time. The women were used to Sophia's loud voice and frantic hand movements, but this was entirely different. They caught words like *bastardo* and *cosca* and mafia. Finally, she calmed down enough to say, "I hope somebody else was taking minutes," she exhaled. "I'm gonna kill that *puttana*!"

"Sophia, what happened?"

"What happened? I'll tell you what happened. I was held up at gunpoint. I was nearly arrested. It's highway robbery, that's what it is. The Mafia has taken over the roads around here."

"You were held up at gunpoint? Who would do that?"

"The Mafia."

"Sophia, we don't have any Mafia here in Georgia."

"Oh no? Well, let me tell you a thing or two. I was coming home from Columbus on Highway 96 and there's a long stretch between Reynolds and Fort Valley. There is no town, nothing around there and then out of nowhere comes this police car. He pulls me over and tells me I was going 20 miles over the speed limit and I owed a $25 fine. Oh yes, and by the way he had a gun.

"Anyway, I asked him how he could tell I was over the speed limit when there was no speed limit on the highway. And he told me I wasn't on the highway; I was on the streets of Fort Valley and I told him he was mistaken."

"My Lord! Weren't you scared?" Earlene asked.

"I was too angry to be scared. The next thing I know, he made me turn around and drive back toward Columbus and about five miles back down the road was this little, bitty sign that read 'Fort Valley, Speed Limit 35 Miles Per Hour.' There were weeds growing all around it. Nobody could see that sign and I told him so.

"Well, he says I was still breaking the law and I could pay the $25 on the spot or I could drive to the court house in Fort Valley and tell my story to a judge... if I could find one. It's extortion! That's what it is, pure and simple."

"That's awful. What did you do?"

"I paid the *brutto figlio di puttana bastardo.* What else could I do?" She threw up her hands in disgust and plopped down in the nearest chair.

The group may not have understood all of Sophia's words, but the meaning was perfectly clear. Sophia was looking for sympathy and understanding and she got it, until Trudy spoke up.

"You know this might be a good thing."

Sophia turned on her, eyes blazing.

"I don't mean it was a good thing it happened to you," Trudy quickly explained. "But think about it. If *you* got caught, how many other people do you think they catch in a day. Five? Six? Ten? And at $25 apiece, how much is the Fort Valley police department making in a week? Or a month? Or a year!?!"

Annabelle made some quick notes. "Well, let's see. Six a day at $25 each would be $150 a day. And for seven days, that's $1050 a week!"

"You reckon they work on Sunday?" Prim asked.

"OK, let's give them Sunday off, that's still *$900 a week.* If we had a setup like that, we could collect enough money for a new fire truck in no time. And then we could just keep making money."

The energy level in the room definitely went up several notches. Everybody was silently trying to remember their multiplication tables as they calculated the possible income. Maybe salvation was in sight.

Eden frowned. "It's a good plan, except for one thing. Highway 96 runs through Fort Valley. We don't have a highway running through Lost River. The closest thing we've got is Highway 23 and that's outside of town. I don't see how this could work for us. We can't move the highway."

That took the wind out of everyone's sails. They looked at one another and finally turned their attention to Mayor Mackie. She was smiling.

"You're right," she said. "We can't move the highway…but we *can* move the city limits!"

Tradition

The City Council wasn't the only group working on a plan. It only took a slight change in temperature and a hint of fall to stir the local boys out of the summer doldrums. "We've gotta do this!" Sonny announced. "We have to do something big before school starts in a couple of weeks and I've got an idea. You know how every year some senior boy climbs to the top of the water tower and signs his name for the whole class. Well, this year we could make history if *all three of us* did it together. Just like the Three Musketeers, but we need to do it now or it'll be too late."

As long as the boys had known each other, Sonny had been the source of countless adventures. They were usually on the risky side, but none had proved fatal...so far.

"I guess you're right," Hank said. "If we don't do it now, somebody might beat us to it."

"Why don't we *not* go and tell everybody we did?" Matt figured that was a better idea all around.

"No, no, no. You've got to go and sign your name. It's a tradition. I'll bet lots of the men in town did it when they were in school. We can look for their names when we get up there." Sonny turned to Matt, "What's the matter, Matt? You're not afraid of heights, are you?"

The simple answer was yes, definitely yes. But instead, Matt said, "I don't know. I've never been any higher than the top of our garage."

"How'd you get up there?"

"On a ladder."

"Then you've got no problem. This is better than a rickety ladder leaning against the garage. This one is bolted to the frame of the tower. Steady as a rock. Just hold on tight all the way up and all the way down. It's not like you'll be swinging through the trees like Tarzan."

Matt tried again. "How are you gonna prove we were up there? Maybe I could stay on the ground and take pictures."

Sonny had that covered too. "My dad just got one of those new Polaroid Land cameras. It develops the picture right in the camera. You just peel the paper and the negative apart and you've got a black and white photograph."

The camera peeked Hank's imagination and once he decided to get involved in the adventure, he started to elaborate. Just signing their names wasn't enough, they needed to do something spectacular. Something nobody had ever thought of before. "We could paint, 'Kilroy Was Here' on the side of the tank. I'll bring the paint and the brushes."

Matt could see his worst nightmare taking shape. Every cell in his body turned to ice. In his dreams he was always falling and he'd wake up covered in sweat with his heart pounding. This couldn't be happening in real life. His heart was beating fast just thinking about it. And he couldn't believe he *was* thinking about it. Without a doubt, he had temporarily lost his mind. But what could he do? If he said no, his friends would think he was a sissy. This wasn't just nightmare fear, this was I'm-gonna-die-for-sure fear. He was trapped. There was no way out.

Everyone in Lost River knew the dogs in town were exceptional. Some folks even believed they were sensitive to changes in weather. What else could account for the fact that in the same way they attended funerals, they came each year to watch The Climb at the water tower. Patiently they waited just in case they might need to get help. So far that hadn't been necessary.

The boys didn't waste any time. Bright and early the next morning they met at the tower. Standing at the bottom, it did look a lot taller than it had from farther away, but nobody— except Matt—was willing to back out. Hank had a canvas bag with a small can of paint and some brushes. Sonny had the camera, a canteen with water and a bunch of sandwiches. "We can have a picnic up there," he announced.

"My last meal," Matt thought. He could feel saliva collecting in his mouth like it always did before he threw up. "Gimme a drink," he said. Maybe some cold water would help.

Sonny handed him the canteen and went to inspect the ladder. The bottom rung was a little too high for the boys to reach, but Hank had brought along a folding chair. Standing on that they could easily get on the ladder. Matt was frozen to the ground.

"There's nothing to worry about," Hank said. "Here, I'll go first." He stepped on the chair, took hold of the ladder and started to climb. It looked easy.

Sonny said. "Matt, you go next. I'll go behind you so if you fall you can fall on me." He laughed. Matt didn't.

Matt closed his eyes and made the sign of the cross. He'd seen Sonny do it, although he didn't know exactly what it meant or whether it would work for a Baptist. He wanted to cry, but instead he stepped up on the chair and almost lost his balance. "Oh my God, I'm not even a foot off the ground and already I'm falling." It took all the nerve he had to make himself take hold of the ladder. He made it up a couple of steps and it wasn't so bad. He wasn't much higher than the top of the garage and he could still see pine trees on either side.

Sonny's voice floated up from below him. "Get a move on, Matt. Hurry up."

"Don't look down, don't look down," Matt kept telling himself. He focused on his hands and talked his way slowly up.

Sonny rolled his eyes. "Good grief, Matt can't you go any faster."

Matt didn't answer. He just kept inching up one step at a time. His legs were shaking, but he didn't dare look up or down. "If I can just make it to the top, I can lie down on the cat walk. Oh please, God let this be over soon." Matt blotted out everything but his hands on the rungs. His palms were sweating. He went a few steps higher and that's when he made a big mistake. He glanced to his right and suddenly realized the trees were gone!

A shiver ran through his body. He couldn't see anything but sky to the right or the left. He had climbed higher than the tree tops! "Oh my God, I'm gonna die." He was trapped, but the only thing he could do was climb higher. He froze. He gave up and prepared to die. At that moment he felt the hand of God grabbing him.

"Hang on Matt." Hank was lying on his stomach on the platform. He grabbed the back of Matt's shirt and pulled him up the last couple of steps. "You made it. I just thought you might need a little help getting up here." Hank rolled over and sat up smiling. Matt felt the solid wooden platform under his body. He crawled a couple of feet toward the tank to get as far away from the edge as possible.

"Oh, thank you God, I'm not going to die," Matt thought. The tank was warm from the sun and he pushed his back against it and stretched his legs out in front of him.

Sonny was right behind him. As if he'd been doing this all his life, he easily stepped up on the platform and joined Hank. They started to walk around exploring and looking for names. Matt concentrated on getting his legs to stop shaking.

The other boys went about their tasks. Hank painted a line around one side of the tank and then drew the hands, head and nose of Kilroy. As he was writing "Kilroy Was Here," Sonny took his picture. Hank painted their names below the drawing and the year, 1949. Sonny took another picture. They walked back to Matt, peeled the paper off the negatives and fanned them in the air to dry them off a little.

"Man, this is great," Sonny said. He passed the pictures around. Then he handed out the sandwiches and passed around the canteen. Matt sat absolutely still. He ate and drank with his arms close to his body. If the other boys noticed, they didn't say anything. They sat on the edge of the platform with their legs hanging out into space. After a while, Hank got up. "Well, I guess we better start down." Sonny gathered up the pictures.

Until that moment, Matt had blocked out the fact that he had to *climb down.* His voice was hardly above a whisper. "I can't do it. I can't stand up and I sure as hell can't get on that ladder again." He was white as a sheet and clearly terrified.

For all his crazy ideas, Sonny recognized a crisis when he saw one. "No problem. We're not in any hurry. The sun's nice, we'll just wait a while." He exchanged a look with Hank and they realized they *did* have a problem. If Matt really couldn't get on the ladder, there was no way any of them could get down.

Hank leaned back against the warm tank trying to look as unconcerned as possible. "Boy, are we gonna have a story to tell everybody when school starts. My dad's name is over there, 1932. He musta been about my age. I can't wait to see what he says when I tell him I saw his name. No way he can deny it. I wonder if Mom knows he came up here."

"Yeah, I found my dad's name up here too. He was a couple of years older than your dad. Funny, I never think about grown-ups doing anything like this. They seem so predictable. So…I don't know, so old."

They continued to talk for a while and finally Hank said, "Matt, you feeling any better?"

"Not really. I'm still scared. I should have told you guys before we started, I just didn't want to sound like a sissy."

"Hey, everybody's afraid of something," Sonny said. "With me it's caves. I'm always afraid the top's gonna fall in on me." Strangely enough, that made Matt feel a little better. Caves didn't bother him at all.

"Look we gotta get down, right? We'll just take it slow and we'll do this together," Hank said. "Matt, all you have to do is get on the ladder and we'll talk you down. You can do this. It's just like holding onto the ladder at the swimming pool over in Macon. Sonny, you go first and let Matt watch you."

"I can't watch him. If I look down, I'm gonna fall."

"Matt, you're not gonna fall. That just happens in your nightmares, you know, like me getting stuck in a cave."

Hank chimed in. "Just hold on tight. Nothing's gonna make you fall and every step you take gets you closer to the ground. Sonny'll go first. Then you. I'll stay up here and hold on to you until you get both feet on the ladder."

It sounded simple enough. But it took all the courage Matt could muster to move away from the safety of the tank. "I can't do it, I'll fall."

The fear in his voice was beginning to frighten his friends. "I know getting on the ladder may be a little scary," Hank said, "but once you do that, the rest is easy. Sonny'll go down first to help you get started and I'll stay up here with you. OK?"

Matt felt a chunk of ice filling up the middle of his chest. His mouth was dry and his hands were shaking, but he forced himself to stretch his leg out to reach the ladder and just when he was sure he was a goner, he felt Sonny's strong hands grab his foot. "I got you."

"Now shift your weight down to the first step." Hank and Sonny held on to him and finally Matt felt his foot touch the first rung. He brought his other foot down and found the ladder. He had made it over the side.

"You did it!" Hank said. From below he heard Sonny yell, "Yeah, you got it, Man. Now one at a time, bring your hands down, then bring your feet down." Matt took a deep breath and slowly started to work his way down. Each time he made it down a step, he stopped, exhaled and took another breath.

Hank let Matt get a good head start and then he began to climb down. It took them more than half an hour to get part way down. Sonny guided his feet and Matt never took his eyes off his hands on the ladder in front of him. He kept telling himself each step brought him closer to having both feet on solid ground.

Hank and Sonny stayed with him until they were almost all the way down. "Matt, I'm on the ground and you're almost there," Sonny said. "Just one more step and you'll be on the bottom rung. Then you'll be close enough to drop to the ground. Just like climbing out of that magnolia tree in your front yard. You got this."

Matt glanced to the side and saw he was way below the tree tops. He almost cried. Just one more step. "I guess I can do it."

As Sonny stepped away from the ladder, he heard a scream. Matt missed the last step and fell. In an instant, the dogs were all over him. Boot put his nose close to Matt's nose to see if he was still breathing. He was. Good. Boot gave him a big, sloppy lick to make him feel better. The other dogs sniffed around to make sure nothing was broken.

In his head, Matt fell 1000 feet. In truth, he fell about five. Nevertheless, it knocked the wind out of him, but when he opened his eyes and saw Boot, he knew he was on the ground and all right. When Hank and Sonny got there, they realized Matt had landed on a sharp piece of tin, torn his jeans and cut a gash in the back of his right leg.

Matt petted Boot and his friends. He was so glad to be lying on the ground, covered with dogs, he didn't even care that his pants were soaked with blood. Hank took off his shirt and wrapped it around Matt's leg. "Look, Moon's is pretty close by. If we help you, do you think you can walk that far? Once we get there, Gibby'll know what to do."

Walk? Of course, he could walk. He had both feet on the ground. No ladder, no problem. Sonny and Hank sort of carried Matt between them and they made it to Moon's without too much trouble. Boot and the other dogs followed. Gibby saw them coming and walked out to meet them. She made Matt sit down on the back porch steps and unwrapped his leg. "Lord have mercy, Child. What have you done to yourself? This looks bad, I think you need a doctor."

"Oh no, Ma'am. Maybe you could just wash it off, put some iodine and a Band-Aid on it like Mama does," Matt said.

"That's a deep cut. Once it's all cleaned up, you may need some stitches. I think Dr. Nichols is outta town, but his nurse Victoria oughta be able to handle that. Hank, go get my car and I'll drive y'all over there."

Nurse Vicki figured prominently in the fantasies of most of Lost River's teen-age boys. She was young, pretty and remarkably well-endowed. Suddenly Matt thought going to the doctor might be a good idea after all. "Well, if you think I oughta go, I reckon I should." He tried not to sound too excited.

When they got to the doctor's office, Hank and Sonny each took one of Matt's arms and practically carried him in. Nurse

Vicki came out to meet them. They had never been this close to her before and they didn't want to miss a thing. She was perfect from her white oxfords, and shapely legs in white stockings, to the uniform that emphasized her tiny waist, her ample bosom and finally her blue eyes. They each decided to get sick more often.

Gibby quickly made introductions all around. Hank nodded politely, but Sonny insisted on shaking hands. Nurse Vicki gave the boys a knowing smile and showed them into an examining room. Gibby explained what had happened.

"All right, Matt, take off your pants and let's see what's going on." Matt froze and Hank and Sonny nearly strangled to keep from laughing. They knew exactly what was going on and there was no way Matt could—or would—take off his pants.

When Matt got his voice back, he said, "Just cut off the leg, my pant leg, I mean. These jeans are old anyway and I can just wear them as shorts."

"All right. Just lie back on the table." With a few decisive cuts, Nurse Vicki exposed Matt's wound, gently examined his injury and cleaned away the blood. "I'm going to put some Lidocaine on this. It's a local anesthetic and it'll take a few minutes to numb your leg."

While they were waiting, Gibby said, "Did you boys climb up the water tower?"

"Yes Ma'am. We were doing fine until the last minute when Matt missed a step and fell on a piece of tin." Sonny explained all he thought Gibby ought to know.

Nurse Vicki tapped on Matt's leg. "Can you feel that?"

"I don't feel anything," Matt said. With that settled, she disinfected the cut, put in a few stitches and applied a bandage.

"Now I'm going to give you a tetanus shot, just to be on the safe side. You aren't afraid of needles, are you?"

He wasn't, but even if he had been, Matt would never have admitted it.

"When you get home, take two Aspirin and call me in the morning to let me know how you're feeling. Tell your mother there's nothing to worry about."

Gibby loaded the boys into the car and took them all home. Then she headed back to Moon's. "Damn fool kids. I knew it was just a matter of time before somebody got hurt climbing that thing." She parked the car, and rounded up some scraps for the dogs who were waiting patiently by the back door.

Sonny wasted no time. When school started the following week, he tacked the Polaroid pictures of their water tower adventure to the main bulletin board in the front hall. The Three Musketeers were on top of the world. They were seniors and instant heroes.

Story #10, "Kilroy Was Here"
(Massachusetts 1939)

Most folks around here call me Jim. I live in Quincy, Massachusetts and during the war, I worked at the Quincy Fore River Shipyard. We built every kind of warship: aircraft carriers, battleships, cruisers, destroyers, even submarines. Our goal was to turn out as many ships as possible for the war effort.

I was an inspector and one of the things I checked was the rivets that held the ships together. Here's how it worked. It takes two people to put in a rivet. A worker on one side pushes a red-hot rivet through a pre-drilled hole in two pieces of metal and a worker on the other side hammers it into place. As it cools, the rivet pulls the pieces together. As you can imagine, shipyards were noisy places, what with all that banging going on.

Just to give you some idea of what my job was like and how many rivets might go into each ship, the Titanic required three million rivets, the Eiffel Tower needed two and a half million.

Of course, we were building war ships, so the count would be different, but you get the idea. There were rivets all over the ships, in tight spaces, down inside holding tanks, and we had to check every one.

Rosie the Riveter was the most famous female worker, but she wasn't the only woman around. Lots of them worked in the yards and like the men, they were paid on a piecework basis, in other words, paid by the number of rivets installed.

In order to keep up, we inspectors counted the blocks of rivets as we went and then left a waxy chalk mark to indicate where we stopped. However, sometimes the workers would erase our marks so that the next inspector would count the same area twice. Extra rivets meant extra pay.

To get around that, I signed my name and just for fun I started drawing a long-nosed, bald fellow looking over a fence. I used a marker that was a lot harder to erase. It took a while, but eventually the workers got the message, "Don't tamper with the inspection count."

Under normal circumstances all our inspection marks would have been covered when the ship was painted just before it was launched. At that point, however the war effort needed the ships so fast, they started shipping them out with the inspection notes still visible in various places on the ship.

When G.I.'s arrived at a new location or a new duty station in Europe or the South Pacific, they saw what they thought was a secret message meaning that the Americans had already been there. It became a morale builder. I've heard that lots of them left the same message in odd places for other G.I.'s to find. Soldiers made it a contest to see how many places they could spot the drawing. That wasn't why I did it, but if it made some poor guy a long way from home feel better, that was fine with me.

About three years ago, in 1946, the American Transit Association ran a radio contest to identify the person who started it all. The prize was a trolley car. About 40 men sent in stories. Mine won...because it was true.

They delivered the trolley car to my yard. By that time my family and I were living in Halifax, Massachusetts, and all nine of my kids had a fine time playing on it.

My name is James J. Kilroy.

Percy Patrol

While the boys were busy with their Water Tower adventure, the City Council was busy with an adventure of its own. However, before they could go any farther with their speed-trap plans, they decided they better run the proposal by Sheriff Latham. The Council could take care of moving the city limits, but in order for the scheme to work, J.W. would have to hire and train a deputy.

Mayor Mackie called Lucy and made an appointment with the sheriff. She spent the rest of the morning making apple strudel. As she was taking the pastries out of the oven, she remembered the last time she had been in J.W.'s office. A lot had changed in her life in a few short months. When she heard the news about Warren Jr., she thought her life was over. Now here she was, *Mayor* Mackie. Amazing!

She walked into J.W.'s office wearing *eau de cinnamon and nutmeg* which immediately got his attention. It is almost impossible to resist a request from a woman offering fresh-baked apple strudel. "Good morning, Your Honor. What can I do for you?"

"I think the Council may have found a solution to the town's financial problems." While Lucy brought coffee and she and the sheriff devoured strudel, the mayor explained what the Fort Valley police department was doing and what the Council wanted to do in Lost River.

The whole thing took J.W. by surprise. The plan was highly irregular and totally brilliant. He wasn't entirely convinced they could pull it off, but he was more than willing to give it a try. Morris had been extremely generous, but he couldn't go on paying the city's bills forever.

Since the election, J.W. had decided the best way to handle this new City Council was to get out of the way and let the ladies take charge. "If you take care of the preliminary work, I'll take care of the deputy," he offered. They struck a deal and Agnes gave the word to the rest of the Council.

Now that the sheriff was on board, Sophia Conti visited Morris Fullerton. He seemed the logical choice to make some speed-limit signs. She emphasized the importance of keeping everything a secret. Morris smiled and assured her he was very good at keeping secrets.

Next Sophia talked to her brother-in-law Salvador and he got them a good deal on a second-hand, black Ford. Junior painted an official logo and "Sheriff's Department, Lost River" on the side of the car in big letters.

Helen Kirkland got Leon to print speeding tickets. Annabelle Knox volunteered to search the court records to see who owned the land that was about to become part of Lost River.

Before he had a chance to finish the last of the strudel, Percy Barns walked in looking rather pleased with himself.

"I know you're gonna need one, so I've come to volunteer my services as Deputy Sheriff," he said with a big smile.

J.W. wondered if there was any official position in Lost River that Percy hadn't volunteered for at one time or another. "What makes you think I need a deputy?"

"For the new speed trap, of course."

"And how do you know about that?"

"Oh Sheriff, everybody in town is talking about it. It's a stroke of genius and I want to do my part to make it a big success. I've already arranged for somebody to take over my job at the G & G. And I bought my uniform," he said as he pulled a pair of khaki pants and a matching shirt out of a bag from Conti's General Store. "I think I'll tailor them a little bit 'cause I want to look my best representing the city, you know. I've been looking for one of those Smokey Bear hats, but 'till I find one, I'll just wear a black baseball cap. With your approval, of course."

Percy carefully folded his new uniform and put it back in the bag. "Before I go, there's just one more thing. I'll need a badge to make it all official. Once I get that, we're in business. Oh yeah, Junior helped me scrounge up some walkie-talkies.

One for me, one for you and one for Lucy. That way we can all stay in touch."

J.W. was slightly annoyed that Percy had just assumed he was going to get the job. His first instinct was to send him packing, but the town *did* need a deputy and it didn't escape J.W.'s attention that Percy hadn't asked how much the job paid.

Somewhere in the back of his mind, J.W. remembered stories about how Ma Barns had established a multi-state delivery service during Prohibition and how that supported Percy and the rest of her family very well. Some folks said the service was still in business. J.W. had his suspicions about how Percy managed to live as well as he did on just his part-time job at the G&G.

While Percy waited, the sheriff turned all this information over in his mind. No one had ever accused Percy of being unreliable, so without evidence to the contrary, J.W. assumed he could be counted on to show up for work, write tickets and collect fines. Just to give himself some wiggle room in case he needed it, J. W. said, "Before we make this official, I'll have to run your name by the mayor and the City Council to get their approval but I reckon the job is yours if you want it."

"Oh, I do, Sheriff." Percy put on his baseball cap and started to leave the office. "By the way, do I get to carry a gun?"

"No, absolutely not. We just want you to write tickets, not arrest folks at gunpoint."

"OK then, I just thought I'd ask."

During her first couple of weeks in office, people greeted Agnes as Mr. Mayor, probably out of habit. Then they'd try to correct themselves, but somehow Miss or Mrs. Mayor didn't sound quite right. Eventually folks settled on just "Mayor" and that sounded fine to Agnes. "Lord, Warren, I wish you could see me now. Better yet, I wish *your mother* could see me. Wouldn't she be surprised?"

Mayor Mackie met with the City Council. "Sheriff Latham called me to say he had a volunteer for the deputy's job." She paused. "Percy Barns. Apparently, we have to approve him before the sheriff can put him on the payroll. I'm almost afraid to ask, but what do you think?"

"Percy Barns? You're kidding."

"No, I'm not. According to the sheriff, he's bought his uniform and everything."

The Council was at a loss for words. "OK, instead of sniping at him, does anyone have a real reason why we *shouldn't* approve Percy?" Eden asked. There were a lot of smirks and smiles around the room, but no objections. Trudy Latham made a motion, Sophia Conti seconded it and the Council unanimously approved Percy Barns as Deputy Sheriff. "Now, as long as we're all here, how are you coming along with your assignments?"

Annabelle was the last to report. "I searched the tax rolls and Vincent Conti has paid the taxes on that property every year. Highway 23 runs right down the middle of the land. Then I contacted the Clerk of Superior Court in Atlanta and you're never gonna believe who actually owns it." They waited. "Gibby! It belongs to Gibby Moon."

Story #11, Gibby (Georgia 1918)

They called him Blue because his name was Agamemnon. With a big smile, he would always introduce himself as, "Agamemnon Moone, but everybody calls me Blue." He'd wait and nine times out of ten folks would smile. It was a joke and Blue never bothered with the folks who didn't get it.

When his first child was born, he decided to pass along the tradition, so he named her Gibbous. Some people got it, most people didn't. At first, Blue would explain that a gibbous moon was more than a half moon, but less than full. Folks just looked confused and called her Gibby. The family lived on a farm and Gibby was equally happy riding on the tractor and working with her dad as she was working in the kitchen with her mama.

Gibby met Adam Conti at Lost River's summer picnic. He was the youngest son of Vincent and Isabella Conti and the handsomest boy she'd ever seen. He had brown hair, blue eyes, full lips and a great smile. For Gibby, it was love at first sight. For Adam, she was just the cute kid who hung around with his little sister.

After high school, Adam went to the University of Georgia in Athens. By the time he was a sophomore, Gibby was a junior in high school and she wasn't a kid anymore. When he saw her on summer vacation, he was the one who was smitten. They started dating and planned to get married when they both graduated.

Their families were delighted. Gibby would be marrying into one of the principal families of Lost River and his parents hoped she might settle Adam down a bit. With an eye to the future, they gave the young couple a plot of land on the edge of town hoping they would build a house there someday. They put the deed in both their names.

Then halfway around the world, Austria-Hungary declared war on Serbia, and within a week, Russia, Belgium, France, Great Britain and Serbia had lined up against Austria-Hungary and Germany. It was July 1914 and World War I had begun.

The U.S. managed to remain neutral for nearly three years until German submarines sank five American merchant ships. That did it! On April 6, 1917 the United States declared war on Germany.

Adam was called up in the first registration of June 1917 and was assigned to Camp Gordon just outside of Atlanta. Like thousands of other young couples, Adam and Gibby decided to get married immediately. Father Sullivan performed the ceremony at St. Philip's Catholic Church. The newlyweds moved in with his parents and then before they knew it, Private Adam Conti had to report for duty.

In March 1918, another Army private in Ft. Riley, Kansas reported symptoms of fever, sore throat and headache. By lunch that day, more than 100 soldiers on the base had fallen sick with what was called Spanish influenza. In less than a year, the disease had spread to other military installations throughout the United States.

Newspapers all over the country looked to the Associated Press wire service for daily reports. Because Boston was a major transfer station for both soldiers and supplies, it was especially hard hit. More than 2,900 cases were reported in the second wave of the flu. Hospitals everywhere were overflowing and nurses were in very short supply.

Leon and Helen Kirkland had also recently gotten married and they were working at the Herald *together. Leon was rejected for military service because he had had encephalitis as a child.*

Right from the beginning, they shared the workload. Helen checked the AP wire service every day and she thought the details about the flu epidemic were too awful to print. Leon thought folks in Lost River needed to know as much as possible about what to expect.

"In addition to normal flu symptoms of fever, nausea, aches and diarrhea, patients may develop severe pneumonia. Dark spots can appear on the cheeks and in severe cases patients turn blue and suffocate from a lack of oxygen."

Throughout the country, citizens were warned to avoid crowds. Schools, churches, movie houses, buses and trains—

any place crowds gathered—were potentially dangerous. The clergy in Lost River urged their congregations to stay home and pray.

In September, Gibby got a letter from Adam telling her that everyone at Camp Gordon was quarantined. "They've moved our cots outside into the fresh air and everybody has to wear a mask. It's scary. This kind of flu doesn't usually hit kids and old people, it goes for young, healthy people like soldiers. I sure hope I don't get sent overseas any time soon because nobody wants to get stuck in an overcrowded troop ship. The flu is all anybody talks about. If this thing keeps going, it might end up covering the whole world."

In general, small towns fared better than big cities. But as reports came in from Savannah, Atlanta and Macon, it was inevitable that it would reach Lost River too. Not only did the flu spread quickly, it was incredibly aggressive. It was said a person could be healthy at breakfast and dead by supper time. The war and the epidemic dragged on for months.

"Helen, are you about finished?" Leon asked gently because he knew how much she hated writing obituaries. Reluctantly she handed him the material she had been working on.

Conti, Adam Christopher 1896-1918.

Private First Class, Adam Christopher Conti, the youngest son of Vincent and Isabella Conti, was the first person in our community to be struck down by the deadly Spanish influenza. He was 22 years old and had been stationed at Camp Gordon near Atlanta. In addition to his wife Gibby, he is survived by his parents and his grandmother, Mrs. Carmelina Conti. Other members of his family include Salvador and Nina Conti and Anthony and Sophia Conti. A funeral mass will be held at 11:00 on Saturday at St. Philip's Catholic Church.

Moone, Agamemnon (Blue), 1878 -1918.

Blue, as he was known to friends and family, was the second person in our community to die as a result of the Spanish flu pandemic. He was a well-known personality in Lost River and will be missed. He passed away at his home, November 25. He was only 40 years old. He is survived by his wife, Eliza and his daughter Gibby. Services will be held at 11:00 on Friday at Bethel Baptist Church.

In one week, Gibby lost her father and her husband. She became a widow almost before she had a chance to be a wife. The citizens of Lost River were stunned. They never expected the epidemic to reach into their community. They had felt isolated and safe, protected by the trees that surrounded the town.

All of a sudden, it seemed they no sooner got home from one funeral, then they had to attend another one. The Conti family closed their grocery store, the general store and the Ford dealership. Zach Stubbs gave everyone at the sawmill both days off to attend the funerals. Boot and the rest of the town dogs paid their respects as usual.

The Spanish flu killed at least 50 million people worldwide, one-third of the world's population at that time. In the United

States, 675,000 died, 30,000 in Georgia, 829 in Atlanta and 2 in Lost River. It only lasted 15 months, but it killed more people than World War I killed in four years.

With Adam gone, Gibby decided to move back home. Because Blue wasn't there to run the farm, she and her mother sold out and bought two abandoned railroad cars near the high school. Morris Fullerton helped them outfit one as an apartment. There was plenty of room for two bedrooms, a living room, closets and a large bathroom. No need to take up space with a kitchen. They had a perfectly good one in the other car which eventually became a diner. They dropped the "e" and opened Moon's Diner.

Gibby didn't exactly drop the name Conti, it was just that she had never had time to adjust to being Mrs. Adam Conti. As far as Lost River was concerned, she would always be Gibby Moon.

In her heart, Gibby had always wanted to have a house full of children, but when Adam died, she gave up on that dream. Ironically, she became the surrogate mother to a whole town full of children.

A Little Strip of Land

With no new cars to take for joy rides, no circuses to attend and no more towers to climb, the boys were right back where they started and Lost River was back to being boring. To the adults, a lack of excitement meant a chance to catch their breath. Having an all-female City Council took some getting used to, even for the council members.

When Mayor Mackie approached Gibby about the land, she seemed confused. She hadn't thought about that piece of property on the edge of town for more than 30 years and she was more than a little surprised to find that Highway 23 ran through the middle of it. It took her and Mama a couple of days, but they finally found the deed rolled up in a piece of oilcloth and stuck in the back of the linen closet. She had no problem giving Lost River the right to annex the property. It would give her access to city services—should that ever apply—and it gave Lost River control over the land, which, of course, included the five-mile stretch along Highway 23.

Now the Council was ready to put their plan into action. They were anxious to get started, but when Mayor Mackie asked if there was any other new business, Annabelle Knox spoke up. "Don't y'all think we oughta find out who has been paying the city's bills and pay back that loan?"

That prompted a call to Sheriff Latham. He said he wasn't at liberty to give them that information and suggested they talk to Sidney Cumberland at the bank. Sidney said he wasn't at liberty to help either, but he would make some phone calls.

Sidney called Morris Fullerton who stood by his original plan. He still didn't want anybody to know about the loan. "If you tell tttthem where the money came from, they're gonna wanta ttttalk to me and I don't want tttthat. How about if I just make the money a gift? Tttthat way nobody has to pay it back."

Sid said he understood, "But Morris I have a feeling the women aren't going to give up on doing what they think is the right thing. They want to know who to thank."

"Maybe we could just make up a name like Joe Btfsplk or something?"

"We could do that, but the money will still have to go… somewhere." There was silence on the line for a minute or two, then Sid came up with an idea. "Morris, how would you feel about setting up a college scholarship in the name of Joe Btfsplk? I think folks would understand that the donor wanted to remain anonymous, but it would still put that money to good use."

Morris thought that was a great idea. "I'd kinda like to make it to Georgia Tech, that's where I went, but what if the winner didn't want to major in engineering? Could we let the person who wins, pick the school, as long as the college is here in Georgia?"

"It's your scholarship, Morris, you can set it up any way you want to. I'll tell the City Council about the decision."

The ladies understood that the benefactor didn't want to be identified, but they drew the line at naming the scholarship after Joe Btfsplk. "Nobody can pronounce Joe…whatever it is," Trudy said. "We need to come up with a better name. Why don't we just call it the Lost River Scholarship?"

Sid and Morris worked out the details. Morris' secret was safe and he smiled when he read the official story in the *Lost River Herald.*

Story 12, Percy Barns

Percy's story was the best kept secret in town. Everybody knew it, but nobody talked about it. The main reason was that they couldn't tell his story without telling Ma Barns' story and telling stories about her was—generally speaking—not a good idea. Percy's part of the story started with Prohibition. At the time, he was too young to drink, but not too young to realize that a lot of law-abiding citizens were playing fast and loose with the current laws.

Adults started using unfamiliar words like moonshiners and bootleggers and being a curious kid, Percy asked his mama what they meant. "Look it up," she said. He did. Turns out moonshiners made illegal whiskey and bootleggers delivered and sold it. But he didn't let it go at that. He kept asking questions and one old-timer explained that the government didn't care whether people drank or not, what made booze illegal was that nobody paid government taxes on it.

Percy also learned from his father and uncles that no man could consider himself a proper Southern gentleman without a steady supply of bourbon to enjoy at his leisure and to share with his friends. Prohibition was putting a crimp in their style. Moonshine was easily available and some folks were satisfied with white lightning which was hardly aged long enough to get it into a fruit jar.

Bourbon, on the other hand, was a different story. It required time and talent and that's what gentlemen wanted. Basically, the solution was to add some charred oak chips, then age the whiskey in oak barrels and wait about three months. It was a slow process, but once they got the system working, moonshiners could produce a steady stream of acceptable bourbon, which was available to select customers at a premium price, of course.

Percy's mama—affectionately known to all as Ma Barns— saw an opportunity to set up a family business. In addition to having a head for business, she could out cuss, out drive, out haggle, out drink and out smoke any man in four counties. According to local lore, most of the professional men in that part of the state earned money to go to college working for Ma Barns.

She had a brigade of bootleggers on the roads at all times. She was no ordinary whiskey distributor, no sir. It was common knowledge that none of her "boys" ever got caught or if they did, none of them ever spent time in jail.

There were numerous rumors about how she accomplished that. Clearly it wasn't her charm. She usually went out of her way not to call attention to herself. She wore baggy house dresses, brown lace-up oxfords and no makeup. However, as the old expression goes, she did clean up nice. When it was necessary, she put on a low-necked dress, curled her hair, dragged out her nylon stockings and her high heels and pranced into whatever local police station was holding one of her drivers. She always resolved the issue to everyone's mutual satisfaction.

Percy adored her. From the time he was ten, he would tear into anybody who said anything against her, or who made a snide remark they thought he was too young to understand. Percy didn't have to understand the words, he just loved his mama.

The other thing Percy loved was numbers. He might have been too young to drink or drive, but he had a natural way with math. Ma was quick to spot his talent and when he turned 12, she made him the family bookkeeper. He ordered and paid for supplies and tracked sales and revenues. He also maintained a lard can of cash under the sink in his mama's kitchen. Bribes were an essential part of any successful bootlegging enterprise. Percy kept the lard can filled and Ma Barns used the funds wisely.

It was truly a family business. Ma ran the organization and made all the executive decisions. She always said one of the keys to her success was that her drivers made all their deliveries in broad daylight. Law enforcement associated illegal booze with bootleggers driving fast cars, on dirt roads, in the middle of the night. Not Ma's boys. To drive for her, boys had to have a suit and tie and a respectable looking car or at least have access to one. No souped-up whiskey cars for Ma. That was just asking for trouble.

The Barns' drivers did have an edge however. Pa Barns was head of the Maintenance and Transportation Department. He was a master mechanic and Percy was his assistant. Together they modified each engine to run a little better, a little quieter and a little faster than anything else on the road. Families supplying cars for The Enterprise, as they called it, never had car trouble...of any kind. "Y'all be careful now, no speeding," Ma would caution as she waved each driver on his way.

Over the years, Ma watched Percy and the rest of her boys go off to college, graduate with honors and become successful men throughout the county and the state. They were well placed in education, religion, government, medicine and law. She knew all she had to do was pick up the phone to call in a favor. Just like Percy's lard can hidden under the sink, it always pays to have something stashed away for a rainy day.

Working in the family business taught Percy a lot about negotiating and about dealing with different kinds of people. The most important thing he learned was to always do the unexpected. "Think ahead," Pa said. "just like working on an engine. Figure it out."

Ma said, "No need to run, hide or fight. No need to make an enemy when you can make a friend." They both agreed that the most important thing was to have fun along the way. "You gotta like what you're doing or it just ain't worth doing it."

Prohibition lasted until 1933 and they had fun all the way. When Ma passed on, Percy and Pa scaled down the operation somewhat. Currently they just dealt with special customers who appreciated sidestepping the government while getting a quality product at a reasonable price delivered directly to their doors. It had been 16 years since his father died, but Percy was still having fun. Only these days, he wore a uniform and was enforcing the law...more or less.

Hiding in Plain Sight

"Ethyl, there's a colored man out front who says he's looking for somebody called Lucille. I told him there wasn't anybody here by that name, but he won't go away," Junior was confused and a little bit curious. "I thought maybe if *you* talked to him, he'd get the message."

Ethyl's heart stopped and she nearly dropped the bottle of Jack Daniel's she was holding. It had to be Leroy, but why was he showing up now? And what made him stop at the Gas and Grill? Oh God, he could ruin everything.

Obviously, she had to talk to him. She dried her hands on the bar towel and tried to look as casual as possible. "Show me where he is, I'll talk to him."

She followed Junior up to the front of the G & G. Leroy was standing beside the front door, waiting. He was looking good and Ethyl felt a jolt of electricity run through her body when she saw him. Before he could say anything, she walked over to him. "Junior tells me you're looking for somebody called Lucille. Nobody here by that name, but maybe I can help you.

Why don't you sit down?" She indicated a stool at the end of the lunch counter. Junior returned to the garage and the car he was working on.

When they were alone, Ethyl said, "Leroy, what are you doing here?"

He looked her up and down. She was wearing her usual work uniform, black slacks with a satin stripe, starched white shirt with diamond studs, a short black jacket with satin lapels, red cummerbund and a bow tie. "Better question is what are *you* doing here?

"I work here. I'm the manager."

"You manage a truck stop and a lunch counter? That ain't exactly your style, Lucille."

"I manage that and the restaurant and the bar and the card games… look, Leroy, this is not Chicago and this is not a black and tan establishment. You don't belong here."

"Far as I can see, neither do you. What's going on with you, Girl? I haven't seen another black face in this whole town. This is *the south*, so where are all the colored folks?"

"It's a long story."

"Then you better start talking, 'specially if this is one of those be-gone by sundown towns."

Ethyl got two cups of coffee. "How did you find me anyway?"

"I went back to the house where we stayed and asked about you. Turns out one black woman in a white town wasn't too hard to locate. You gonna tell me how this happened?"

Ethyl took a deep breath and told him the whole story from the day he left her in the house of the folks they found through the Green Book. She told him about meeting Gibby and how she had introduced her to J.W. Turned out they were both from Chicago and when he asked where she had worked before, she told him about her job at the Palmer House. Almost before she knew it, he offered her a job managing both the bar and the restaurant. The deal included an apartment upstairs.

"It was almost too good to be true. There I was with no money, no job, nowhere to live, no particular place to go and nobody to help. I didn't know where you took yourself off to, all I knew was I was on my own. So, yeah, I took him up on his offer and I never looked back. I've been here the whole time. I'm part of this town. I got friends."

"Black friends?"

"Listen to me, Leroy, I didn't know whether that white man you hit over the head lived or died. I didn't know if maybe the law was after you... and me. Anyway, I figured the safest place for me was right here. I mean, who in the world would come looking for a black woman in the middle of a white town in south Georgia?"

Leroy laughed. "Yeah, you got a point. Just so you know, I didn't kill nobody. Gave him a hell of a headache, but he lived. Police came to the club, but they just asked a few questions and left. I guess they figured if a white guy was stupid enough to go dancing on the South Side, he deserved what he got. So how come you ain't Lucille anymore?"

"Well, you gonna get a kick outa this one. J.W. Latham, the man who owns this place, is also the sheriff. He already knew I was from Chicago and when he asked my name, I didn't think I wanted to tell him the truth… just in case we was wanted somewhere. When I looked out this window," she gestured to the gas pump outside, "and I saw that sign advertising Ethyl No-Nox gas and so I told him my name was Ethyl Williams."

Leroy laughed some more "Ethyl No-Nox, huh? Lord God, Woman, couldn't you come up with something better'n that?"

"Seems to be working just fine, so don't be givin' me a hard time."

Leroy held up his hands in surrender. "OK, OK, that clears up one thing, but Lu.. Ethyl, I still don't understand why there ain't no black folks around here."

Ethyl had wondered the same thing when she first got to Lost River. As it turned out, down the road about five miles was Scottlandville. It was an all-black town, no whites around. The way Ethyl heard the story, the land was originally a plantation. The owner's wife died and several years later so did he. They never had children. In his will, he freed the slaves working on his land and left the property to them free and clear. As word spread, more black folks moved in.

"They got everything Lost River has: churches, a school, dance hall, all kinds of stores, filling station, car repair, post office, they even got a colored sheriff. Some of the men come over to work in the saw mill, but that's all."

"So, what do you do when you get lonely?"

"What makes you think I *get* lonely?"

"Come on Lucille, everybody get lonely from time to time."

"I got no time to be lonely. I got a good job, I eat at my own restaurant, I live rent-free and if I get lonely, I invite Mr. Jim Beam to spend the night. If he's busy, I try Mr. Jack Daniels. I'm building me a future here, Leroy. I'm saving my money and one of these days I'm gonna own a place like this… or maybe I'll just buy this one and call it Ethyl's Place."

They talked for a while longer. Leroy told her he was working for the school press at Dillard University in New Orleans. "It ain't like the *Defender*, but it's a good job and New Orleans is a happening place. Dixieland jazz and all. I reckon I'll stay there, but I wanted to know what happened to you and if you was all right. I can see that you are. I'm glad of that."

Before he left, he leaned across the table and kissed her good-bye. When he drove away, Lucille went with him, that just left Ethyl. When she told Leroy she was part of Lost River, she realized she had made a choice for her life. There was no turning back now.

High Cotton

Early Monday morning, a week after Percy Barns became Lost River's first deputy sheriff, he walked into J.W.'s office and saluted. He was wearing starched khakis with military creases, brass buttons, spit-shined shoes and a Smokey-the-Bear hat. J.W. didn't know whether to laugh or return his salute.

Percy wasn't even officially on the payroll yet, but he had been hard at work. He picked up the speed-limit signs from Morris and planted several along Highway 23 going both north and south. He didn't put out enough to be too obvious, just enough to be legal. He also picked up the pads of speeding tickets from the print shop. One pad was clearly visible in his breast pocket next to a shiny new pen. He bought an official-looking black notebook in which he had calculated a number of fines corresponding to miles-per-hour over the speed limit. The fines ranged from $15 to $75. He stopped by the bank and got $50 in fives to make change, if necessary.

"Sheriff, I'm calling this Operation 23 and I've given it considerable thought. I'm ready to do my part to help Lost River recoup what the old mayor absconded with. All I need is official approval and a badge. Oh yeah, and $50 to reimburse me for setting up my bank."

They both knew the City Council had approved him, but J. W. went through the charade of saying it out loud. Then he opened his desk drawer, took out a badge and handed it to Percy.

"Don't you need to swear me in or something?"

The sheriff started to dismiss the idea, but then thought better about it. "Lucy, have we got a Bible around here somewhere?" It took a minute, but she finally found one on a bottom shelf under a stack of old phone books.

J.W. walked to the front of his desk and held the Bible out to Percy. "Lucy, you be the witness. All right Percy, left hand on the Bible, raise your right hand. Percy Barns, do you swear to uphold and enforce the laws of the United States of America, the sovereign state of Georgia, the official county of Bleckley and the municipality of Lost River, so help you God?"

"I do." Percy handed the badge back to the sheriff. "I think you oughta pin this on just to make it official." The sheriff complied. Lucy rolled her eyes and went back to work.

"Percy, I know you're anxious to get started, but we're not quite prepared yet. We don't have another police car and I can't..."

"Oh we got a car. Sal Conti found one and the City Council bought it and gave it to me. Didn't nobody tell you?"

JW shook his head. "Why would anybody tell me anything, I'm just the sheriff?" he thought. "OK, so you've got a car but I haven't had time to lay speed detector strips across the road..."

"Oh, you don't need to do that either, Sheriff. I've got a system all figured out."

J.W. started to ask what that entailed, but decided in the long run, he didn't really want to know. Percy assured him everything was under control and against his better judgement, the sheriff sent him on his way. Nobody heard anything from Percy until the following Monday when he came by the office at 8:05 and dumped a cardboard suitcase full of money on J.W.'s desk.

Lucy walked over to the desk and ran her hands through the bills. "There's got to be $1000 here!"

"Naw, it's just $630," Percy said.

"You collected $630 in one week!?" J.W. was obviously impressed. "Percy, what's going on?"

Percy poured coffee for all three of them. "Y'all get comfortable and I'll tell you the whole story. First of all, I figured out that we ought not to ever charge any fines over $15. See, if I started writing tickets for $75 or even just $25, the word would spread and folks might stop driving down Highway 23 and that would defeat the purpose. But $15, well, most folks can handle that.

"Then I got to thinking about what happens when you get pulled over. Folks get scared and they start making up excuses. So instead of chasing them down, I went and bought me a black and white checkered flag like the one they use at stockcar races, you know like that new NASCAR thing.

"Now every time I see somebody going real fast around that big curve just outside of town, I flag them down and I ask to see their license and registration. When I read the name on the license, I say something like, 'I thought you might be Lee Petty or Red Byron, you know, one of those famous race drivers.'

"If it's a lady, I mention Sara Christian, 'cause she's real famous over at the Macon Speedway. Then I say, 'I mean, the way you handled that curve was *outstanding*. How fast do you think you were going anyway?'

"And you know what? *They tell me*. In fact, I think some of them add five or ten miles an hour just to make themselves look good. Then I take out the black notebook, and check out what the fine should be. And I shake my head and tell them how sorry I am to have to fine them $75 because I know that's a lot of money."

J.W. and Lucy forgot to drink their coffee. They just sat there with their mouths hanging open. Percy took a swallow and then launched into the next chapter of his story.

"Finally, I take out my book of tickets and I fill in their name and how fast they told me they were going, but I stop before I finish writing. That's when I say something like, 'Since you're such a good driver and since this is your first offense, I'll just write this up for $15. How does that sound?' They all think that sounds great and they pay me on the spot. I mark their ticket 'paid,' give them one copy and I keep a copy. They're in that paper bag over yonder.

"As I finish up the ticket, I ask them some questions about where they live and where they're going. If they're headed to Florida, I tell 'em about a good rest stop down there around Hazlehurst, you know just before 23 turns due south. If they're headed north to Atlanta, I suggest they take a break and head over to Moon's for what we all know are the best hamburgers east of the Mississippi. I didn't bother to tell them her secret is fried green tomatoes."

Percy finally got back to explaining his system. "Half a day I work the cars headed south, the other half I catch the ones going north. It's been pretty steady work. I do take half an hour off for lunch. I bring it with me along with a thermos of coffee.

"Monday was pretty busy with folks headed home from down south but Friday, Saturday and Sunday were the busiest days with folks going both ways. Seems like everybody wants to go to Florida, but they all got to head home sometime. I collected a bunch of money and you know the best part? Nobody got mad at me. In fact, some of them even waved bye when they drove off."

When Percy finally got to the end of his story, J.W. and Lucy were still sitting there speechless.

"I haven't had this much fun since Prohibition," Percy said. "All that talk about Moon's has made me hungry. I think I'll go get me a burger. Y'all want some more coffee before I leave?" When he left, Lucy said, "Well, if that don't just beat all?" J.W. shook his head.

From that first week, the money just kept rolling in. Lost River collected on an average of $600 a week, $2400 a month! That was nearly as much as an average family made in a year. Workers at Stubbs Mill made $55 a week. Percy suggested he get paid $25 a week and J.W. agreed that was more than fair. With a steady source of income, the City Council got busy.

First of all, Sidney Cumberland signed Annabelle Knox to manage the Lost River Scholarship account. Ten percent of each week's income from Operation 23 went into that fund. The next item was a new fire truck. However, the price of a new pumper truck was $13,000. The Council decided that was way too much to spend on equipment they hoped would only be used once in a while.

Every woman on the Council knew the value of hand-me-downs, so they put out the word that Lost River was in the market for a used truck. The next week, Mayor Mackie got a call from the fire chief in Macon. That fire department was getting a new pumper and agreed to sell Lost River their present one for $500.

Junior checked it out and said both the motor and the pump were in good condition. Since there were no buildings in Lost River more than two stories high, it was all they needed. Junior and Inky drove the old fire truck over to where the orphanage used to be, removed the distributor cap and left the old truck for the kids to play on. That worked out so well, the Council cleaned up the grounds, used some of their new income to buy playground equipment and gave the area a proper name, Fire Truck Park.

With their immediate obligations taken care of, the Council got down to the exciting business of spending money. They made a wish list which included—in no particular order—a firehouse with an alarm system, a swimming pool, a gym for the high school, a town library, more paved streets, new sidewalks, decorative street lights and a bandstand for Oak Park downtown.

"This is like making up a Christmas list out of the Sears Roebuck catalogue," Helen Kirkland said. The Council knew eventually they would have to set some priorities, but at the moment they were just having fun. After all, it didn't cost anything to put an item on the list.

Operation 23 was responsible for some other changes in Lost River. Travelers in trouble were delighted to find gas and a competent mechanic in what they considered the back of nowhere. J.W. seriously considered hiring another attendant to help Junior at the Gas and Grill. Gibby started seeing more out-of-town and out-of-state customers at Moon's. Tourists who would normally have passed right by the town, now took the time to drive over and do some shopping. For some reason they thought buying home-grown tomatoes at Conti's Grocery or a cotton work shirt at the General Store was an adventure.

Mystery Solved

1950 started out cold and wet. Boot was looking forward to warm coffee and bread with Mrs. Conti. But as soon as he got to the edge of the garden, he knew something was wrong. Ever since he came to Lost River, he had gotten up early and made a pilgrimage to the garden. At first, he wandered up and down the rows, sniffing and pawing to see if there was anything worth digging up. The only thing that interested him was garlic. It smelled wild and reminded him of the stews cooked up by Texas Bill and his hobo friends riding the rails.

Mrs. Conti was another early-riser. She lived in a private wing on the back of her son Tony's house. Before daybreak every Thursday she went into the main kitchen and made six loaves of bread, two for each of her daughters-in-law. While she waited for them to rise, she brought her coffee and a piece of bread out to her garden.

That's how they met. Boot was busy digging up a garlic plant, when the old woman came running toward him flapping her apron and yelling, *"Statti! Vatinni!"* Boot didn't understand the words, but her meaning was clear. He high-tailed it out of the garden, but the next morning he was back. So was the old woman.

This went on for several days until Boot decided to try a different approach. He had noticed that each day the old woman sat on a three-legged stool in front of her small garden shed and drank her coffee. When he saw her sit down, he sat down on the other side of the garden. They waited, sizing each other up. *"Bon jornu,"* she finally said.

More strange words, but at least she wasn't yelling, so Boot took that as an invitation to come over and get acquainted. He walked up, sat down in front of her and gave her The Look. It was an expression perfected by dogs over thousands of years of dealing with humans. It was a little bit pitiful and a little bit pleading, but most of all it said, "I think I like you and I would really like to share whatever it is you are eating."

"You want *coffe macchiato?"*

He wagged his tail and came a little bit closer. The old woman broke off a piece of bread, put it in her saucer and poured coffee over it. Then she put it on the ground and waited.

Boot came closer, sniffed at the food, then lapped it up and asked for more.

"Ahhhh, you like?" She tapped her chest, "My bread. Sicilian coffee." She smiled and Boot smiled back.

From that day on, they had breakfast together every day and soon struck up a friendship. Mrs. Conti's daughters-in-law didn't speak Sicilian—except for some well-chosen curses they picked up from their husbands—and her sons were too busy to talk with her, so she talked to Boot. He didn't understand the words, but he liked the sound of her voice and he was a very good listener.

Most of the time, she just talked, but one day she cried. Boot came over and put his head in her lap. *"Grazij,"* she said as she stroked his head and scratched behind his ears. She seemed to appreciate having someone to talk to and Boot definitely liked her bread and coffee. She planted extra garlic for him and they got along just fine.

But this day was different. When Boot walked through the garden, Mrs. Conti wasn't there. At first, he thought she might be sitting inside the shed to get out of the drizzle, but she wasn't there. He waited for her all morning, but she never came. For several hours, he lay by the three-legged stool with his head on his paws. He was very sad.

Many people accept the fact that dogs have a sixth sense. They recognize sadness and joy and sometime even pick up on early signs of illness. It was obvious to Boot that something was very wrong in his universe. Late in the afternoon he walked over to Tony Conti's grocery store. It was closed and there was a white wreath with black ribbons on the door. Boot saw the same thing on Vinny's general store and Salvador's Ford dealership.

The news of Carmelina Conti's death at 97 spread as quickly as a flash of summer lightning. She was older than anybody else in Lost River and folks couldn't imagine the town without her. Most people remembered seeing her standing in front of a door waiting for someone to open it. Other than that, they realized they didn't know her at all.

A funeral mass was scheduled for 11:00 on Saturday at St. Philip's Catholic Church. Neither the Conti family nor Father Sullivan was prepared for the number of people who came to pay their respects. The story of Carmelina Lombardi and her mother and brothers coming to America and settling in Lost River was apparently well known to Sicilians throughout the southeast.

Normally, on the day of the funeral, Boot would have waited outside the church with the other dogs, but not this time. He followed the Conti family down the aisle and went to sit as close to his friend in the coffin as he could. He didn't lie down, he sat tall throughout the entire mass. After the grave-yard service, the other dogs went home. Boot stayed.

An old man who looked to be about Carmelina's age came up to Tony. "I am so sorry for the loss of your mother. I was from her village, Palermo, and I knew all the Lombardi family. I was friends with her brothers. Before we left, it was a very bad time in Sicily. Terrible thing for a young girl to see what they did to Mr. Esposito," he hesitated. When Tony didn't respond, he asked, "You know that story, yes?"

"No Sir, my mother never talked about that. Can you tell me what happened that day? What happened to her father and the rest of her family?"

The old man found a bench and sat down. Tony joined him. "My name is Luca Marino. We lived in the house next door to the Lombardis. My mother remembered and she told me the story. Carmelina and her mother were in the square that morning and saw the soldiers shoot Mr. Esposito. He was the principal at our school. After that, everyone in the village was afraid to go out into the streets. Carmelina's family was one of the lucky ones. They already had their papers and they left Palermo soon after that morning."

"Her father didn't come with them," Tony said. "They never knew what happened to him. Do you know anything about that?"

Mr. Marino shifted his gaze from Tony to the black hat in his lap. At first Tony thought he hadn't heard the question or that maybe he was embarrassed to admit he didn't know anything.

"I know," he said quietly. "I was hiding in my house and I saw Mr. Lombardi. He was all covered with blood and he was running from the soldiers. He tried to get into his house, but they caught him. They beat him with clubs and then dragged him away. I am sorry that is all I know. I do not know where they took him and what happened next. Many men in our village were... taken away. We left shortly after that horrible day. One of my brothers was...taken away too."

Tony felt like someone had opened a door just enough for him to see a little of the brutality his family had escaped from. No wonder they never talked about it. Sicily had always seemed to him like a make-believe place. He realized bad things happened there, but it was like the bad things that happen in a fairytale. Not a real place, not where real people were beaten with clubs. Not a place where his relatives died.

Mr. Marino sat very still and Tony thought he saw a tear run down his cheek. He reached over and patted the man's hand. "Thank you for telling me your story. Since you are here, I assume some of your family made it out safely. Are they living near here?"

"My mother lived with us, but she passed away seven years ago. She had a good life in this country. She loved America. She said our home in Tallahassee reminded her of summers in Sicily. Like Carmelina, she had a family, children—me and my two sisters—and grandchildren, even one great grandchild. The difference was, my mother talked about her old life a lot. She said it was important for us to know about the evil in the world so we would appreciate what living in peace meant. I hope it was not wrong to tell you about the bad things that happened."

Tony smiled. "No Sir, it wasn't wrong. In fact, Mr. Marino, it explains something that has puzzled me all my life." And he told the old man about his mother's aversion to doorknobs.

Beware of Ordinary Days

Principal Slonacher made his normal daily announcements, and then sat back in his chair, put his feet on the desk and settled in for his morning nap.

Students filled the halls and then sorted themselves out into their assigned homerooms. Everything was pretty much the same, except for Matt. He had grown three inches over the summer holidays and he was still getting used to being tall. He had always been the shortest one of the Three Musketeers, now he was as tall as Hank…maybe even a little taller. The only problem was he kept bumping his head. His two friends just laughed. On the other hand, Matt was getting a lot more attention from the girls.

Hank slid into his desk in homeroom just before the last bell rang. He had been doing that a lot lately, which was totally out of character. Matt and Sonny wondered if something was going on with him.

Hank might be late, but there was no way he—or any of the other boys—were going to miss homeroom. The previous teacher, Miss Cardwell had finally retired. And in her place was Miss Lawson. She was single, she was pretty and she was *young*. Her first job right out of college was the word going around town. The older teachers were taking bets on how long she would last. Hank gave Miss Lawson a big smile as he gathered his long legs under his desk.

"You ready for that history test third period?" Matt asked.

Hank looked annoyed. "How can Miss Thompson give us a test now?"

"That's what I said," Sonny added. "She oughta know we've forgotten everything over summer vacation. It's not fair!"

Hank agreed.

"What are you talking about, Hank? History's your best subject. What's up with you anyway? You've been acting weird ever since school started this year."

Hank opened his mouth to answer just as the last bell rang. Miss Lawson smiled, "All right, boys. Settle down now."

School meant confinement to the students, but mothers all over Lost River breathed a sigh of relief. The kids were out of the house, off the streets and hopefully out of trouble. For the hours from 8:30 to 3:30 the town was significantly quieter. Time for mothers to get housework done. Labor-saving devices, like electric washers and dryers were becoming popular. Washers were fine, but most women still preferred hanging their clothes in the open air assuming the rain stopped long enough for them to get dry. As they say, "A woman's work is never done."

Like everybody else, Tony Conti had a Monday morning routine. He set up crates of vegetables and fruit in front of his store. He remembered the first day he met Boot standing around looking lost and hungry. At the time he would never have guessed his mother and that dog would become such good friends.

Mr. K. and Inky were working on a layout showing the high-school football schedule for the coming year. Their first game was with Freehand High School over in Empire. High school football was big news and folks counted on the *Herald* to cover all the games.

Because none of the churches had paid custodians, early Monday morning various ladies from the congregations came to dust, vacuum and straighten up. Florence Cumberland organized a little inter-denominational coffee time at Trinity Episcopal. What better way to catch up on local gossip after their church duties were done?

On that particular day, anybody who could get away for an hour or so, was waiting at 10:00 at Conti's Ford Dealership to see the local allotment of shiny 1950 models roll off the truck. It was an annual social event in Lost River. Junior and Ethyl walked over from the Gas and Grill and joined Sid Cumberland, Morris Fullerton and Zach Stubbs. As he was waiting for the car carrier to show up, Zach noticed the water tower over the tree tops. Although his son Hank wasn't big on the details, he had made a point of telling his father that while they were up there, they found his name. Zach had to smile at the boys' reaction. They seemed genuinely surprised that he had done something so wild in his youth. Hard to remember a time when he and his friends all believed they were invincible and nobody worried about consequences.

Finally, the carrier pulled up in front of the dealership. The first car off the truck was a bright red Crestliner, two-door-sports sedan. "Thank God Detroit's back in business. I was getting tired of those old pre-war models," Junior said and everyone agreed.

The next model was the County Squire Wagon. The polished wood side panels gleamed in the sun. "That's the one everybody's calling the Woodie," Sal announced. It was followed by a two-toned aqua Tudor sedan. Sal was partial to the red Crestliner, but the one that got the most comments was the last one off the truck. A mint-green Club Coupe. All in all, it was quite a show.

Sheriff Latham missed all the excitement because he was checking out Percy's Operation 23. The Do-or-Dye was closed on Monday, so Trudy decided to ride along with him. The speed trap was working so well, Percy had become something of a local hero. They watched him flag down a speeder, but didn't interrupt his well-timed performance.

Just another ordinary Monday. The kids were in school, the new Fords had arrived and Percy was raking in the cash. Then out of the blue, Boot walked into the middle of Jefferson Street in front of Conti's Grocery and turned in circles several times. Finally, he sat down, faced west toward The Grove where Mrs. Conti used to live and started to howl. That attracted attention because Boot was normally a very quiet dog. He didn't bark much and now this? People decided it was probably his way of mourning Mrs. Conti's death.

But that wasn't it at all.

Something in The Air

Boot knew something was coming, he could feel it in the air. He tried to warn them, but they didn't understand. The other dogs understood and went to find shelter. By mid-afternoon, there wasn't a dog to be seen anywhere in Lost River, but nobody noticed.

The sky was getting darker, but afternoon thunder storms were nothing new. A few people noticed the clouds that day were blacker than usual and they hung low across the whole sky. They weren't the normal soft, slow-moving clouds folks were accustomed to. They were rolling around like thick grits ready to boil over. Even with all that going on, hardly anyone took time to stop and really pay attention to the sky and the weather.

As the day wore on, the black clouds continued to gather until they reached all across the sky from East to West as far as anyone could see. However, below the dark clouds and above the trees, there was a strip of blue sky. Again, hardly anybody noticed. Buried in the high clouds, lightning bounced back and forth, but instead of sharp thunder claps, this thunder growled, deep and angry like a caged animal.

On the far end of Highway 23, J.W. and Trudy watched as the wind picked up items that were never meant to fly and sent them sailing into the air. Wooden shingles from an old barn half a mile away, Percy's newly planted speed-limit signs, pieces of tin from an abandoned billboard.

"I've never seen a wind like this," Trudy said. "It's like the sky's raining trash. Wonder what's going on?"

J.W. was a city boy. He knew about street riots, gangsters and predictable snow storms. Weird wind storms were a mystery to him. "I have no idea, but it doesn't look good. I'm gonna give Lucy a call."

He picked up the walkie-talkie and hit the push-to-talk. "Breaker 1-9. Lucy, can you hear me?" He felt a little silly using the truckers' lingo. "Listen, the storm is looking kinda bad out here. Lots of things blowing around. Just to be on the safe side, why don't you get hold of Hazel in the mayor's office. If this situation turns out to be dangerous, you two can hide in the Ladies' Room in the middle to the building. And while you're at it, please turn on the air-raid siren. Over."

Lucy's voice came through loud and clear. "OK, but not much is happening over here. Now about that siren. We've had it all through the war, but we've never used it. I'll see if I can find the thing, but I'm not sure it will still work. And if it does, it's gonna scare the b'Jesus out of everybody. They'll probably think the war's started again. Over."

"You may be right, but I'd feel better if you did it anyway. Out."

Lucy shook her head, but she walked into the back room, found the siren and switched it on. Then she found Hazel, who was not thrilled about the idea of hiding in the restroom. Over the noise of the siren she shouted, "What do you mean, 'hug a commode?' I'm not hugging any toilet…" About that time the windows on the west side of the building shattered. Both women headed toward the restroom at a dead run.

Lucy and Hazel might not have known what to expect, but Morris Fullerton did. He didn't need to *see* the storm, he felt it in his bones. The wound in his leg had healed, but the wound in his mind was still fresh and raw. When the sky darkened and the air got still and heavy, Morris was back in the Philippines, back in the Bataan prison camp. He had seen more than one typhoon come charging across the water and tear into the land. In the camp, he met the storms with open arms and prayed he might die by the hand of God rather than at the hand of some vicious prison guard.

Now he watched the storm approaching Lost River. He stood perfectly still, felt the temperature drop and listened as hail started to bounce off the sidewalk. In a few seconds, he saw mail boxes, gardening tools and flower pots go swirling through the air. His first thought was typhoon. His second thought was *run,* but he couldn't run. The wind picked him up and slammed him into a ditch beside the road.

At about the same time, Curtis Leland looked out the window and saw a huge wall of debris headed toward the funeral home. He called to Mildred as he ran out the door. "Call the G & G and tell everybody to meet me out front." He jumped in the big black hearse and made a bee-line for the Gulf station. When he got there, he threw open the back door. "Get in here. Hurry!" By then the wind was howling so loud he couldn't hear his own voice. Junior and Ethyl and half-a-dozen customers were waiting. "Everybody in?" Curtis yelled and slammed the door. "Hold on!"

Signboards and bicycles and anything that wasn't nailed down was flying around. Hail hit the windshield and collected on the side of the road like snow. Curtis made it back to the funeral home just in time to get everyone down the stairs to the basement. It sounded like pieces of the building upstairs were being ripped off. Then they heard a crash that shook the whole structure and instantly the air was filled with the smell of pine.

They braced for another crash, but nothing happened. All the noise stopped. The air got still. There was no sound, no wind, no insects, no birds. "Don't move," Curtis warned. "The storm's not over, it's just changing direction. It'll be back."

In the next instant, the tornado touched down with all its pent-up fury.

One Way or Another

There are two ways to experience a tornado. From the pages of a book... "A tornado is a violent, rotating column of air reaching from the base of a thunderstorm to the ground."

The other way to experience a tornado is up close and personal. Folks in Lost River were caught totally by surprise. Tornadoes, when they happened, were normally in the extreme southern part of the state and it was the wrong time of year all together.

Night came early to Lost River. Falling trees brought down telephone and electric lines. Fierce lightning deep in the clouds split the darkness for an instant. In spite of the danger, some folks couldn't resist going outside to watch the raw power of the storm.

From a distance, the funnel cloud looked like a giant Mixmaster running at full speed and out of control. Small objects offered no more resistance than an egg yolk folded into cake batter. The storm tumbled everything together and hurled globs of debris in all directions.

The wind stripped all the leaves off the oak trees in the square and left the branches clinging modestly to whisps of Spanish moss. The pine trees hung on to their needles, but even some of the two-foot-thick trunks snapped as easily as breaking a kitchen match. The smell of pine sap mixed with the hot metallic smell of exploding transformers. Downed power lines spewed sparks that started little bonfires everywhere.

Common knowledge says what goes up must come down and it did. Some of the flying debris ended up miles away, some of it slammed back into the ground with such force that all that was left were bits and pieces. Wreckage stacked up against buildings and in the gutters like cracker crumbs in the bottom of a box.

The town was covered with mounds of trash and downed trees. Most of the buildings were intact, but all that energy had to go somewhere and it settled on Church Corner. The storm ripped the steeple off St. Philip's Catholic church and sent a statue of the Virgin Mary flying up to heaven. It took the new roof off Wesley United Methodist. The shingles were last seen headed in the general direction of Savannah.

Bethel Baptist had held a baptismal service on Sunday and no one had drained the pool yet. With surgical precision, the tornado ripped the pool out of the wall and deposited it on the corner of Oak Park under the naked trees. Not a drop of water was spilled. Remarkable since it weighted about 1,500 pounds.

Several of the beautiful stained-glass windows of Trinity Episcopal were shattered into so many Mardi Gras beads. On its way out of town, the tornado picked up the Quonset hut at the G&G. Sometime later it was found unharmed in the next county.

As bad as the mayhem was, the scariest part of the storm was the noise, which was so loud it was like a physical presence. It reminded some folks of the biblical battle of Jericho when the noise from the Israelites' trumpets brought down the walls of the city.

They say a tornado sounds like a freight train. What they fail to mention is that the train isn't way off in the distance. It sounds close enough to touch, terrifying enough to make the hair on the back of your neck stand up.

For the citizens of Lost River, the storm went on forever, but actually it lasted less than ten minutes. As suddenly as it touched down, it was all over. Like a cruel joke, the sky cleared and the sun came out bright and cheerful, like nothing had happened.

The town was a mess, but apparently nobody had been killed or seriously injured. The one fatality was mourned by Sal Conti who stood in front of his Ford showroom and wept at the sight the brand-new 1950 Ford Crestliner sports sedan wrapped around a light post.

Downside Up

Morris Fullerton's body was cold and clammy. He lay perfectly still and felt the cold seep into his bones. "I guess I must be dead." He lay there and thought about that for a while. Then he felt warmth on his back like someone slowly pulling a blanket over his shoulders. It felt good and he thought about *that* for a while.

"If I can feel warm and cold, then I'm probably not dead. But if I'm not dead, what the hell am I doing lying face down in a ditch?" Then something cold touched the back of his neck. He jerked away and did his best to roll over and sit up. There was Boot looking him in the eye as if to say, "Why are you in the ditch. Are you OK?"

Morris gave Boot a pat and stood up. The pain in his leg was familiar and strangely comforting. At least something was normal. Like the Pied Piper of Hamelin, Morris hobbled in the general direction of downtown and Boot and his friends happily followed along.

On the other side of town, J.W. helped Trudy up the ladder welded into the side of the grease pit at the G&G where they had taken shelter. He looked around expecting to see the Quonset hut, but it was nowhere in sight. At least he and Trudy weren't hurt. "Are you OK?"

Trudy turned on him. "Let's see. I'm soaking wet, smeared with axel grease, I've got a bruise the size of New Jersey on my side and I'm still shaking. But other than that, I'm just fine."

J.W. couldn't help but laugh. He reached out and hugged her quickly before she could hit him with a tire iron. "Come on, True, let's see if we can find anybody else."

When they got to City Hall, Sid Cumberland, the bank staff, Lucy, Hazel, half-a-dozen bank customers and other shoppers were standing out front looking at the pile of bricks that used to be the façade of the bank and the space in the air where the clock tower should have been.

As soon as she saw him, Hazel confronted the sheriff. "I was holding on to a toilet...*a toilet* for God's sake and I was scared to death I was gonna get sucked up in the air." Her eyes were big and her hands were shaking. "I thought my eardrums would burst, but the scariest thing was when the water in the toilet was sucked straight up through a hole in the roof. It was eerie, like some black magic kind of thing. Evil." She shivered. Trudy put her arms around Hazel's shoulders and tried to calm her down.

When other people saw the sheriff, they started to congregate. Everybody wanted news, but J.W. could only report on what he had seen. Lots of the bystanders had cuts and minor injuries from flying glass and other debris. Sid's car was nearby so he volunteered to take anyone who needed help over to Dr. Nichols' office.

As they were leaving, Percy drove up and everyone turned to him with questions. He reported what he had seen. "I went by the lumber yard and there were 2x4's lying around like Pick-up Sticks. Two logging trucks were turned over and the roof blew off one shed, but nobody got hurt. By the way, Mr. Stubbs, your car is OK.

"Moon's is OK too. Moved the whole train car a couple of feet off its tracks, but the salt and pepper shakers were still on the tables if you can believe that. There was no way to lift the train car back up on its rails, but believe it or not, it landed on a concrete slab nearby. Junior and some guys from the G&G were working to reconnect gas and water lines, so Moon's oughta be back in business pretty soon."

Downed trees and live wires made driving difficult, but Hank, Matt and Sonny got through on their bikes. "Sheriff, we just came over from the school. I think the kids are OK, but nobody knows where Miss Eudalee is. The last time anybody saw her, she had gone back in the building to get a couple of first-graders. Seems like y'all oughta get over there quick as you can."

Lost River High School had started as a one-room wooden structure. Over the years a number of other rooms were added until in 1900 the original school was replaced by a two-story red brick building that housed all 11 grades. By 1940 the school board added a 12th grade and workers moved the cafeteria from the bottom floor of the main building to a new addition. Lost River High School now boasted a brand-new gym paid for with speed-trap money.

Picking their way around downed trees and live wires, the crowd headed over to the school. From a distance, the building looked normal, but around back, it was a different story. A yellow school bus was stuck upside down in the corner of the building with cracks radiating in all directions. The bus looked like a dead bug with its wheels in the air. Boot and his friends immediately started sniffing around the rubble.

Teachers had done a remarkable job of getting all the students out safely and it wasn't until they took a head-count they realized Miss Eudalee was missing. As they stood looking at the damage, someone yelled, "Look out!" and more beams and bricks came down in a cloud of dust and smoke.

The boys started to run toward the crash. "Hold it!" Zach Stubbs stopped them before they got too close. "That walls unstable. If you go tromping around that pile of stuff, your weight could bring the whole thing down."

As if they understood the problem, Boot and his friends took up the search. Using their noses to guide them, they sniffed at every crack and opening. It took a while, but eventually they zeroed in on a huge pile of debris and set up a cry for help. "Come on, guys. We found her. She's down here." They barked as loud as they could so Miss Eudalee would know help was on the way.

Someone thought they heard faint moans, but that was all. "She sounds like she's hurt," Matt said. "What if she can hear us, but she can't answer. Or maybe she can't even hear us."

J.W. turned to Percy, "Drive over to the office and see if you can find a bullhorn somewhere back in the store room? It'll be on the top shelf way in the back in a box marked riot gear." J.W. remembered being amused when he put the box away. He'd seen his share of riots in Chicago, but even if everybody in Lost River decided to participate, there wouldn't be enough people to put together a proper mob.

While they waited for Percy to get back, J. W. sized up the situation. They needed to clear away the rubble, but some of the pieces were too big to be moved by hand. Reaching Miss Eudalee was going to take time and he wasn't sure how much time they had.

Zach Stubbs offered to bring the bulldozer over from the lumber yard. When he first started working with his dad, handling the heavy equipment was his favorite job. He didn't get to play with the big toys much anymore. Sid gave him a ride to the lumber yard.

When word got around that a rescue was underway, everybody came to watch. Miss Eudalee had taught almost everybody in town. She was like family.

J.W. aimed the bullhorn at the pile of rubble, "Miss Eudalee, we know where you are and we're working to get you out. The noise you hear is a bulldozer. We're using it to clear away some of the big stuff. Just hang on. Help is on the way."

Zach used the dozer to remove as much of the rubble as he dared. There was no shortage of helpers willing to remove bricks, boards, broken furniture and hunks of plaster. It was slow going because they didn't want to cause a cave-in. Finally, they got close enough to see that Miss Eudalee was alive. "I'm all right, except for my arm. I think maybe it's broken."

The Three Musketeers immediately sprang into action. They climbed over the last pile of wreckage and slowly helped her make her way to safety without any further damage. When she was finally free, she realized her best suit was torn and covered with dirt and ashes.

"Oh shit!"

When she looked up, she was facing a sea of astonished faces. Without a moment's hesitation, she shook her finger at the crowd and adopted her best settle-down-and-pay-attention voice. "I did not say that, and you did not hear it. Is that clear?"

"Yes, Miss Eudalee," they mumbled.

Sid helped her into his car and drove over to Dr. Nichols' office. Before the crowd broke up, Brother Bob offered a short prayer of thanks that Miss Eudalee had been rescued and no one else had been seriously hurt. The crowd lingered. When no one was looking, Morris Fullerton told the sheriff he was willing to feed the multitude. He volunteered to pick up the tab. The crowd moved across the street to Moon's and Gibby and Mama served burgers and pie until they ran out of food.

"That's it for us, folks," Gibby said. "Looks like it's Stone Soup from here on."

"What's stone soup?"

Gibby smiled. "It's a long story."

"Tell it."

Everyone was still pumped up and nobody wanted to go home and deal with whatever awaited them. In no time, the Three Musketeers gathered scrap wood for a bonfire. Some of old folks remembered back in the days before radio when storytelling was their only form of entertainment. The crowd gathered around the fire and Gibby began.

Stone Soup

"This is an old story. It's been around for hundreds of years and everybody who tells it has their own version. This is the Lost River version.

"Back before Boot came to Lost River, he didn't have a home. He just wondered from town to town looking for food. Somewhere along the way, he met up with a man—we'll call him Bill—and for a while they traveled together. Whenever their food was running low, Bill and Boot would go into the nearest town looking for a meal. They never begged because Bill had a magic stone that made soup.

"This is the way it worked. He and Boot politely asked for help at several houses. Housewives always pleaded poverty and turned them down. Bill understood. It was, after all, hard times. Then Bill explained that he didn't really need food, all he needed was a pot of water and some fire wood. By that time, of course, he made sure a crowd of curious onlookers had gathered to see what was going on.

"Someone always provided the pot, and once Bill had a roaring fire going, he carefully filled the pot half full of water and positioned it just right over the fire. He took his time and made sure he had everyone's undivided attention. Then Bill made a big show of taking a large, white stone out of his knapsack, cleaning it off and putting it into the water. After that, he carefully put the lid on the pot and he and Boot sat down to wait.

"After a proper amount of time, Bill tasted the soup and offered some to Boot. 'I think it's just about right, what do you think?' Boot shook his head. Then Bill handed the spoon to one of the townswomen. 'What do you think?'

"All she tasted was hot water, but she wasn't about to admit that a man might have a better sense of taste than she did. She smacked her lips, looked thoughtful and said, 'It needs some salt and pepper.' And she added them to the pot.

"Not to be outdone, another woman grabbed the spoon. She fancied herself the best cook in the village. When she tasted the soup, she shook her head sadly. 'Why anyone can tell it needs onions. They're the most important ingredient. I always put six onions in my soup.' And she added them to the pot.

"Granny Grump toddled over to the pot with her apron full of something. 'Onions are nice but real soup needs celery and carrots,' she pointed out. She took a knife out of her pocket and proceeded to chop a bunch of carrots and a big stalk of celery into the pot. 'Now, that's better,' she said as she shook the garden dirt out of her apron.

"At this point, Bill tasted the soup again and looked thoughtful. 'Well, the salt and pepper, the onions, the celery and the carrots did help the flavor, but the stone has made better soup, there still seems to be something not quite right. I wonder what we're missing?'

"That was an open invitation for everyone to get involved. The women in the village didn't have much to brag about, but for goodness's sake, they all knew how to make soup and secretly each one considered her soup superior to anybody else's.

"'In my day, we always started with soup bones. Every good cook knows that.' The butcher's wife, opened a bag and dumped all but one bone into the pot. She tossed the last one to Boot.

"The local schoolmarm got involved too. 'That's all fine, but what about potatoes?' she asked. 'You can't make soup without potatoes and she added several handfuls to the pot.

"The mayor's wife wasn't about to be left out. 'You can't possibly make soup without tomatoes!' she said. Tomatoes were considered exotic, so of course only the mayor's wife could afford them. With a flourish, she added them to the pot.

"Several little girls came with their hands full of garlic cloves and dropped in each clove one at a time.

"The pot was beginning to fill up. 'This may not be the richest village around, but we can always find meat for a pot of soup,' said Sister Felicity, who did the cooking for the local priest. She added several pieces of prime beef to the pot.

"No one wanted to be left out and so they added sausage and beans and hot peppers and squash and herbs. By this time the huge pot was nearly overflowing and the soup smelled wonderful. Bill took the wooden spoon and gave the soup several lusty stirs. Once again, he poured a little out for Boot to taste and sampled a spoonful himself. His face immediately lit up. 'Oh my, no doubt about it, this is the best soup the stone has ever made!' Boot agreed.

"Everyone went home to get bowls or cups and what-have-you. Bill served each and every one and they all agreed it was exceptional soup. Delicious. When they had all had their fill, Bill scooped the stone out of the bottom of the pot. He washed it off, dried it carefully and stored it safely in his backpack. He and Boot thanked the ladies for their help, wished the men of the village good health and headed to the next town. And that is the story of Stone Soup."

The crowd applauded and everyone headed for home. It had been a long day. With a little sleep they would be able to tackle the work that lay ahead of them.

The Wrong Dream

The tornado in Lost River made the news on WSB radio in Atlanta. When word got around, offers of help came in from everywhere. The quartermaster at Camp Wheeler asked Mayor Mackie if the town needed anything. She explained that other than the school and a few buildings downtown, they were fine. "Everybody's pitching in, but we could use some help cleaning up." That afternoon a large truck and a detachment of men rolled into town and went to work alongside the men who had come over from the lumber yard.

The air was soon full of the sound of saws and the smell of fresh sawdust. Once the trees were out of the way, Georgia Power and Southern Bell crews went to work. Everyone who had a shovel and a pickup truck hauled trash.

Mildred Leland and her group from the WMU joined teachers and students to salvage furniture, books and supplies from the school. The Conti wives worked with the lunchroom ladies to make enough spaghetti and meatballs to feed the entire town.

Florence Cumberland went searching for somebody to organize. Southern Bell had worked miracles and as soon as the phones were back in service, she called the Episcopal Church Women. "Girls, it is up to us to take the lead in caring for the volunteers. Junior Ottley helped me locate an extra coffee maker and I hope I can count on each of you to bake up something delicious. We'll set up an aid station at City Hall where everyone can see us. We'll serve fresh, hot coffee and pastries. I think that will add a touch of class and be an appropriate way to show our appreciation. So, hop to, Ladies. We have a lot of work to do."

Bright and early that morning Hank borrowed a pickup from the mill and picked up Matt and Sonny. At eight o'clock they were hard at work clearing trash and downed trees from the mayor's yard. It was mid-afternoon before they finished and they were dirty, hot, tired and hungry. They headed over to Moon's to eat and to see if Gibby needed any help.

The boys ordered their usual but instead of gobbling his food, Hank just sat looking at his plate. At first Matt and Sonny were too busy to notice. Finally, Matt hesitated long enough to pay attention. "You're not eating. What's the matter?"

"Nothing."

"This is us you're talking to," Sonny said. "It's got to be something really serious if it's more important than Gibby's burgers."

"Yeah, you're been acting weird lately. What's up?"

"It's nothing…I mean it's nothing I can do anything about."

"Well, that's clear as mud."

"It's my Dad."

That got their attention. "Is he sick?"

"What? No, it's not that. It's just that he's got my whole life planned out. Graduate from high school, go to UGA, major in forestry, come home, get married, have kids, work in the mill, get old and die. I don't want that, not any of it. For starters, I don't want to go to college."

"You don't *want* to go to college!!?" Matt spat out the words. "I can't believe you. You've got it all and you don't *want* to go? That's all I've ever wanted to do."

It was true, Hank, Sonny and Matt had always talked about how great it would be when they went away to college. Matt's family didn't have a lot of money, but he knew his parents had set up a college fund for him. Sonny, on the other hand, never worried about money. Now he was worried about grades. Getting by on his good looks and personality had worked pretty well in high school, but he wasn't sure they would cut it at college.

Of the three of them, Hank had it made. His dad owned the mill, he was captain of the football team, president of the student council and an "A" student who was a shoo-in for valedictorian. He should be happy, but instead he looked totally miserable. "You guys don't understand. I really don't want to go to college."

"That's nuts. We've always talked about going to college together. Like the Three Musketeers. It'll be a blast," Sonny said.

"We'll be living the dream," Matt said.

"The trouble is it's not *my* dream. I don't want to go to college and I don't want to be in the lumber business."

Not going to college was one thing, but not taking over the family business was something else. "Have you told your dad?"

"Are you kidding!? That's what I was trying to tell you. I'm stuck. There's no way out."

***

On the other side of town, clean-up was in full swing. The whole town was covered in a thick carpet of leaves. Almost as quickly as the leaves were raked up, kids flung themselves into the middle of the piles scattering the leaves in all directions. Adults tolerated the mayhem at first and then got down to the serious business of burning huge piles of leaves. For the next couple of days there wasn't a mosquito to be found in Lost River.

Inky got his broom and started on his usual round of sweeping sidewalks. He started with Washington Street and had worked his way down to the Do-or Dye Salon, when Mr. K.

stopped him. "When you're done here, Helen could use some help back at the shop."

Leon Kirkland didn't believe in filing cabinets. "You put something in the wrong file and it's lost forever. Makes a lot more sense to stack things out in the open where you can see them." Normally the system worked just fine, but the storm had seriously rearranged Leon's well-ordered piles and now the inside of the Print Shop was covered with papers. Helen was standing in the middle of the floor shaking her head. How could she put things back in order when she had no idea where they belonged to start with?

Inky devised his own system. Hand-written notes went in one pile. School news went into another. Farm news and prices went into a third stack. He gave all the social stuff to Helen and tossed pictures into a box. He only glanced at the written material long enough to decide where to put it, but he found the pictures fascinating. There was one faded snapshot that caught his attention. He didn't recognize the name on the back so he decided to ask Helen about it later.

They finally took a break and headed to Moon's for lunch. Halfway through his first burger Inky remembered the picture. He held it out to Helen, "Who's Blossom?"

Helen smiled at the skinny kid in the baseball uniform. "That's Leon when he was about your age. He played professionally for a while and dreamed of playing in the major leagues, but it didn't work out."

Story #13, Blossom (Atlanta Circa 1924)

His family called him Lee and he was a scrawny kid. His favorite job in his father's print shop was cleaning the type and putting each letter back in its proper place in the wooden case. His hands, arms, clothes and often his face were a masterpiece of black-ink smears. Like all the kids in town, Lee was expected to do chores and to help out in the family business. But the minute he was free, he headed for the sand lot behind the saw mill.

He started playing ball as soon as he was big enough to pick up a bat or a stick if nothing else was handy. He was younger than most of the other kids in his neighborhood and he was usually the last to be chosen because he couldn't throw worth a damn. But when he came up to bat, it was a whole different ball game. High, low, inside, outside, curves or sliders, he could hit anything and he was fast.

By the time he was 15, he was 5' 11" and had gained some weight. That put some power behind his hitting and the scouts began to take notice. Two years later he was signed by the Atlanta Crackers.

The afternoon he ran onto the field wearing a Crackers uniform was the proudest moment of his life. It was the opening game of the 1924 season and the first game to be played in the new stadium on Ponce de Leon Avenue. Built by R. J. Spiller, the new ball park cost $250,000 and was steel and concrete with bucket seats, not bleachers. It held 20,000 fans, and one Atlanta newspaper called it "the most magnificent park in the minor leagues."

All that was fine, but the thing that made the stadium really famous was a stately magnolia tree in the middle of center field. If a ball hit the tree and bounced back into the field, it was still in play. If it stuck in the tree or went all the way through, it was a home run.

Lee said the secret to his hitting was that he always chose something specific to aim at and his favorite target was the big white flowers on that tree. Whenever he hit one, the announcer would say, "Hey-ho, another blossom bites the dust. Way to go kid." That's how he earned the nickname Blossom Kirkland. Everyone said he was headed for a career in the majors, but then his father died. The dream was over because he had to quit and come home.

Amen

Brother Bob Blalock's time had come. It was spring, getting close to the end of the school year, sap was rising, fresh green leaves were on the trees, warm breezes promised better weather and revival was in the air. The Rev. Mr. Robert Blalock, pastor of Bethel Baptist Church, was not like most Baptist preachers. Brother Bob loved the blues and played poker, although he didn't gamble.

Ethyl kept his stash of $50 in her office at the G&G. The total never varied. If he lost, he made up the difference out of his own pocket. If he won, he put anything over $50 in the poor box at church, ergo, no gambling.

His congregation treasured him because he knew each and every member of his flock. He was a good pastor, but he wasn't a very good preacher. However, his annual revivals made up for that. He was the Cecil B. DeMille of revival meetings. They were the perfect combination of religious fervor and top-notch entertainment.

Brother Bob was always on the look-out for just the right person to be the headliner of his revival meetings. In 1950 he found the perfect candidate on Beale Street in Memphis. The man was known throughout the region as the Guitar Preacher. He was tall, skinny as a rail and his long curly black hair had a wild, untamed look about it. Brother Bob hoped the young people would see a cool street musician and the older folks would see the Prophet Jeremiah.

The Guitar Preacher's real name was Anthony Dubois. He had been born and raised in Bogalusa, Louisiana, and his father pastored a little church in the unincorporated community of Cross Roads. He learned to play guitar by the time he was six. When he was 13, he got into some trouble with the local sheriff and ran away from home. That was the basis of his testimony.

Brother Bob made a special trip to Memphis and hung out on Beale Street to watch the Guitar Preacher in action. He was perfect. He never failed to draw a crowd and lost souls were saved on the spot. As he was packing up his guitar late one night, Brother Bob approached him with an offer. The opportunity to preach in an actual church with a captive audience appealed to Anthony…at least on a short-term basis.

Once Brother Bob got a firm commitment from Anthony, he drove back to Lost River and went to work putting together the rest of the program. He approached Ethyl with the offer of a three-day paying job playing piano at the services. That was guaranteed to liven things up. In Empire he found a girls' trio whose close harmony sounded almost as good as the Andrew

Sisters. They called themselves the Belles of Heaven. Brother Bob drew up flyers and Leon Kirkland printed them.

Matt was put in charge of distribution. He couldn't wait to tell Hank and Sonny that the Belles of Haven were the same three girls they had met at the circus. Suddenly the boys decided their souls could use a little reviving. Things were shaping up nicely from everybody's point of view. In no time at all, revival flyers were plastered all over town.

To show their religious fervor, Hank and Sonny came with Matt to Wednesday night prayer meeting. They lifted their voices in song and prayed seriously for the success of the revival. However, when the sermon dragged on a bit too long, they started having a little too much fun with the hymn books. Brother Bob knew exactly what was going on and sent one of the deacons to put a stop to it.

In his slightly miss-spent youth, Bob Blalock had done the same thing. Grab a hymnal, flip through the pages, read out a title and add "between the sheets." He still remembered some of the better ones. "Jesus Loves Me"—between the sheets. "I Surrender All"—between the sheets. And the one that finally got him kicked out of a similar Wednesday night service when he was 15. "Jesus Is Coming"—between the sheets.

The revival officially began the next night. Thursday was designated Kids Night with free hotdogs and Cokes. That never failed to draw a crowd and where kids go, parents go. Several children came forward to say they wanted to be baptized and join the church. Things were off to a good start.

Excitement was building as word about the Guitar Preacher got around. Friday night was Youth Night and to ensure a good crowd, every teenage member of Bethel with access to a car was encouraged to spend Friday afternoon driving around the county picking up kids to bring to the night's service. An added incentive was a free spaghetti dinner.

That night the Guitar Preacher started off playing low-down, it's-a-hard-life blues, then preached the healing power of the Lord Jesus and ended up with a rousing gospel song of forgiveness and redemption. Ethyl got the old church piano rocking. It was a program guaranteed to appeal to all.

Of course, it appealed to some folks more than others. A teenage girl wearing a tight black skirt and a red nylon see-through blouse caused quite a stir when she came striding down the aisle. She was crying and her black mascara ran in streaks down her face. As she neared the alter, she pulled off her long dangle earrings and flung them into the congregation. Sonny was immediately intrigued. "Don't get all excited," Matt said, "she does that every year."

"How come I've never seen her before?"

"Don't know. I guess you just weren't looking in the right place."

Sonny decided to pay more attention in the future. He might be missing out on a good thing.

Thursday and Friday nights laid the groundwork for the big finish of Saturday night's sermon, "God's Lost and Found."

The Guitar Preacher gave his testimony embellished with lots of scandalous details. "It all started when I stole money from the collection plate and had to run away from home. I was 13 and I went into a far country—New Orleans—where I joined a zydeco band and played in honky-tonks and road houses all over south Louisiana. I wallowed in sin and corruption down in the miry clay. Yes I did. I wasted my substance with riotous living, spent every cent I made and began to be in want. That's when I went to work for a farmer feeding the pigs. I was so hungry, I ate some of the slop meant for the pigs.

"Finally, I came to myself and said, I will arise and go to my father and admit that I sinned against heaven and against him and ask for forgiveness. And do you know what? My father forgave me. Just like the Prodigal Son, because in God's lost and found, nobody is ever really lost."

It was a familiar parable guaranteed to touch hearts and get folks walking the aisles. Toward the end of the service, the choir stood to sing the invitational hymn, "Softly and Tenderly Jesus is Calling." A fair number of folks came to be saved or to rededicate their lives. The revival was going well so far. Then out of the corner of his eye, Brother Bob saw something that caught his attention.

The choir sounded particularly angelic as they sang, "Come home, come home, Ye who are weary come home…"

There was something oddly familiar about the man making his way down the aisle and shuffling to the front. The face was lined and wrinkled. The man was thin and his clothes looked like he had slept in them. No, they looked like he had *been* sleeping in them for quite a while. It wasn't until he spoke, that Brother Bob realized the man was Mike Sweeney.

The preacher reached out to shake his hand and for several seconds the two men looked at each other in total silence. Finally, Brother Bob found his voice. "Mike, are you coming to make a profession of faith?"

"No."

"Then what the hell are you doing here?" Brother Bob thought, but what he said was, "Then how can I help you?"

"Confession."

"Alright, we'll go to my office as soon as this service is over."

"No. I need to confess to everybody, in church tomorrow." With that, Sweeney slumped down on the front pew, covered his face with his hands and began to sob.

That pretty much brought the service to an abrupt halt. Brother Bob managed to acknowledge the people who came forward. Then he said, "Brothers and sisters, some of you may recognize this man," he indicated Mike. "His name is Mike Sweeney. He is a… he's a long-time resident of Lost River and he has requested time in tomorrow morning's Sunday service to make his confession. I hope you will come to hear what he has to say."

He might as well have saved his breath. Wild horses couldn't have kept any of them away.

Testimony

The church was packed. Extra seats had been added in the choir loft, a row of extra chairs was added down both the center and the side aisles. The back of the church was standing room only. Clearly "Sweeney's Confession" was the hottest ticket in town.

Back-row Baptists surprised everyone by arriving early and filling up the front pews. Prim Blalock and the rest of the WMU ladies—and husbands—were among the first to claim their places. After all, it was their church and they didn't want to miss a word. The Methodists filled in the next rows in the center; the Episcopalians sat farther back.

It was considered a sin for Catholics to attend a protestant service. However, this was a unique situation and Father Sullivan was not about to have his people left out. Since he didn't have time to get proper dispensation from the Pope, he declared the service a "town meeting" that just happened to be held in the Baptist church building. The Conti clan and every other Catholic in the county showed up.

Normally the Sunday morning worship service would have been the climax of the whole revival. Rev. Blalock and Brother Anthony knew it was Mike Sweeney folks had come to hear and it would be a waste of time trying to preach under those circumstances. Therefore, they kept the preliminaries to a minimum. The regular service started at precisely 11:00 with a welcome to guests, a short prayer and the doxology.

Rev. Blalock addressed the congregation. "Brothers and Sisters, we are gathered here this morning in the sight of God and man at the request of Mike Sweeney. There will be no preaching other than this message from Ephesians 4:32, 'Be kind to one another, tenderhearted, forgiving one another, as God in Christ forgave you.'" He nodded to Mike and took his seat.

Apparently, there was to be no other introduction. Mike took a deep breath, stood up and approached the pulpit. He was thankful for something to hold on to and to hide behind.

His former air of confidence was gone. The man facing the congregation was a far cry from the Mike Sweeney they had all known. He no longer looked like a prosperous Southern politician, but he did look slightly better than he had the night before. He had bathed, shaved and done his best to give himself a haircut. He had on a white shirt that had seen better days. He'd lost so much weight there was a noticeable gap between his collar and his neck. A collection of stains stood out in vivid contrast to his faded suit. His sky-blue silk tie was knotted carefully in a full Windsor. It looked totally out of place, but he had obviously taken great care to preserve at least one small part of his former self.

"Thank you for giving me time to talk to you today. I'm not quite sure where to start, but I guess I just oughta start at the beginning. As most of you know, my family has been part of Lost River since it started. You've probably heard stories and rumors about the Sweeneys, not all of them good, I'm afraid."

Eudalee leaned over to Helen Kirkland, "You can say that again."

"My family made lots of money when cotton was king, but the Civil War and the boll weevil pretty much took care of that. From cotton they switched to trees, and they made money there too. In fact, they made so much money they got above their raisin'. They started investing in the stock market and when The Crash came, they lost almost everything."

That came as a surprise to most of the audience.

"They sold off enough land to keep going for a while, but that's when they started borrowing money and taking out second mortgages. As far as anybody knew, we Sweeneys were doing fine. Truth was, my mama was the one who kept us afloat by selling her jewels and some of the valuable antiques around the house; anything to keep up appearances."

Mike could almost hear the quick intake of breath as the shocked audience absorbed all that information.

"They managed to hold it together—living in genteel poverty—until my mama passed on and not long after that my father died. Rebecca and I had just gotten married and I closed up my law office in Savannah and came home to manage the estate. But there was no estate. It had all been smoke and mirrors. There was no money, just a mountain of debt."

"My God, I can't believe that was going on right under our noses," Daniel Barlow whispered to his wife.

"Like my mama, Rebecca was a strong-willed woman. When she learned everything Mama had done to keep up a brave front, she took over. There was no way she was going to let folks know how bad things were. She set up a bare-bones budget. We sold the big house and the land around it and moved into town. Rebecca went to work at the high school and I opened my law office here. We ate a lot of beans and rice in order to look good in public. Eventually I became mayor.

"The one extravagance we kept was my weekly poker games. Rebecca figured that was important to keep up the charade. There were strict limits. It was just nickel and dime stuff among friends. The high stakes game was strictly off limits. No one questioned my decision to stay out of that because everybody knew I wasn't the world's best poker player," he acknowledged the smiles, "but I always paid off my markers.

"Then Rebecca died and it all fell apart. She had always been my rock and without her, well you can see what finally happened. For me, I just needed to win once in a while to convince myself that my luck would change. But it didn't. I continued to lose, but I didn't stop gambling. As a matter of fact, I couldn't stop. That's when I started using city money to pay my gambling debts. At first it was just once in a while and never for more than $20 or $30. But by the time I got to that last game I was in way over my head.

"You've got to understand, for a gambler it's always about the next game, the next hand. As far as I could see, my only hope was to win big in the high-stakes game. Just one good win and I could pay it all back. So, I took $500 from the Fire-Truck Fund to buy in.

"At first, Lady Luck smiled on me and I won a hand or two. That was enough to convince me my luck had finally changed. On one level, I knew I was betting money I didn't have, but that wasn't the point. I was holding *a winning hand*, a straight flush, Jack high. I simply couldn't lose.

"But I did.

"Those big games brought in a lot of shady characters like this guy Russo from New Orleans. Not the kind of person you want to mess with. No need to go into all the details, but I ended up owing him $500 I didn't have. When I lost, I panicked. I convinced him to give me until the next morning to cover the bet. I knew there was $500 left in the Fire-Truck Fund and I stole that too. I put it in an envelope on my desk, told Hazel to give it to him and I left town.

"I think I had some crazy idea that I'd get a job and pay it all back…but I was kidding myself. I knew in my heart that was never gonna happen."

The room got very quiet. Mike wanted to stop, but he knew he had to tell it all, no matter what.

"I managed to get a few menial jobs, but the minute I got my hands on some money, I found a game. I kept chasing the big win and I kept losing. Before long I'd lost my car, my clothes, my watch, even my wedding ring.

"I ended up washing dishes and scrubbing toilets in a truck stop on the Dixie Highway halfway down to Miami. I had a room and I ate whatever was left on the plates that came back from the lunch counter. One night I stole some money from the cash register and I got fired.

"I started walking north. After a couple of hours, it started to rain and this truck driver picked me up. We got to talking and he told him my sad story. He told me I was a fool to have wasted all I'd been given. I tried to find some excuse, but he was right. I had no excuse. I had hit bottom.

"That's when I remembered the story of the Prodigal son and I decided to come home.

So, here I am. I'm not asking for your forgiveness. I don't deserve it. I'm just here to say I'm sorry."

***

Brother Blalock may have urged forgiveness, but that didn't mean you couldn't talk about the sinner first. Mike Sweeney had uncovered *generations* of sin and corruption, bless his heart. It was just too good to pass up. He provided something to satisfy everybody's righteous indignation and there is nothing like coming face-to-face with a real sinner to make ordinary folks feel positively virtuous.

Citizens forgot to listen to "Jack Benny" or "The FBI in Peace and War" or any of their other Sunday night radio shows. Who needs radio drama when they were living in the middle of the real thing? Lost River hadn't had this much fun since the weekend everybody thought Mike Sweeney had run off with Annabelle Knox.

In His Own Words

Mike Sweeney opened his journal and began to write. It wasn't as good as talking to Rebecca, but it helped.

"Well, I did it. I told all the family secrets and I'm not one bit sorry. I've been carrying that garbage around all my life and worse than that, I made you carry it too. I thought if I didn't get arrested, then maybe I could just stay. Turns out, it wasn't my decision.

"Everybody was talking about my confession and arguing about what ought to be done to me. Some people folks thought I'd suffered enough, but others were still mad about the money I stole.

"What happened was this. JW gave me a choice. Sign over the deed to our house and the corner lot to the city or go to jail. I signed the papers. The City Council suggested they divide the lot in two, keep the house and sell the other lot separately. That money paid off my debt to the city and they're turning the house into a library. They auctioned off most of our stuff to pay for the renovations, but I saved a few keepsakes. So, it's all gone. I didn't get arrested, but I ended up owning nothing. On the other hand, my record is clear and that's a lot."

***

"No more gambling for me and you know what? I don't miss it. What I do miss is being mayor. I liked having folks give me a wave and a friendly hello. Truth is, I liked being a big shot. Well, that's all over now."

***

"I have a new job. The janitor at the school retired and I took his place. I don't start work until after 3:30 when the kids go home. That means I have a lot of time on my hands in the morning, so I started showing up early and sitting in the school library. It's better than sitting in my room staring at the wallpaper.

"Last week I was reading *Huckleberry Finn* and this little kid with a real deep voice came over to me. 'Hey Mayor, you know anything about arithmetic?'

"At first I thought he was making a joke, but no, he just wanted help with his homework. His third-grade class was studying fractions and they were giving him a headache.

"We never had kids and I still don't particularly like them, but this kid was so serious he was funny and he called me mayor, so how could I refuse? I remember you used to say 'show don't tell' so I drew a picture of a pie. Then we talked about cutting it in half and then in half again. He was amazed to see that two fourths and one half looked the same. I got a kick out of the smile on his face when he finally got it. Maybe that's why you liked teaching.

"Now the word has gotten around school that I'm in the library every day and if somebody drops by, I'll help them with their homework. Once in a while, one of the older boys will stop by looking for advice. Graduation is getting close and the seniors will be striking out on their own. Freedom can be a scary thing when you actually get your hands on it.

"It's not just the kids. Sometimes old friends stop by to swap stories or talk about what's bothering them. I guess folks feel comfortable talking about their sins with a fellow sinner. No judgement, you know. I've heard so many confessions I wonder if I'm horning in on Father Sullivan's territory."

***

I've rented a small apartment. Junior Ottley helped me find some second-hand furniture and stuff. I'm telling you the kid— he's 26 so I guess he's not really a kid anymore—has a talent for scrounging.

"Well my love, that's my new life. It's not what we planned, but it's not so bad."

Story #13, Junior Ottley (Camp Wheeler, WWII)

Junior was the youngest of 12 children. It was hard to make your mark in a crowd of that many kids. His sisters pampered him; his brothers mostly ignored him. But that never stopped him. He realized the other kids would tolerate him if he made himself useful. When he overstayed his welcome and got on somebody's nerves, he just moved on to another sister or brother who was doing something that looked interesting.

One of his sisters taught him to read when he was about five. With that many kids in school, there were always books around and Junior tried to read them all. He started out with Dick and Jane and worked his way up from there. Sometimes the books made sense, sometimes they were too complicated, but Junior didn't mind. He read what he could and made up a story for the parts he didn't understand.

History was all right, but it was the stories he liked best. He liked Sherlock Holmes and all his adventures and he liked Agatha Christi although he didn't always understand her stories. Junior knew the chances were slim, but he dreamed that someday he would be able to go to college and study all the great books ever written.

When the war started, Junior was 17 and with six brothers already in the Army, he was exempt. He got a civilian job at Warner Robbins Air Force Base and learned to be a field repair mechanic. He worked on almost every kind of plane from B-17s, C-47s, B-29s, B-24s, P-38s, P-47s to P-52s. He learned something new every day and he loved it.

When Camp Wheeler near Macon re-opened in 1943, he was transferred to the motor pool there. Now he was working on trucks instead of airplanes, but to the military's way of thinking, a motor was a motor. The main difference was the camp itself. Wheeler was a POW camp with a 1,000-bed hospital.

That was a shock. Junior knew about POWs in a general way, but it never occurred to him there would be a camp on American soil and certainly not one that close to home. He assumed the prisoners would be beaten, angry old men so he avoided them.

The first POWs sent to Wheeler were Italians. The next year, it was Germans. Wheeler held nearly 2,000 captives. By the end of the war, there were five other camps in Georgia where 4,700 POWs were held.

The POWs did yard work and made minor repairs around the camp. Junior watched them carefully and was surprised that they seemed almost happy to be there. Most of them came expecting the same brutal treatment they had heard about in other POW camps. Instead, they were given food, housing, uniforms and were even paid a small wage. No one seemed to mind the big "PW" on the back of their shirts. They didn't look beaten or angry and they weren't old. In fact, most of the prisoners were Junior's age. He was curious.

He had grown up with a couple of the Conti boys, so he spoke a little Sicilian. It wasn't Italian, but it was close enough for him to communicate. One day he saw a young soldier reading Little House on the Prairie. *"Good book," Junior said.*

The boy nodded. "Yes. I try to learn about America," he said. "I am Luigi."

Junior burst out laughing. The soldier looked puzzled.

"It's not you," Junior said. "It's just that every Saturday night I listen to a show on the radio called 'Life with Luigi.' It's about this guy from Italy who comes over here and every week he writes a letter to his Mama Mia. His name is Luigi Basco. Understand?"

"No. What is radio?"

"Wireless. I think that's what you call it over there. I'll ask Sarge if I can bring my radio in and maybe we can listen together." From then on, they met occasionally around the camp.

Officially Junior worked in the motor pool, but it wasn't long before he got a reputation for finding things. Even in the military, automotive parts were scarce. However, if a soldier needed something they couldn't find or weren't authorized to have, Junior would find a way to procure it. He cobbled together devices that weren't always up to military regulations, but they worked.

When the war was over, Luigi and the rest of the POWs were sent home. That was another surprise. Junior thought they would just be released. The boys made plans to write and maybe even visit someday, but Junior wondered if he would ever see Luigi again.

Junior went to work as the mechanic at the G&G. Folks had been holding their cars together with bubble gum and bailing wire all during the war. New cars weren't available yet and parts were still scarcer than hen's teeth. Junior took that as a challenge. What he couldn't beg, borrow or "procure," he made. Junior had a nice little side business to add to what he made at the G&G. He worked hard, lived at home and saved his money. Although he never mentioned it to anybody, he still held out hope that he could go to college someday. You never know, stranger things have happened.

See the World

The door was open, but Hank just stood outside. It wasn't the first time he had been by, but he'd never actually talked to anyone. The colorful posters on the walls made the place look friendly and inviting, but he wasn't sure what he wanted to do.

After several minutes the man sitting at the desk looked up and smiled. "Nice to see you back again. I'm here to help, so let me know if you have any questions." He went back to the work in front of him and left Hank on his own.

Hank took his time, but eventually he sat down at the man's desk. They talked for a while and Hank liked the fact that he was treated like an adult, not like a kid who couldn't make up his mind. After all, he'd done his homework.

"You know I couldn't start until the middle of June."

"I understand. As soon as you sign here, we'll take care of everything. Then you can relax and enjoy your graduation. You're making a good choice. Welcome aboard."

The Best Laid Plans

Hank's heart was beating a mile-a-minute. He took his time walking over to Moon's. He was hoping to be on his own for a while, but no such luck. Matt and Sonny were in a booth and they waved him over. They both had a bad case of graduation fever. That's all they could think or talk about.

In fact, most of the town was caught up in the excitement. There wasn't a yard of crepe paper, a string of lights, a single balloon or a mirror ball still available anywhere in the county. Prom dresses and white sports coats were hanging in closets, ready and waiting for the big night.

Families were standing by with Kodaks to record the event.

"I can't believe we made it!" Matt said.

"Yeah, the prom, then graduation and then we're off to college. The Three Musketeers, just like we planned," Sonny added. Hank didn't join in, but his friends didn't notice.

"Reckon they'll let us room together?" Matt wondered. "Do we have to know what we want to major in or will they tell us that?"

The phone next to the cash register rang and Gibby answered. She listened a moment and her face turned white. "I'll get him," she said and something in the tone of her voice caused nearby customers to stop talking. She walked over to the booth. "Matt, there's a call for you. It's the sheriff. Something about your dad." He looked at Gibby and instantly knew something was wrong.

He picked up the receiver, "Sheriff? It's me. Has something happened to my dad?"

By this time, everyone in the small diner was listening. They watched Matt's face dissolve into tears. He slumped into the nearest chair and handed the phone to Gibby. "Sheriff, it's me, Gibby...yes, of course, I'll take care of it." She hung up. Everyone was watching her. "It's Matt's father. He's been in a bad car wreck. Dr. Nichols is with him and Zach sent over the ambulance they keep at the sawmill. They're on the way to the trauma unit at Medical Center in Macon."

Hank and Sonny were there with Matt. "What can we do?"

"The three of you take my car, go pick up Matt's mother and then drive to Macon. I'll call your parents and tell them where you are."

Just after dark, Hank dropped Sonny at home and then returned Gibby's car and walked home. He could hardly believe that earlier that afternoon they were all talking about graduation and going off to college. Everything could change in a minute and without any warning. Just a driver going a little too fast and not paying attention. That's all it took.

When he got home, his parents were having supper. Hank told them that Matt's dad had a back injury and his legs were temporarily paralyzed. The doctors said he would recover, but learning to use his legs again would take some time and physical therapy.

"What a terrible thing to happen," Eden said. "The church will probably be there to help, but I guess this will change things for Matt. I know how much you boys were looking forward to starting college together, but you know with hospital bills and everything…"

"I can't see him going to college now," Zach said. "Too bad."

Very quietly Hank said, "Maybe we could help. Since I'm not going to college, maybe we…"

Zach cut him short. "It's a nice thought, Son, but I don't want to hear any more of this nonsense about you not going to college. You're going, and that's all there is to it."

"Actually, Dad, I can't go. I joined the Navy." Hank hadn't planned to blurt it out like that, but it was too late to take it back now.

"The hell you have! Besides, you're too young to make it legal."

"Dad, there's a new law that says at 17 I'm old enough to make my own decisions. I signed the papers and everything."

"God damn it!!" Zach slammed his hand down on the table hard enough to make the dishes jump. That was scary, but it was even scarier to hear his father curse.

"Mom?"

She was close to tears. "Hank, how could you do such a thing without talking to us first?"

It was clear he wasn't going to get any sympathy from his mother. Hank left the table, went to his room and closed the door.

Matt was having a similar conversation about college with *his* mother. "The deacons assure me that your dad will continue to get his regular salary and the WMU will help all they can, but I'm afraid college will have to wait. We'll have to use your college money to pay the doctors and the hospital. I'm so sorry, Matty, but I don't see any other way out."

Some time after midnight, Hank heard a knock on his door. "Can I come in?" Zach said as he opened the door. "I want to show you something." He opened a folder and covered Hank's study desk with old yellowed drawings. Cars. Round ones, sleek ones, three-wheel ones, cars with wings, cars with fins, cars with no windows and cars with nothing but windows.

"When I was your age, this was my dream, to design cars. I had it all planned out. Go to Georgia Tech, study automotive engineering… but things happened and well, here I am. Maybe I gave up on my dream too easily."

"Are you sorry?"

"Sometimes. But if I had made different decisions, you wouldn't be here. So I guess it all worked out for the best. I can't say I'm happy about your decision, but I understand."

"Thanks, Dad." Hank wanted to hug his dad, but they weren't a hugging family, so he let it pass.

Boot and his friends attended graduation like they did every year. The ceremony went off without a hitch. The one surprise was that Junior Ottley was awarded the first Lost River Scholarship. It was a miracle. He was 26, but he was finally going to college. With all the vets on the GI bill, maybe he wouldn't be the oldest freshman in history.

Time was running out so the Three Musketeers decided to meet at Moon's for one last Saturday morning pancake feast. Matt sat down with a big smile. "Guess what? I'm gonna be a cowboy."

Hank and Sonny looked at him as if he'd lost his mind.

"No, no. It's true. We have to use my collage money to pay the doctors, but my dad has a brother who lives near Oklahoma City. The two of them don't get along very well, but when he heard about dad's accident, he called and said I could come stay with his family and work on their ranch for a year or two to earn some money. Anyway, I'm going."

Sonny was the first to respond. "I can't believe this. Hank, you're going off to see the world compliments of the US Navy and Matt you're going out west to be a cowboy and here I am stuck in Georgia. I was supposed to go to college with you guys and now I find out I'm going with Junior Ottley. He's gotta be at least ten years older than me. This isn't the way things were supposed to work."

Matt looked at his friends. "Y'all remember when I said Georgia was boring? Well, I take it back. It's been a wild year and you just never know what's gonna happen next, do you?"

About the Author

Grace Hawthorne is an award-winning author. She began her career working for a newspaper and has written everything from ad copy for septic tanks, to the libretto for an opera, corporate histories and lyrics for Sesame Street.

She was born in New Jersey, grew up in Louisiana, went to high school in Texas, lived in Europe and worked in New York City. Now she and her husband, Jim Freeman, live in Atlanta with a rescue cat named Boots.

Shorter's Way

Chapter One

Willie Shorter's office smelled like shit. Manure to be polite, horse manure to be specific. The odor drifted up from the deserted Morganton Livery Stable downstairs but Willie hardly noticed any more. The afternoon heat however, was inescapable. The black oscillating fan simply moved the heavy air around the room and Willie found it hard to stay awake. He pushed himself out of his rump-sprung chair, headed out the door and down the back stairs in search of a breeze.

"Villie! Come, come!" Sol Goldman urgently summoned him.

Willie walked across the street to Gold's Mercantile where Sol stood beside a black man wearing faded overalls.

"This is Mr. Cunningham. He's a good customer, but he's got himself some big trouble." Sol looked at Cunningham and jerked his thumb toward Willie. "Tell him."

Experience had taught Nelse Cunningham to avoid dealing with white men whenever he could, but Mr. Goldman had always treated him with respect, so he couldn't very well refuse.

"Well Sir, Mr. Bull Rutledge, he hired me…"

"Harman Rutledge's son?"

"Yes Sir. You know him?"

"I know *of* him," Willie said.

Sol looked disgusted. "Bad man, he vould kick a dog just to hear him yowl. Go on, tell Villie what he done."

"Well Sir, he said he'd pay me $5 to clean out a couple'a acres back'a his house and I done it. Then he said I'd busted up part of his fence. Now he's not gonna pay me. 'Sides that, he's gonna take my mule to pay for the fence. How I'm gonna farm without that mule?"

"You are lawyer, Protector of Poor, Villie, so you help him, yeah?"

"Sure, I'll help."

Nelse shook his head. "I 'ppreciate your help Mr. Goldman, but I ain't got no money to buy a lawyer."

Willie smiled. "Don't worry about that, I'll think of something."

From the time he first opened his law office, Willie's main thought was his political future. In gold letters he introduced himself to the world, "Willie Shorter, Attorney at Law. Protector of the Poor."

How could he possibly say no? Willie had known men like Bull Rutledge and Nelse Cunningham all his life. And God knows he knew about being poor. He'd been born out of wedlock and by the time he was three, his 18-year-old mother, gave him to a widowed neighbor, climbed aboard a Greyhound bus and disappeared.

Aubrey Shorter was left with a skinny, silent child. Aubrey had a knack for saving lost, injured animals and Willie certainly looked the part. He carried the boy into the kitchen and pulled a chair up to the big wooden table. He padded the seat with a couple of Sears Roebuck catalogues and sat Willie on top. The boy watched as Aubrey mashed up some cornbread in pot likker and offered it to him. "Go ahead try it, Boy," Aubrey said gently. "You'll like it."

That was the beginning. Aubrey not only gave Willie his first taste of real food, he also gave him comfort, a home and a last name.

Waterproof Justice

Chapter One
(Waterproof, Louisiana 1946)

The pale winter sun came through the glass in the top of the front door and wrote "Waterproof Sheriff's Office" in shadows on the floor. Nate Houston braced his hands on the arms of his chair and carefully shifted his position. Then slowly he opened his desk drawer and looked down at the bottle inside. He hesitated several minutes pretending he had a choice. Finally, he took the heavy, brown bottle out and set it on the edge of his desk.

So this is what I've come to, not my proudest moment.

The pain persisted, working its way up from a dull ache to a knife edge. Not to worry, he knew how to take care of that, at least for a while. He hated to admit that he needed the doses more often now than when he first began using, but he still had the situation under control. He opened the bottle and poured out a generous amount. The fumes burned his nose, but that was a small price to pay for the soothing warmth to come.

Horse liniment.

The only thing that tamed the pain in his knee. A little souvenir from Germany. A fragment so tiny the doctors missed it, but big enough to get his attention on a daily basis. He massaged the liniment into his knee and relaxed as the heat began to drive out the pain. Nate put the top back on the liniment and stashed it in his desk.

When he first got home, he thought taking the job as sheriff was a good idea. But he soon found out that having seen war and death up close, it was hard to take a Saturday night bar fight seriously. It was harder yet to deal with what "normal" folks considered threats of life and death. As if on cue, the phone rang.

"Sheriff, come quick! Bud Garvey's got Luther up a tree and he's threatening to kill him." Nate recognized Lucy Castle's voice although it was pitched several octaves higher than usual.

"Does Bud have a gun?"

"No Sir, but he's got a baseball bat. I'm tellin' you it's a matter of life and death, Sheriff. You've gotta get over here right now."

Nate shook his head. He didn't see how Bud Garvey on the ground with a baseball bat posed any immediate danger to Luther up a tree. Oh well, welcome to law enforcement in Waterproof.

He grabbed his cane and headed for the door. The patrol car was a pre-war Chevy that smelled of cigarette smoke, Burma Shave, and Old Spice. It was a little past its prime but well suited for patrols through the rolling hills of West Feliciana Parish. A stranger—if ever there was one hanging around—would have had no reason to suspect he was looking at law enforcement. There were no markings on the car, not because of stealth, but because Nate had never found anybody to paint it.

Similarly, he refused to wear a uniform ever again. Instead, he wore a khaki shirt and pants, and an ancient Panama hat with a sweat-stained hatband. His one concession was the small sheriff's badge pinned to his left shirt pocket, which was totally unnecessary because everyone knew him.

He'd lived in Waterproof most of his life. His father had worked a small farm on the edge of town and his mother had worked at Parchment Products, which canned Grade A Louisiana yams—not to be confused with ordinary sweet potatoes. The culls of the yams were ground up, roasted, and mixed with cottonseed meal to make animal feed. Waterproof always smelled like a sweet potato pie that had overflowed and burned on the bottom of the oven.

Crossing the Moss Line

Chapter One

"We'll take the whole lot, the whole shipload."

The broker studied the two young men standing in front of
him and shook his head. *"Foolishness, total foolishness,"* he
thought to himself. *"The whole boatload?"* But then, who was
he to turn down money...and a lot of it too. Cash on the
barrelhead, up front. That's the way he liked doing business.

The 300-ton *Windward* rode at anchor in the small harbor
at Bunce Island. The trading site was in the Sierra Leone River
about 20 miles upriver from Freetown. It was a small island in
the country's largest natural harbor, which made it an ideal
base for the large ocean-going ships of European traders.

Due to the conditions aboard and the length of the voyage,
he knew the buyers would lose at least ten percent of the cargo
in the crossing and that was probably on the low side. However,
once the papers were signed and he had his money, he'd be on
his way. Not his responsibility any more.

Caleb Harding and Patrick Donegan exchanged worried
glances and tried to maintain an air of confidence. They knew
they were on shaky ground; they just hoped it wasn't too
obvious. Normally they would have dealt with a business agent
in Savannah, but to save some money, they decided to handle
the transaction themselves.

They pooled every cent they had, negotiated what they thought was a good price at $500 a head, and set very specific guidelines about exactly what they wanted. They also promised the captain a bonus if he delivered the cargo in good condition. If everything turned out as they hoped, they were on their way to owning the richest rice plantation in Georgia. If not... well, one way or the other, it was too late to turn back now. They followed the agent into his office to conclude their business.

The crew aboard the Windward paid no attention to them. They had enough to do with loading supplies and getting the ship ready for the long voyage ahead. In addition to spare sails, ropes, nails, pitch, tar, coal and oil, they loaded food supplies including ship's biscuits.

Jonesy, the new cabin boy, was as curious as he was green. "Here you go, try one of these," a craggy old sailor said and tossed him what looked like a cookie. Jonesy tried to take a bite and nearly broke all his teeth.

"Ahh come on, what's this?" he asked.

"Hardtack, me boy. Sealed up tight, it'll last for months at sea and there'll come a time you'll be glad to get it. Best soak it in your tea to soften it up a bit before you try to eat it, but don't forget to bang it on the table a couple of times first."

"Why would I do that?"

"To knock out the beetles and the weevils and any other nasty little beasties who've made a home for themselves in your biscuit." Jonesy looked a little sick and the crew laughed.

The seamen continued to load on the salt pork, dried fish and various grains. Finally, Jonesy stopped and looked toward the hold. "How do you stand the noise?"

"Just ignore it. It'll quiet down. The first week is the worst. After that, things get quiet, sometimes too quiet."

Jonesy tried, but he didn't think he would ever be able to ignore the cries and wails coming from the hold. They made the hair on the back of his neck stand up. No language that he could understand, just mournful, eerie sounds.

"That's the way it started way back there in 1802," Granny Johnson said.

Thunder and White Lightning

Chapter One

"Freeze!"

Duncan McLagan stopped dead still. Other than the black locust wood crackling under the cooker and the bees buzzing in the mountain laurel, there was no other sound for miles through the quiet Georgia hills. The voice didn't have a threat in it, but the gun pointed at his chest told a different story.

The tall man slowly put the gun back in his holster. "You're Duncan McLagan, that right? I'm Homer Webster. I'm a federal agent."

"I know who you are, Homer. Glad you put your gun away. Was you plannin' to shoot me?"

"Naw, the gun's mostly for show. We're just gonna bust up your still and then we're gonna take you to jail."

That was about what Duncan expected from what he knew about Homer. However, he was relieved not to have a gun pointed at him. He walked over to wash his hands in the creek and took his time rolling a cigarette from the tin of Prince Albert tobacco he kept in his overall pocket. This gave him a little time to think. He knew he'd been caught red-handed, but Homer sounded friendly enough, so Duncan decided to follow his lead.

"Homer, if I'd known you were comin', I wouldn't have wasted my time patchin' up leaks. But you know, since you're causin' me all this trouble, you oughta let me keep at least one jar. Lord knows, I deserve a drink."

Homer just laughed and nodded to his men.

Duncan managed a sad smile and sat down on a nearby rock to watch as the revenuers took an ax and a sledgehammer and destroyed his still. It broke his heart to see it go. His father had helped him build the still shortly after his son Gus was born. That was 15 years ago now.

By the time it was all over, the sun was beginning to set. Homer sized up the situation and looked at Duncan. "It's gettin' late and there's no sense in takin' you to jail now. You go on home tonight, but be at the courthouse by 9:00 sharp tomorrow. You know where the courthouse is, don't you?"

Duncan nodded. He'd been making shine more than 30 years and in all that time, he'd never been caught. Early the next morning, Duncan and Gus loaded up their wagon with a lot of hay and a dozen or so Mason jars of shine. When the shine was secure, they piled into the wagon and headed to Dawsonville.

While Duncan went inside the courthouse to take care of business, Gus got busy. In no time he had sold their supply of shine. When Duncan came back outside, Gus gave him the money and Duncan went back to pay the bondsman.

Finally, Federal Judge Edwin Dunbar got things underway. Homer Webster presented his evidence. Then the judge called on Duncan, who unfolded his six-foot-three frame and faced the judge.

"Judge, I'm sure you know that is was needin' money to pay for The Civil War that gave the gov'ment the idea to tax whiskey and that's when moonshine became illegal. I just want to say that I might be what you call a tax evader, but I am *not* a criminal. I bought the land, I bought the stuff to build the still, I bought everything I needed to make the shine and I worked long hours up in those woods. I never stole nothin' and as far as I can see, I'm not guilty of nothin'. Duncan bowed and sat down. The audience laughed, rose to their feet and gave him a hardy round of applause.

"Mr. McLagan since this is your first offense, or at least the first time you've been caught, I'm inclined to be lenient. If I let you off with a caution, do you think you could refrain from making illegal whiskey?"

Duncan knew what he *should* say, but the momentum of his speech and the sweet sound of the applause temporarily robbed him of all reason. "Judge, I could promise to do my best, but to tell you the honest-to-God truth, I just don't think I can manage to give up moonshining."

The courtroom broke into laughter again. And so it was, that in the Year of Our Lord 1940, Duncan McLagan was sentenced to a year and a day to be served in the Federal Penitentiary in Atlanta.